A FUNERAL IN MANTOVA
The Fifth Rick Montoya Italian Mystery

"Following *Return to Umbria*, Wagner's fifth series outing features a likable amateur sleuth who carefully analyzes other people. Rich in details of the food and culture of Italy's Lombardy region, this atmospheric mystery will be appreciated by fans of Martin Walker's French-flavored "Bruno" mysteries. Readers of Frances Mayes's Under the Tuscan Sun may enjoy the colorful descriptions."

—*Library Journal*

"Wagner's fifth series entry provides his usual deft mix of art, travel, and suspense."

—*Kirkus Reviews*

"...the many details of meals that Rick enjoys on his trip are a highlight, as are the author's appended notes on the food and wines of the area..."

—Henrietta Verma, *Booklist*

"This is a book for armchair travelers as much as it is for mystery lovers."

—*Publishers Weekly*

RETURN TO UMBRIA
The Fourth Rick Montoya Italian Mystery

"Translator Rick Montoya is in Orvieto to persuade his cousin to return home to Rome when he gets drawn into investigating the murder of American Rhonda Van Fleet. Did Rhonda's past in Orvieto, studying ceramics, lead to her death? The setting almost overwhelms the plot, but Rick is a charming and appealing amateur sleuth."

—Library Journal

"Wagner skillfully inserts nuggets of local culture without slowing down the narrative pace, and perhaps even more importantly, he gets Italy right. He understands the nuances of Italian manners and mentality as well as the glorious national preoccupation with food."

—Publishers Weekly

"With taut pacing and enough credible suspects to keep the reader guessing until the end, *Return to Umbria* makes for an engaging read."

—Shelf Awareness

MURDER MOST UNFORTUNATE
The Third Rick Montoya Italian Mystery

"Returning in his third outing, Rick Montoya travels to Bassano del Grappa to work as a translator at an art seminar. When one of the attendees ends up dead, Rick can't keep himself from investigating, along with Betta Innocenti, the daughter of a local gallery owner. Rick, as always, is a charming sleuth."

—*Library Journal*

"Though he spent his childhood in Rome, Montoya proudly kicks around Italy in the cowboy boots he brought with him from the years he spent in New Mexico. He is an easygoing, empathetic protagonist—with just enough American irreverence to keep his Italian colleagues entertained."

—Karen Keefe, *Booklist*

DEATH IN THE DOLOMITES
The Second Rick Montoya Italian Mystery

"Like *Cold Tuscan Stone*, the novel is light on its feet, with a protagonist who will strike readers as a good guy to hang around with."

—David Pitt, *Booklist*

COLD TUSCAN STONE
The First Rick Montoya Italian Mystery

"David P. Wagner gives us a compelling new character in a setting so romantic and redolent of history it pulls us in immediately and holds us until the surprising ending.... This is a wonderful start to a series, which should have immediate legs, and surely will thrill everyone who has lived in Italy, been to Italy, or would like to visit. As a boy I lived in both Firenze and Napoli, and reading Wagner takes me back deeply and instantly."

—Joseph Heywood, author of *The Woods Cop Mysteries*,
The Snowfly and *The Berkut*

"If you are interested in Italian art and artifacts, Italian history and culture, Italian food and wine, or even just good storytelling, then *Cold Tuscan Stone* will be right up your cobblestone alleyway. Set in the ancient Tuscan town of Volterra, David P. Wagner's atmospheric debut novel delivers all of the above and more... Simply put, this exciting, intriguing, well-written mystery extends an offer no reader should refuse. Capiche?"

—Amanda Matetsky, author of *The Paige Turner Mysteries*

"Wagner hits all the right notes in this debut. His likable protagonist engages, plus the Italian angle is always appealing. Perfect for readers who enjoy a complex puzzle, a bit of humor, and a fairly gentle procedural. Don't miss this one."

—*Library Journal* (starred review)

"Like the Etruscan urns he seeks, Rick's debut is well-proportioned and nicely crafted."

—*Kirkus Reviews*

"The intriguing art milieu, mouthwatering cuisine, and the team of the ironic Conti and the bemused but agile Montoya are bound to attract fans."

—*Publishers Weekly*

ROMAN
COUNT
DOWN

Books by David P. Wagner

The Rick Montoya Italian Mysteries
Cold Tuscan Stone
Death in the Dolomites
Murder Most Unfortunate
Return to Umbria
A Funeral in Mantova
Roman Count Down

ROMAN COUNT DOWN

A RICK MONTOYA ITALIAN MYSTERY

DAVID P. WAGNER

Poisoned Pen
PRESS

Copyright © 2019 by David P. Wagner
Cover and internal design © 2019 by Sourcebooks
Cover design by The Book Designers
Cover images/illustrations © Tomasz Wozniak/Shutterstock

Library of Congress Cataloging-in-Publication data is on file with the publisher.

Published by Poisoned Pen Press, an imprint of Sourcebooks
P.O. Box 4410, Naperville, Illinois 60563-4410
(630) 961-3900
sourcebooks.com

Printed and bound in the United States of America.
SB 10 9 8 7 6 5 4 3 2

In loving memory of Baffi, my feline muse
for this book and all the others.

No man is lonely while eating spaghetti.

—*Robert Morley*

Chapter One

Count Umberto Zimbardi was surprised when the bus slowed down and pulled ahead of him. He'd expected to climb on through the front door, but fortunately there was enough light from a nearby street lamp to see "Entrance" stenciled above the back doors that banged open when the bus stopped. He stepped from the curb to the door, clutching the metal railing. As his foot touched the second step the door slammed shut behind him and the bus started up. Fortunately, he managed to grip the pole at the top of the steps.

Now came the part he was most concerned about. He looked around for someone to take his ticket and saw only a few passengers staring out the windows. Far in front he could make out the head of the driver, and written on the metal barrier behind him was an official admonition that he should not be bothered. The count kept the ticket at arm's length, wondering what to do next, and then spotted a box attached to a pole ahead of him. Could it be? He staggered toward it, hands moving from pole to pole to steady himself while grasping the ticket between his fingers. Yes, the instructions above the metal contraption were clear, and he followed them carefully, inserting his ticket in a small opening. It made a *kerchunk*, almost loud enough to startle him, and when he pulled it out, he could see the time stamp.

He'd done it.

Suddenly, he was back in school. The headmaster sat at his desk and stared at young Umberto with dark, piercing eyes, sinister even through the thick glasses. What a disappointment. A lad with such potential. What would your parents think of what you did? The count had successfully repressed the memory of that humiliating meeting for years, and now it flowed back.

Calming himself as best he could, he took a window seat in the middle of the bus and gazed at Rome by night. The view was quite different from what he saw regularly from the backseat of his car when he was usually reading the newspaper while Rocco dealt with the traffic. He'd glanced out of the window of his car, as often as not staring at the side of a bus. Now he was inside the bus, admitting that, except for the hard, plastic seat, it was not unpleasant. A plus—he could see over all the cars. Even late at night there was a thick stream of traffic with drivers alternately charging madly ahead or impatiently growling while stopped at a traffic light. Beyond the cars' roofs the sidewalk ran along the Tiber River. He watched a young couple, oblivious to the sounds of the street, leaning on the stone wall and looking at the water. It was too dark to see any debris floating down from the northern part of the city, so their romantic moment was not spoiled.

Umberto sighed deeply as he recalled strolling along the Thames embankment all those decades ago with his first love, Samantha Peabody. Whatever became of Samantha? She would be married, no question about that, probably various times, with a brood of children. And grandchildren. He smiled to remember the weekend he escaped from school and took the train into London to see her. Once again he thought of the headmaster. The old goat made sure Umberto paid dearly for that escapade, but it was worth it. Well worth it. He never told his wife about Samantha, not that some minor incident in his youth was anything to hide from the countess. She'd probably had a fling or two herself, when she was a girl. Well, perhaps not...

The bus started moving, and his thoughts returned to the issue at hand. The Zimbardis always stood for honesty, so he knew what his decision had to be. *Probitas* was the only word on the family crest, after all, inscribed under the crossed lances and the unicorn. The single exception to this family fixation on honesty was his Uncle Guidobaldo who, rather than face the music and the judge, decamped to the Sudan where he set up a pizzeria that did quite well. Guidobaldo's name did not come up often when the Zimbardi clan gathered during Umberto's childhood, and then only in hushed conversation. When Umberto misbehaved, the worst threat he could receive from his mother was, "If you keep that up we may have to send you to the Sudan."

The phrase had sent shivers down his small spine, but it also piqued his interest in the black sheep of the family. He pictured giant fans wielded by nubile maidens, cooling his uncle as he kneaded his pizza dough—an image inspired by a copy of *National Geographic* that Umberto kept under his mattress. It was about that time when he was sent to school in England, where he never mentioned his uncle to any of his schoolmates. Nor to Samantha Peabody.

He must be getting close to what would be his stop, but since he never took the bus, he wasn't sure. It would be close to the bridge across Tiberina Island, he assumed. He saw a passenger pull the cord and the bus stopped; could he just do the same when he got to where he wanted to get off? Unsure of the protocol, he decided it would be better simply to be ready for the scheduled stop, wherever it might come. He got to his feet and walked unsteadily down the aisle toward the front of the bus where other passengers had gotten off previously. There were only three other people remaining, in addition to the driver. One was asleep, and the second, who looked North African, stared out the window. The third, who'd squeezed through the door as it was closing, just after the count got on, was wedged in the rear seat out of sight. He wanted to get a better look at the man in back, but decided it would be better not to stare. It could draw unwanted attention, which was the last thing he needed. It crossed Umberto's mind that the second man could be from the Sudan. When he got home he would check his office globe to get the country's exact location. Near Egypt, if he remembered correctly.

Sure enough, the bus ground to a halt and the front and rear doors banged open. The driver braked with such suddenness that Umberto had to grab a seat back to keep himself upright. Once he got his balance he walked past the driver and stepped down to the pavement. Something caught his eye in the darkness, maybe someone exiting from the rear of the bus. That confused him, since he was under the impression that leaving by the driver door was required. Could it be the man in the backseat? Once again he supressed the urge to look, taking deep breaths to calm his nerves. At least now he was off the bus, his feet on solid pavement, and his destination would soon come into view. Knowing he was returning to familiar surroundings helped him relax, as did the thought of enjoying a tumbler of whiskey in his study. The driver put the bus into gear and groaned ahead as the count watched. Should he have thanked the driver? Perhaps a gratuity? No, likely not. He would ask Gonzalo, his butler, about bus protocol, though, in fact, he was not planning on riding another one any time soon.

He was left standing on the sidewalk, surrounded by the fumes of the departing bus along with the slightly less toxic exhaust of the cars. Ahead was the traffic light at the narrow bridge over the river, the only way to get a vehicle on and off the island. Isola Tiberina looked like a ship floating in the middle of the Tiber. In ancient times, the Romans, who knew a thing or two about monumental architecture, built a huge prow of a boat at the northern end of the isle, now long gone. The island still kept part of its original vocation—healing—being the site of a large hospital. As Umberto walked across the bridge an ambulance shot past him, siren blaring, toward the Emergency Room entrance. He edged toward the rail and pitied the poor devil inside. Despite its proximity to the Zimbardi residence, Umberto had never been in this hospital. Like most wealthy Romans, he used a private clinic when needed, eschewing the Italian National Health Service. He walked past the side of the hospital where the cars and mopeds of the night-shift staff parked in jumbled lines.

To his right was a small *piazza*, beyond which beckoned the facade of the San Bartolomeo Church, which he always called Saint Bartholomew. Sora Lela, the restaurant, was closed at this hour, without so much as a light visible through the dingy windows. The light was also dim on the bridge that would take him across the other arm of the Tiber split by the island. He could almost see the ancient Teatro Marcello, site of the Zimbardi residence.

As he started across the bridge he noticed a group of feral cats gathered around paper plates, licking the sauce off spaghetti left there by one of the city's mysterious cat ladies.

Suddenly, he stopped. "What are you doing here?"

It might be said that if one were going to be the victim of a physical attack, what better place to have it happen than a few steps from a hospital? But the proximity of medical help was of no use to the count. The emergency room doctor at the Ospedale Fatebenefratelli estimated that the victim left the world at the instant his head hit the bridge pavement. The irony, which would not have been lost on Count Umberto Zimbardi, was that his first visit to the hospital on Tiberina Island would also be his last.

Chapter Two

"Are you going to eat that or just stare at it?"

For the moment, at least, Rick was merely going to stare at the plate in front of him. It wasn't exactly a plate, but a red plastic basket, lined with checkered paper and containing a green chile cheeseburger and fries. His sister was already two bites into her lunch, a large chef's salad with Thousand Island dressing. She stabbed at a slice of tomato with her fork and waited for her brother to answer. She was in no hurry. They sat in a booth on plastic seats, a small jukebox on the wall between them. Outside, it was a perfect day, typical for New Mexico, which would still be the Sunshine State had Florida not stolen the name. But Land of Enchantment worked just as well.

"Anna, this may be the last green chile cheeseburger I'll eat for years. It never occurred to me that they won't have green chile cheeseburgers in Rome."

"That city is a culinary backwater, Rick. You'll probably waste away to nothing."

He picked up his glass and held it out, studying the brown liquid. "And Alien Ale. They won't have it, either."

"You'll have to drink water. But you've always been ingenious; you'll find a way to survive." She opened a packet of Saltines.

"You're right, I'll muddle through somehow. But will I be able to make it without my dear sister constantly…?"

"Giving you excellent advice?"

"*Nagging* was the word that came to mind."

"Mom and Dad are in Brazil, someone had to do it." She poked at the salad. "You're not really nervous about making this move, are you, Rick?"

He finally bit into his cheeseburger, and she waited for him to swallow.

"Boy, that's good," said Rick. "The best this side of San Antonio." He took a sip of beer. "Why should I be nervous? I've sold all my belongings and taken my savings out of the bank so I can move to another country with the tenuous hope of restarting a business which, I might add, was doing quite well here in Albuquerque."

"We've been through this, Rick. You know a lot of people there, and Uncle Piero will help."

He took another drink of beer, this one longer. "Piero will probably start on his thing about me becoming a cop."

"I thought that was just a joke."

"I'm not so sure, Anna. The e-mails I've been getting from him keep mentioning cases he's working on that I might find interesting."

"He has nobody to talk to about his work except the other cops. You'll fill the void."

Rick shrugged and picked up a French fry in his fingers. "This may be the last time for a while that I can eat one of these with my fingers. It's considered quite the *bruta figura* not to use a fork in Italy, as you'll remember."

Anna rolled her eyes. "Enough already with the food stuff. What about the real issue of importance, dear brother?"

"And what would that be?"

"When are you going to find a nice girl and settle down?" She said it with a slight Italian accent.

"Your Mamma imitation is creepy."

"Years of practice. You are past thirty. I already had two children at your age."

"And great kids they are. You took a lot of heat off me with Mamma by getting married and having those two. Don't think I don't appreciate it."

She sipped her iced tea. "The pressure will start building up again, Rick. Mamma was only temporarily distracted. She wants the best for her bambino as well as her daughter. Have you been in touch with your classmates from the American School?"

"Art Verardo. He knows I'm coming. That's about it. I'll find out about others when I get there."

"Including the girls. What about *la bella* Lidia? You two were quite a number back in the day.

"Art hasn't mentioned her in his e-mails."

He chewed his last bite of burger and thought about Lidia. If she is still in Rome and is single, it might be worth giving up green chile cheeseburgers for a while.

• • ● • •

In the backseat of the bus, two tourists from Texas craned their necks to see what the tour guide was talking about over the loud-speaker. The woman seated nearest the window held her camera at the ready, while her husband peered over her shoulder. Along with the rest of the tour group, the two had just gotten back on after a rushed loop around the inside of the Colosseum, where she'd spent most of the time taking pictures of the feral cats basking on the stones. The bus made a wide turn around the street that circled the arena and now headed down the six-lane Via dei Fori Imperiali, named for the ruins that flanked it. Every Roman emperor worth his salt had built a forum, and those that weren't visible along this street were buried under it.

"We know that the violin had not been invented until well after Nero's time," said the voice over the loudspeaker. It belonged to a man wearing a wrinkled white shirt with a name tag slightly askew. A thin tie hung loosely from an open collar. His eyes were hidden behind dark aviator Ray-Bans. "In fact, historians now agree that while Rome burned, the emperor was playing a zither."

"You know, Wade," said the woman from Texas, "I'm beginning to wonder about this tour guide."

"Why, Glenda?"

"What he said about soccer games in the Colosseum."

"Why not? These Italians love soccer."

"Okay, but saying that Jerry Jones came over here and studied the Colosseum before building Cowboy stadium? I don't remember reading about that back in Dallas."

The loudspeaker crackled to life again. "Julius Caesar himself marched down this street with his legions. It was after one of those parades that he went back to his villa and invented what we now know as the Caesar salad."

"See what I mean?" Glenda poked her husband in the ribs.

"Maybe you're right.

"But what he said about the Baths of Caracalla having the largest bathtub ring in recorded history, that made sense to me."

The bus moved down the street as the guide continued his running commentary. When it reached the huge monument to Italy's first king, it swung to the left and climbed past the steps leading up to city hall. Passing more ruins, it came to the river.

"For many years," said the voice on the loudspeaker, "a troll lived under this bridge, demanding payment to let people cross. The authorities eventually put a stop to it, and last I heard he was working a bridge over the Arno, in a rural area east of Florence. His name is Otto." The woman from Texas dutifully took a photograph of the bridge as they crossed on the way to the Vatican.

When the bus approached St. Peters Basilica, the guide's commentary turned to the papacy. "It is from that tiny chimney that the cardinals signal whether they have come to a decision on a new pope. White smoke indicates that they have elected one, black smoke means they left the pizza in the oven too long. Of course, in the Middle Ages, the pontiff was selected by an arm-wrestling competition among the cardinals." Phones and a few real cameras clicked away as the bus stopped at the edge of the square before swinging a looping U-turn and going back toward the river.

An hour later, as the tour was coming to its conclusion, the couple in the backseat had decided that the tour wasn't so bad after all, despite what the guide had said about Jerry Jones.

"We sure are learning a lot about ancient history, Glenda. I always thought that Cleopatra ended her days in Egypt, but apparently she fell on her asp while riding on a sedan chair right here in Rome."

"And it was just after watching the elephant races at the Circus Maximus," she said to her husband. "Don't forget that part."

"That shows you how Hollywood doesn't care about historical accuracy. The chariot scene in Ben Hur was just plain made up."

The tour ended on a street near the Spanish Steps. The guide, the young man with dark sunglasses, thanked each of the passengers as they stepped off the bus. Most of them said nothing to the guide, or if they did, the comment was less than positive. Glenda and Wade told him how informative the tour was, tipped the man five euros, and started toward Piazza di Spagna. As they neared the bottom of the Spanish Steps, the crowds thickened.

"Look at all these people, Wade. It's like Kyle Field on a fall Saturday. Maybe we should just go back to the hotel. We could get pickpocketed."

"Not on your life. I want to see the Spanish Steps, where he said that international Slinky competition takes place. What a shame that we missed it by two weeks. We could have cheered on the American team."

• • ● • •

They ordered steak, as would be expected in Buenos Aires. No meal in Argentina was complete without a slab of meat from a cow raised on the sweet grass of the Pampas, and certainly not a business lunch. The choice wasn't just a matter of national pride, it was a taste cultivated over generations of Argentines who considered themselves gauchos, even if they'd only seen horses in movies. There were sharp knives set at each place on the crisp white tablecloth, but the steak would be so tender it could be cut with a spoon. The knives proved useful to slice off bites of yellow *provoleta* cheese, grilled to perfection and served as an appetizer, another standard in Argentine restaurants. This one was among the more elegant eateries in the city, and an appropriate setting to consummate an important business deal. The other diners, mostly men in tailored suits, talked in low voices as they sliced their steak and discussed the usual topics: politics and making money. The two were often connected. At this table the talk was strictly business.

Juan Alberto Sanguinetti sipped his wine, a red from Mendoza trying hard to be robust, and he was surprised to find that it wasn't bad. Though it was not one of the more famous labels of that region, his host made a point of ordering it. Of course he was the marketing manager for the winery that produced it. Juan Alberto wondered if the man had checked to be sure it was on the restaurant's wine list before reserving their table. He wouldn't ask. Instead, he listened patiently while his host extolled the climate of the valley where the grapes had come to maturity, although Juan's mind began to wander when soil acidity took over from climate. He understood that he should know about such things if he was going to sell their wine in Italy, but as he had done throughout his thirty or so years, he assumed he would rely on his wits and personality to get the job done. How hard could it be to sell Argentine wine? He'd been drinking it himself since he was a toddler, when his grandmother let him sip from her glass, so he should be able to extol its qualities. Only during his short sojourn in America was it difficult to find wines from home, and he was forced to drink wine from California and even—he shuddered at the memory—New Mexico.

The host was now describing the angles of the sun's rays at various times of the year, and what it meant for the maturation of the grape. Juan Alberto fought off a yawn. He'd been up late the previous night, woke up mid-morning with no appetite for breakfast, and now the wine was hitting his empty stomach. He took a sip from his water glass, wishing he could splash some of it in his face to liven himself up. His cell phone saved him. He pulled it out and checked the number.

"I really must take this, if you don't mind. One of my contacts in Rome."

The man grinned and waved him away with his hand. "Of course, of course."

Juan Alberto got to his feet and walked quickly toward the *caballeros* door at the opposite side of the dining room, just missing a man coming out while straightening his tie. He put the phone to his ear as he entered the bathroom.

"*Hola*, Mina. You called at the perfect time." He walked to the sink and checked himself out in the mirror before pushing back a few strands of his thick black hair, the only ones out of place.

"You didn't say goodbye this morning, Juancito." He didn't need to see her face to know it held the signature pout.

"You were still asleep, *mijita*, I could not bear to wake you." She sniffed. "I am going to miss you so."

"Don't start, Mina. You know it will only be for a few weeks."

"Enough time to meet some Italian *desvergonzada*."

He hoped it would take only a few days to meet one. "I have to go, my new boss is waiting. See you tonight." He hung up, slipped the phone into his pocket, and turned on the cold water tap. Carefully, so as not to get any drops on his shirt or tie, he rubbed the cool water into his face before taking one of the cloth towels from the basket and patting himself dry. Good enough to keep awake through coffee.

He arrived back at the table at the same time as their steaks, each one barely fitting on the expanse of its plate and oozing red juices. The aroma of the *parilla* wafted up from the dark grill marks seared into the crusted surface of the meat.

"What is it the Italians say for *buen provecho*?"

"*Bon appetite*," answered Juan Alberto, earning a puzzled look from his host.

He would make a point of learning the correct Italian phrase early on. Rick would know.

● ● ● ● ●

O'Shea's Irish Pub sat at ground level on a narrow street, a few blocks from the Tiber, in a part of town considered old even by local standards. The street had been laid out originally by the Romans, but Romans who wore togas and sandals rather than Armani suits and Bruno Magli shoes. Now the area had a distinctly medieval feel to it. Even the dirt—which municipal street-sweepers regularly and lovingly moved from one side of the pavement to the other—dated to the fifteenth century. The low buildings at the edge of the cobblestones were just as old. Developers would love to tear them down to put in something more modern, but eliminating anything old in this city almost required an act of Parliament. New buildings in this part of Rome were as scarce as Tex-Mex restaurants.

It was a typical weekday evening at O'Shea's, and Guido O'Shea stood behind the bar surveying the sparse crowd. His outfit was the same every night: black pants, a white shirt, and a white apron blemished by a few beer spots. He was clean shaven, and his hair carefully combed. The very picture of a professional tavern owner, he thought. As he looked out over the room, he wondered, as he always did when the place wasn't full, what could be done to bring in a better clientele. By better, he meant larger, since his goal was selling more beer, and it didn't matter who bought it as long as they paid and didn't trash the place after doing so. O'Shea's was already a regular watering hole among some circles of younger English-speaking expats. He served up warm beer to the Brits and Irish and, thanks to an ear for languages, he could affect an appropriate British Isles accent when required. For his fellow Americans the brews were always served cold, and for those who truly wanted to feel at home, in the bottle. To go along with the alcohol he had a cook in the back—chef would be too generous a term—making snacks, mostly fried, which the regulars described in less than glowing terms, though not so Guido could hear.

TV monitors hung at various strategic positions around the room, their modernity contrasting with a décor that could be described as mid-century modern, that century being the seventeenth. Wood was the dominant feature of the place: wood floors, wood tables and benches, a long wood bar, and dark wood beams crossing the low ceiling. Long John Silver could have clomped in, ordered a tankard of ale, and felt at home. The TVs were the big draw, and Guido knew it. His best nights were those when some sporting event was featured on the flat screens. Beer and football went together, as well as beer and soccer, and certainly beer and Australian-rules football. The satellite charges were outrageous but worth it to bring in thirsty customers looking for a piece of the homeland.

Tonight the best he could muster was a rerun of the NBA semi-finals from the previous season, and the numbers at the tables showed it. Two women sitting in one corner of the room were not paying any attention to the game on the screen above them. One, dressed in a smart business suit, looked like she had come directly from the office. She nursed a glass of Peroni, taking an occasional stale peanut from a small bowl Guido had put between them, and dropping the shells on the floor. The other wore jeans and a sweater, and sipped from a bottle of Miller Lite. The two had been friends since they were students at the American Overseas School of Rome. One had an Italian father and British mother, the other an Italian mother and American father. Both had left Italy to go to the university, one in England and the other in the States, and both had returned. They were part of a core of AOSR alums who gathered on occasion at Guido's to talk about the good old days in high school, but tonight the mood at their table was somber.

"I'm at my wit's end," said Giulia, who ran a tour bus company. "I had to fire one of my guides and I can't find anyone to replace him. If I don't get someone soon, I'll have to cut back on my tours. I can't afford to do that."

The other woman sipped from her bottle and put it down. "Why did you can him?"

"He drank too much and when he picked up the microphone at the front of the bus he'd start spouting all sort of stuff. A few of the clients liked it, but those who knew anything about Rome got annoyed."

"Really? What kind of stuff?"

The first woman shook her head in disgust. "The last straw was when he was at the Vatican and told the group that it was called a basilica because the pope grew basil in planters hanging from the side windows." She took another pull from her beer.

"That's pretty clever."

"But not what people want to hear on what they think is a serious bus tour of the city." She drained her glass and signaled Guido for a refill. "They want a commentary that brings the ruins to life. But with facts." Giulia glanced up at the screen where two players were arguing with a ref, then back at her companion and frowned. "I don't see what's so funny, *cara*."

"Sorry. I was just thinking. There just may be someone who could step in temporarily." She shook her head. "Though he'll probably be too busy." She shrugged. "But you never know. I think he gets into Rome in a few days."

"I'd take almost anyone. Don't keep me in suspense. Someone I might know?"

"You may remember him. He was in our class."

"Aha. I wondered when all your computer searches of our classmates would come in handy. It isn't that nerdy Timothy Testa, is it? He was always trying to get me to go out with him."

"No, Timothy is working at a bank in London."

"Jason Failla? He always aced the history tests. He could work."

"Nope. Jason's Facebook page puts him in Miami, selling insurance."

The new Peroni arrived and she took a long pull. "Don't keep me in suspense."

"Let's see, what's his name again?" A pause. "Oh yeah, Rick Montoya."

The beer spilled when the other woman banged the table. Peanuts fell to the floor. People at the nearest table looked over in surprise. It even got Guido's attention.

"Get out! Rick? You've got to be kidding." She grabbed a tiny napkin and tried to soak up the beer before it dripped in her lap.

"Not kidding. I heard it from a good source. He's moving to Rome to start his own business, translating and interpreting."

"He never gave me the time of day. He was always with Lidia." She shook her head. "Isn't that ironic?"

They both thought about Lidia, the best-looking girl in the class.

"Did I mention that Rick is still single?"

• • ● • •

"Your police have done nothing to find my husband's murderer."

Commissario Piero Fontana tapped a finger on the armrest of the sumptuous chair as he looked directly at the woman sitting across from him, trying his best to avoid saying something rude. She was, after all, the Countess Zimbardi, the last of a long line of Roman nobility, and such things still counted for something in Italy, especially in Rome. When said nobility was combined with wealth, it counted for quite a lot. As such, the countess was able to pick up the telephone in her *palazzo* and call a high-level official in the Interior Ministry, who happened to have been a friend of her late husband the count. The result was the visit by Commissario Fontana, who normally would not be involved in a case which the police dismissed as a simple mugging gone bad and consigned to the file of homicides likely not to be solved. The file was not so-named officially, but everyone in the division knew that's what it contained. Not that they hadn't tried to find the murderer when the body had been found. Thanks to the count's notoriety—at least in some social circles—the investigation had been extensive. Despite serious efforts, the police came up with no suspects. They assumed the killing was perpetrated by one of the petty criminals who occasionally prowled the city streets. Violent crime was rare in the city's historic center, but it did happen on occasion. Unfortunately for Commissario Fontana, the victim was a count, though it could well be said that it was even more unfortunate for Count Zimbardi himself.

The *commissario* kept the same serious look on his face. "I can understand your frustration, Countess. It is matched by our own. Be assured that we are doing everything possible to find the guilty party, but the randomness of the crime makes our investigation very difficult." It wasn't exactly true, but he hoped it was enough to hold her off while they made another attempt to track down the killer. He disliked rounding up suspects purely for the sake of demonstrating that something was being done, but it might be needed to placate the woman.

She looked back without speaking, giving the policeman the sense that she was weighing her thoughts before responding. He hoped it would not be another disparagement of the police, but the hope was weak. He waited, and her eyes moved around the room. A sumptuous room it was, as would be expected for an apartment at this address.

The Teatro di Marcello started its life two millennia earlier when the Emperor Augustus decided to take over a project started by Julius Caesar, and dedicate it to his late nephew Marco Claudio Marcello. The theater, with its classical half-circle design, had held fifteen thousand spectators, but over the centuries it suffered the fate of so many monuments in the city. Its stone was recycled to construction sites around Rome, became a fortress for powerful families, and fell into various states of disrepair. But real estate values being what they have always been in downtown Rome, it was eventually renovated and became a location which many *per bene* Romans would kill to call home.

"I have discovered something that could help with the investigation."

It was not what the *commissario* had expected, but he was pleased to hear her words. He leaned forward. "And what would that be, Countess?"

"My husband was a traditionalist. Perhaps old-fashioned would be a more accurate way to describe the count. He kept a journal and he wrote letters. In long hand. In going through the papers in his study I came across them in a file. They were not locked up, mind you. Umberto had nothing to hide from me."

The policeman considered the last comment. How could she be so certain that her husband had nothing to hide? He spent a mere ten minutes with the woman and it seemed like an hour. Did the count seek out other companionship? He put the thought out of his mind and returned to what she had said. "We would be interested in the material, Countess. It might be helpful, even though it appears random violence took your husband from you. Have you found anything of interest to the case in these papers?"

"I haven't read them."

"I don't understand."

She spoke slowly, as if talking to a child, or someone who should understand without her telling him. "Commissario, my husband's mother was British, he had a British nanny, and he spent much of his youth, including schooling, in Britain. English was effectively his first language. So his journal is written in English, as were the letters from his British schoolmates."

"And you don't read English."

Her reply was an annoyed frown. "I don't suppose you have anyone on your staff who could do the work? This is not the sports pages of the tabloids, unfortunately. Whenever I see a policeman sitting in his squad car he seems to be either reading the sports pages or a comic book."

Fontana let the comment pass, and an idea jumped into his head. "We have an American who we sometimes contract for translations. He does not come cheap, so if you can pay him directly, it would avoid my having to justify the expense in the bureaucracy."

She waved a hand, as if shooing away a flying insect. "Of course."

The policeman took her answer as a welcome end to the conversation. He got to his feet. "I will have him contact you in the next few days."

"What's his name, Commissario?"

"Montoya. Riccardo Montoya."

The policeman stole a look at his watch. Too late to get to the airport. Damn this woman.

"The line for Italians is that one, *Mister* Montoya"

The agent pushed the passport back through the opening in the glass with one hand and jerked his thumb with the other. Rick was in the wrong line, but did the guy have to be so rude about it? After all, he was still groggy from the flight, since no amount of airline coffee could make up for being jolted awake by the sudden glare of the cabin lights while bouncing over the Alps. And he had merely stood in the line he always used when arriving in Rome, like all those other times when he was using his

American passport. This time, since he was going to be working, it seemed proper to use his Italian one, so could you really blame him for getting in the wrong line?

It was an inauspicious arrival. So much for Rick Montoya, suave international traveler.

He crossed over under puzzled looks from people of many nationalities, especially the Italians of the new line where he took his place. Fortunately, everyone was as tired as he was, and they held their tongues as this column of arrivals, now all Italian, edged forward at the speed of an aging turtle. Several minutes later he realized that he was truly back in Italy when his Italian passport was pushed back by a uniformed agent who paid him no attention whatsoever. And why should he? More important was the conversation about the previous Sunday's soccer game with his colleague in the booth behind him. Rick had no doubt that the agent would be more attentive to the young lady who was next in line. He noticed her as well—long, dark hair and a slim figure—but was too tired to strike up a conversation. He left the cubicle pulling his carry-on bag, stopping only to glance back at the girl. As expected, the agent was checking her document carefully and carrying on a conversation, no doubt to be absolutely sure she wasn't a terrorist using a false passport.

Yes, he was back in Rome.

The various passport control lines merged into a human stream flowing in the direction of the baggage claim area. The Americans moved faster, thinking that after waiting so long in line to get their passports stamped, their bags would already be making turns around the carousels. The Italians, knowing better, took their time, many already talking on their cell phones. Rick stopped and pulled his own from the zippered pocket of his bag. He powered it up and was pleased to see, as promised back in Albuquerque, that it worked. The first message on the screen was a text.

BENVENUTO NIPOTE. UNABLE TO COME TO

AIRPORT. HAD TO MEET WITH A COUNTESS. SENT
A DRIVER. KEY WITH DOORMAN. BACI. ZIO PIERO.

Rick assumed the encounter with a countess had something to
do with his uncle's police work, but he couldn't be sure. Getting
to know Piero better was something he looked forward to on
this adventure, if that's what one could call picking up stakes and
leaving a decent job in Albuquerque to try his hand at working
in Italy. He could do the translation jobs anywhere that had an
Internet connection, so why not move back to the city of his
youth and get on the interpreting circuit? He kept contact with
a classmate of the American School of Rome who'd encouraged
Rick to give it a shot.

His mother, as usual, had mixed feelings—pleased that he
would be reconnecting with her native Italy, but worried about
his leaving a reliable job and jumping into the unknown. That
he would be staying, at least initially, with her brother helped
her accept what his father had said was inevitable.

"Rick is an adult," the elder Montoya had said. "He can make
his own decisions." Which was a very American reaction, as would
be expected, just as his mother's ambivalence was *molto* Italian.
Business as usual in the dual-national Montoya family. Since his
parents were now in Brazil, they couldn't complain about being
separated from their son, and his sister in Albuquerque encouraged
him to take the leap. She would miss him, but with a husband
and kids, she had enough family close by to keep her busy.

Rick checked the electronic boards at the end of each car-
ousel, passing flights arriving from Paris, Dakar, Bogota, and
London before finding his own. The Paris flight was the only
one with a moving belt, but it held only a few bags, and none
that remaining passengers wanted to claim. The suitcases moved
slowly around the loop, disappeared into the hole in the wall,
then reappeared with renewed hope that someone would take
pity and give them a home. He got to his aisle, recognizing
passengers from his plane. Most stared at the flaps covering the

opening of the conveyor, others talked on their cell phones, still others struggled to keep awake.

He pulled out his own phone again to check e-mails. One was from a friend who regretted missing the goodbye party at an Albuquerque watering hole. Just as well that he was out of town, Rick thought. The guy was a notoriously ugly drunk. Another was an inquiry about translating an article for a scientific journal. That was good, since it meant income, though Rick hated translating scientific jargon. A third asked if he'd arrived safely, and she couldn't wait to hear how he was adjusting to life in Rome. He was glad to be out of that relationship.

A loud buzzer and a flashing red light brought him back to the business at hand. The conveyor belt came to life and the people gathered around it began pushing ahead like lemmings nearing a cliff. His bags were among the first to appear, and he elbowed his way to the front, snatching them off under the annoyed looks of fellow travelers. He slung the duffel over his shoulder, pulled out the handles of the carry-on and roller suitcase, and headed for customs.

He went through the "nothing to declare" line without incident before emerging into the hall where lines of people waited along a railing. Like buyers at a cattle auction, they watched the herds of travelers who plodded their way along the line. Several held signs indicating businesses or travel agencies, some with just a name. Toward the end he spotted someone holding a hand-lettered sign: MONTOYA.

He hadn't expected a woman. When Rick owned up that he was Montoya, she shook his hand and introduced herself as Carmella Lamponi. The handshake was firm, as would befit someone who, despite her years, could easily be taken for a professional wrestler. Bleached, close-cropped hair added to the impression. She wore jeans, a Metallica sweatshirt, and red sneakers.

"These all your bags?" Without waiting for an answer she

continued. "Not much for someone who's moving here. The car's out there." She pointed to one of the far doors and started walking.

"I'm having other clothes sent." Rick tried to keep up. "How did you know I was moving here?"

"The *commissario* told me." They reached the door, which opened automatically, and she pointed toward a large, dark blue Alfa Romeo sitting in a space marked with a crossed-out P indicating a no parking zone. "It's that one." She pulled a key from her jeans, pressed it, and the trunk popped open.

"Have you, uh, worked for my uncle before?" He watched while she heaved his larger suitcase into the trunk with one hand, the duffel with the other.

"Put that little one in the backseat," she ordered, pointing at the carry-on bag, and got into the driver's seat.

Rick did as he was told and climbed into the passenger position. "I said—"

"I heard you. Have I worked for your uncle? He's my boss. One of many. I just do this to earn a little extra money when I'm not on duty."

"So you're a policewoman."

She glanced at him before pulling into the traffic. "You're pretty sharp, kid."

They were still inside the airport compound, passing the Leonardo Da Vinci statue, when Rick asked Carmella how she got into police work. It became immediately apparent that she was not averse to sharing her life story with someone she'd just met, even the nephew of her boss. Even the friendliest of New Mexicans would have waited a few encounters before getting into such details. As they passed slower vehicles, which included every other car on this section of *autostrada*, she talked. She spoke with the thick *Romanaccio* accent, almost a dialect, that he remembered hearing on the street when he was a kid. He had to concentrate to get it all.

Been working at the Polizia dello Stato for twenty five years. Just made sergeant. Married and divorced. Her former husband, a cop, was a bum. Her son, who just turned twenty and lived with her, was a student at the university. He was lazy and too often took after his father. She was trying to pound some sense into his thick skull.

Rick wondered if she meant it literally. An Italian mamma who was also a cop—definitely a formidable combination. By the time the car pulled onto Piero's street, she was describing her extended family, but was forced to stop when they reached the door to the building. She got out and opened the trunk.

"When you need a taxi, give me a call." She handed him a card. "My cop shifts change, so I may be available day or night."

"Thanks, Carmella." He reached into his pocket. "What do I owe you?"

"Your uncle got it." She slid into the car and drove off.

Rick pulled his hand out of the pocket, realizing it was just as well the fare was covered since he had forgotten to stop at an ATM at the airport to get euros. It was his second rookie error of the day.

Chapter Three

Rick knew from experience that the trick for beating jet lag was to stay awake the entire day and through the evening. No napping allowed, no matter how tired you got, and then you might be able to sleep through the night. Sometimes it worked, sometimes not. The rule of thumb held that a day was needed to recover from every time zone crossed, meaning it would take him about a week to get his body off a New Mexico clock and functioning on Rome time. He hoped it would be less. So far so good, but the bottle of expensive wine Uncle Piero ordered to celebrate his nephew's arrival wasn't going to keep Rick's eyes open.

Piero had picked a restaurant near his apartment, perhaps in consideration of his nephew's jet lag. *Il* Commissario was well known to the waitstaff, who struck the right balance between the familiarity given to a neighborhood regular and the deference required for a senior policeman. The warmth of their greeting to him this evening had been extended to Rick: they politely made a point of not staring at his cowboy boots. Piero was dressed more casually than during working hours—he wore a tattersall shirt and paisley tie under a blue blazer—but still looked like he'd just left his tailor. Rick, with a sweater and sports shirt, knew from previous encounters with his uncle that he could never match the man's fashion sense. He was sure that if he looked up the term *bella figura* in a dictionary there would be a picture of his Uncle Piero.

"Tell me about this countess, Zio. I was intrigued when I got your message on my phone this morning at the airport."

"It is a curious case, that of Count Zimbardi." Piero took a sip of the wine, a dark red from Piemonte. Unlike Carmella, the man spoke the Italian of a cultured university graduate, which he was. "It is understandable that his widow is frustrated with the lack of progress in the investigation. I am, as well. Let me start at the beginning."

Before he could begin, the pasta course arrived and conversation moved back to food. Rick had ordered his favorite local dish, *spaghetti alla gricia*, made with *pancetta*, olive oil, grated *pecorino* cheese, and black pepper. One bite and he felt at home. Piero had opted for lighter fare, a simple tomato soup. They wished each other *buon appetito* and started to eat. After a reasonable exchange of comments about the dishes, the policeman returned to the subject at hand.

"The night the body was found, the assumption was that Count Zimbardi was the victim of a mugging that went bad, since his wallet and watch were missing. But that could be what the attacker wanted us to think, and it wasn't a mugging at all. The back of his head hit the pavement, and that, according to the medical examiner, caused his death, though there were other bruises which indicated a struggle. We think he was surprised by the attacker but there was no way to know if he tried to flee the pursuer. He hadn't been sweating, according to the autopsy, but of course he was a count, so we don't know."

"I don't follow."

"Italian nobility. Because they have done no manual labor for so many generations, their sweat glands have become vestigial organs."

"Really? I didn't know that."

"It's a joke, Riccardo."

Rick hoped this instance of his gullibility would stay with

his uncle, and not be shared with anyone, especially not with Carmella.

Piero took a spoonful of soup and then patted his mouth with the napkin. "Anyway, three Swedish tourists found him on the Ponte Fabricio. Do you know where that is?"

"One of the oldest bridges over the Tiber, connecting the Tiberina Island with the east side of the river."

"You still know the city well."

"It's a hobby of mine, Roman history." He swallowed a forkful of the spaghetti. "From the way you described it, I get the sense that you think there may be more to it than a mugging."

"Perhaps. There are some puzzling aspects—the most curious one was the bus ride. We found a bus ticket in his pocket, and from the stamp it appears that he rode down the Lungotevere, got out at the island, and was struck down while crossing the river to get to the Teatro Marcello where he lived."

"So a regular route to get home."

"Not according to the countess. She said he never took the bus, always used his own driver or rode taxis. Didn't want to mix with the unwashed masses. His driver was off that night to celebrate the anniversary of the founding of the city. She said the count had called, as he always did, to tell her he'd be home soon, and she assumed he was going to take a taxi."

"So you don't know where he was before he got on the bus?"

"No. That is another puzzling aspect. And it is where you may come in."

Rick's fork paused in midair. "Me?"

"When I spoke to the countess this morning, she told me that her husband had been writing a book. Local history of some sort. Being an amateur historian is what you do when you're a wealthy count and don't have to worry about keeping a job. Apparently, the man kept a journal, and also had made lots of notes for the book. She thinks that something in the notes could help with the investigation."

"I don't understand how—"

Piero raised his hand. "The count received his education in England, thanks to an English mother. All his writing is in English."

"Aha. And you'd like me to read through all that."

"Precisely. The countess has agreed to pick up your fee. Of course if you are too busy with other clients…"

Rick grinned. "I can squeeze the job in somewhere. But I have to say that the count's little project sounds interesting. Reading his notes might be fun for me, since I consider myself an amateur historian as well. And if it helps solve the mystery of his murder, all the better."

"Excellent," said Piero. "She's expecting you tomorrow. You'll enjoy seeing the inside of the Teatro Marcello, though be prepared, the woman does not have an especially warm personality."

"I would expect nothing less of a countess. Roman nobility must maintain their standards, after all."

They finished their first course and the waiter appeared with the menus to make the choice of the *secondo*. Both men went with beef, though of differing types. Piero opted for a simple steak, cooked rare, though it would not be as rare as Rick's *carpaccio*. The waiter took the orders, filled their wineglasses, and disappeared.

"Did Sergeant Lamponi take good care of you?" Piero asked.

"Who?"

"Carmella Lamponi. She picked you up at the airport."

"Oh, Carmella. Of course. She did, and thank you again for covering the cost. An interesting woman."

"She gave you her life story, I suppose?"

"She recounted every sordid detail. I was exhausted when we got to your apartment, and I wasn't sure if it was from hearing her talk or fatigue from the flight."

"Could have been either, or both. She's part of the team working on the count's murder, by the way. So you may encounter her again."

Does that make me part of the team?

Piero took a piece of crusty bread from the basket on the table, broke off half, and ate it. "My sister called me this afternoon at the *questura*."

"Mamma is checking up on me already?"

"She wanted to be sure that her beloved son arrived safely, and didn't want to call you, in case you were napping."

Rick took the rest of the piece of bread. "And?"

Piero chuckled. "We know her well, don't we? She also said that she would like regular reports from me. Do I get the impression that you don't communicate with your mother as much as she would like?"

"To satisfy her I'd have to call twice a day. Minimum. I supposed she asked if I'd met any nice eligible girls yet."

"Not directly. But she did express hope that you would." He held up his hand again, this time as if taking a vow. "Fear not, nephew. I will not probe into your private life, and certainly not act as a spy for my sister. I have enough intrigue in my life through my work."

"I appreciate that, Uncle." He held up his glass. "To Mamma."

Piero raised his own. They took sips and reflected in silence on the subject of mothers and sisters. After a few moments Piero spoke.

"What are your plans for the next few days?"

"Well, my first priority is getting the word out that I've set up a translating and interpreting business here. I thought I'd start by calling some of my high school classmates. I'll also contact the embassy to get listed, since they get inquiries from Americans needing the service. One of my dad's old friends from when he worked here is running the embassy commercial office, so that should help. I translated some articles for professors at several universities here in Italy, when I was back in Albuquerque. I'll give them a call to be sure they know I'm now here in Rome. And I should start looking for a place to live. Your apartment is very comfortable, but I don't want to impose longer than I have to. Perhaps you know of a real estate agent."

"In fact, Riccardo, I have done better than that. Do you remember your Great Aunt Filomena?"

"Rings a bell. Was she at my grandparents' funeral?"

"She was. She owns a small apartment near the Piazza Navona, and the tenants just moved out. I mentioned to her that you are relocating to Rome and she would be overjoyed if you would take it. It's not very big, she says, but it sounds perfect for a bachelor. And she'll give you a family discount."

"When can I move in?"

He looked up. "Let's at least wait until we finish dinner. Our next course has arrived."

Piero's steak was of medium size, oozed juices, and sat alone on its plate. In front of Rick the waiter placed a plate of equal size, but it was covered with paper-thin pink beef over which equally thin slices of Parmigiano-Reggiano cheese were arranged. Drizzled olive oil completed the *carpaccio*.

Rick picked up his knife and fork. "This is something you can't find in America. Americans eat a lot of beef, but they always like to cook it." He pointed his fork at his uncle's steak. "Like that."

Piero noticed that his nephew had said "they" instead of "we," but said nothing.

• • ● ● •

Rick did not arrive at the Countess Zimbardi's apartment until the afternoon. He had woken up during the night and stayed awake for several hours, his body clinging to Mountain Time until it relented and let him fall back to sleep. At mid-morning he stumbled out of bed, showered, and shaved. He left his uncle's apartment near the Piazza del Popolo, and after finding an ATM, had an early stand-up lunch of a *panino* and a coffee at a nearby bar. The weather was pleasant, so he decided a walk would be good for both body and mind. Did he still know his way around the maze of streets of downtown Rome, where he had spent much of his adolescence? Even if he got lost, it would be good to re-immerse himself in the city.

He headed south in the general direction of the Teatro Marcello, toward the countess' apartment. Of the three streets that spread like fingers out of the Piazza del Popolo, he took Via di Ripetta, which stayed relatively straight until it changed its name to Via della Scrofa. At that point a jumble of other streets, most of them narrow, shot out of it from all angles. He started working his way through the urban confusion that was Rome's heart before bursting into Piazza Navona. Its oval shape followed the lines of Diocletian's original stadium, leaving Rick to wonder exactly where Aunt Filomena's apartment was. It was around here somewhere. This would certainly be a great part of Rome to live in, despite the dirt and chaos of traffic, both motorized and pedestrian.

Leaving the piazza he crossed the busy Corso Vittorio Emanuele, choking on bus fumes, and plunged into another hive of streets before reaching Campo dei Fiori where the market was already closing down for the day. He strode through the square, came to Piazza Farnese, walked past the French Embassy, and a few blocks later came out to the river. At a traffic light he crossed the Lungotevere, as always clogged with cars, and walked along its sidewalk under the trees. At this point both he and the Tiber were going south. On his right was the stone gorge built to contain a river that had periodically flooded the city for millennia. A few blocks more and he would be at his destination.

You still know your way around this town.

The sidewalk bent left, revealing the point of Tiberina Island, sitting like a ship that divided the current of the Tiber on either side of its prow. Piero had told him that it was over this island that the count had taken his final steps before being struck down on the Ponte Fabricio, within view of his residence. Rick walked to the middle of the pedestrian bridge, looked down at the ruins of an even older one, and tried to picture what could have happened that night. It wasn't easy, since the sun now shone brightly and the area bustled with people. He walked down off the bridge and waited patiently to traverse the busy street in front of the Teatro Marcello.

The security service person at the gate had his name, which he took as a good sign. He went as directed and eventually found himself in front of an ornate door in a long hallway. The guard must have called ahead, because when he knocked, the door opened immediately. Behind it was an older man dressed in the black uniform of a butler, his expression unreadable.

"Signor Montoya, please come in." He stepped aside and Rick entered.

They stood in a small rectangular hall decorated with modern paintings and a tall piece of sculpture so abstract that it was impossible to tell what, if anything, it represented. A set of double doors directly ahead opened to a living area with a similarly modern décor—black leather and metal in the seating, and swaths of framed color on the walls. In contrast to the art of the room, the window looked out on three tall, Corinthian columns, all that remained of the Temple of Apollo. Green bushes on the other side of Via Teatro di Marcello marked the side of the Campidoglio, the original Capitol Hill. It was a view and location that any Roman would die for, Rick thought, with some irony.

He turned to the man in black. "And you are?"

"Gonzalo." The response came with a slight bow, and before Rick could respond, he continued. "The countess was expecting you earlier this morning. Unfortunately, she had an appointment this afternoon, so she is not here to greet you. But she asked me to bring you into the count's study so that you could begin working. This way, please."

Rick had the impression that the man's speech had been

prepared and practiced ahead of time. Very professional, this Gonzalo fellow, and very butler-like, not that Rick had much experience with the profession. He followed the butler through one of the side doors, down a hallway past two closed doors, and up a narrow circular stairway. At the top was a room which also looked out over the ruins, but with only two small windows.

The count's study could not have contrasted more with the living room downstairs. Climbing the stairs was like stepping back several centuries. The chairs were leather—old, brown, cracking, and framed by wood rather than stainless steel. The desk looked like one found in the captain's cabin of a British ship of the line, and the framed prints of sailing vessels on the wall added to the impression. Continuing the maritime theme was a world globe, as high as the desk, which turned on a carved wood frame that was a work of art in itself. From the countries Rick was able to see, he estimated the globe to be from the nineteenth century. One entire wall was lined with books floor to ceiling. A carved wood step stool sat on the floor ready to help reach the upper shelves.

"This is quite an impressive room, Gonzalo."

The butler retained his professional demeanor, but Rick thought he noticed a touch of sadness in the man's face. "The count spent many hours here. He was proud that his great-great grandfather served in the British navy."

"I suppose he enjoyed sailing himself?"

"The ocean made him terribly seasick, unfortunately. It was one of the great disappointments in his life. He once told me that he'd tried out for crew at Eton, but even being on a small boat was too much for him." Gonzalo shuffled nervously, perhaps realizing that he had revealed too much of the personal life of his deceased employer. "The count's journals and notes are on the desk," he said rapidly. "If you need anything, Signor Montoya, press the button next to the desk lamp. It rings in my room."

Rick watched the butler descend the steps and disappear from sight. He walked to the bookshelf and ran his fingers along the spines of those at eye level, noticing that the titles appeared to be grouped by topic. Naval history was together, as were books on the Roman Empire, British royalty, classical architecture, the Renaissance, and art history. It was not all nonfiction. The count's tastes ran to classic authors, both British and Italian, in both languages. The titles helped form an image of the count in Rick's mind. For all he knew the man had never opened any of them, but if he were trying to impress people, the books would have been in the living room and not his private study. No, the count had been the real deal. He walked to the desk and sat down, the chair creaking as he pulled it forward.

Everything was stacked neatly in front of him. In one pile were files with loose papers, another contained notebooks like Rick used in his courses at the university, and a third had folders held together by elastic, like the archives of an old accountant. The countess, or perhaps Gonzalo, had conveniently provided a legal pad, what the count with his British background may have called foolscap. A tray of pens and sharpened pencils lay at the ready under the gooseneck lamp, and next to it a small, framed photograph of a pigeon.

He wondered about the pigeon, then pulled the chain on the lamp and started to read.

Two hours later he tore off four sheets of yellow paper, folded them, and put them into his pocket. After neatly arranging the papers he turned off the lamp and pressed the butler button. By the time he got to his feet and walked to the top of the stairs he could hear Gonzalo in the hallway of the floor below. He started down the stairs and found the man waiting for him at the bottom.

"I hope you found something that could shed light on the case, Signor Montoya."

"That will be for Commissario Fontana to decide. I will need to come back since there is more material to read, but I found something interesting. The count was doing historical research, if that's the way to describe it. Something about the streets of old Rome. Were you aware of that?"

They were standing in the hallway. Gonzalo made no move to invite him into the living room, but it would not have been his place to do so. They were both hired help, after all.

"Oh, yes. The streets project."

Rick waited for the butler to continue. He didn't.

"It wasn't clear from the count's notes exactly what the project involved. He was interviewing people and there was a lot about the history of various streets, but I couldn't figure out the purpose. Do you have any idea?"

"The count considered himself an amateur historian, and he decided to interview those persons who lived or worked on each of the streets within the city's historic center."

Rick nodded. "That makes sense, given all that I read about the people living on the street and how it had changed over the years."

"He hoped to put it all in a book. When do you think you'll return to finish? The countess will need to know." A touch of impatience had crept into Gonzalo's voice, as if he was uncomfortable standing in the hall chatting. Rick took the hint and moved toward the door. The butler stayed with him as he walked.

"I'll be back tomorrow afternoon about the same time." He reached for the door but stopped before his hand got to the handle. "One more question, Gonzalo, and I'll let you get back to your duties. In his journal the count mentioned a bar where he played cards with friends. Do you know where that is?"

There was no hesitation before answering. "That would be Il Tuffo. I'll give you the address."

Ten minutes later Rick crossed Via Florida and took the sidewalk that ran next to Via Torre Argentina, thinking about the origin of the two street names, neither of which had anything to do with the U.S. state or the South American country. Maybe the count was onto something with his interest in Roman streets. He looked down at the ruins of the *Area Sacra*, a group of temples unearthed during Mussolini's time. As always, it was surrounded by tourists who came to look at the ruins of the temples but were immediately distracted by the hundreds of feral cats that prowled among the stones. He stopped and noticed one which reminded him of Pupa, his family's cat when he was a kid. Perhaps it was time to get a cat himself, now that he was settling down for a while in Rome. There were certainly enough of them that needed homes. His phone rang.

"Montoya."

"Montoya, you *stronzo*. Do you think you can sneak into town without me finding out?"

Rick laughed. Art Verardo, his closest friend in high school.

"Arturo, do you think I want to ruin my first week in Rome by spending some of it with you?"

"Your point is well taken, Rick. But you'll have to get over it sometime. Are you free for dinner this evening?"

"I'll try to fit it into my busy schedule. Where?"

"Let's have a drink first. There's a place where a lot of our classmates sometimes gather. You never know, we might run into a few of them. It's called O'Shea's Pub."

● ● ● ● ●

Rick took a slug of his beer and looked around the room. "Couldn't our classmates have picked a classier place to hang out?"

He was dressed informally, in a lightweight sweater over a long-sleeved polo, blue jeans, and his more casual pair of cowboy boots. In contrast, Art Verardo wore a dark suit, white shirt, and striped tie. His concession to informality was a slight loosening of the neckwear.

"The decision behind the choice of this pub is veiled in the mists of time," answered Art, "and now nobody wants to take responsibility for it. On a certain level the place makes perfect sense. Centrally located. Serves cold beer for those of us with American roots and warm beer for the Brits. American and British sports on the TV. Or the *telly*, if you are so inclined. And the owner, Guido, is an American who is pretending to be Irish." He ran his fingers over the table and then wiped off their stickiness on a paper napkin. "But you have a point. Problem is, if we found someplace that's more elegant, it would be impossible to get everyone on board."

"Group inertia."

"Exactly. You recall how difficult it was to get everyone to agree on doing something in school?" Rick rolled his eyes, which Art took as a yes. "Well, it's even more difficult now that we are in our thirties. Jeez, can you believe how old we are?" He stared at his beer.

"I will take that as a rhetorical question."

A cheer came from a corner of the bar where four Brits were watching a soccer match. It had been played weeks earlier, and they knew the outcome, but it was the only game in town at the moment. Guido, at his place behind the bar, didn't look up from his yellow-covered paperback. The only other occupied table held two young British women drinking what looked like lemonade. They watched the British men, and Rick wondered if they had all come in together. He took another drink from his glass. The beer, a local lager, wasn't Alien Ale, but it wasn't bad.

"All right, Arturo, bring me up to date on our classmates living in Rome. Start with the guys. Actually, start with yourself."

Art sighed. "A most mundane tale is mine. I'm still working for the accounting firm, spending my days looking at numbers on a screen and evenings searching for something, anything, that can brighten my drab existence."

"Like women."

"Mostly women, in fact. You recall that my marriage to Marisa did not work out as planned. Clash of cultures. She thought that an accounting firm run by Americans would have heavy social obligations—cocktail parties, lavish dinners, that kind of thing. Clearly she had not met many accountants."

"She thought they were all like you."

"Perhaps that was it. She finally decided she couldn't make

it through another tax season, when she wouldn't see me for weeks." He contemplated taking another drink of his beer. "I heard she's engaged to a librarian."

"Lots of glitz in that profession, that's for sure. What about Beppo?"

"Beppo. Good question. We all assume he joined the family business and is making piles of money, but I haven't heard from him in years. Do you remember Francesco Oliveri?"

"Of course. The guy who crashed his father's Mercedes into the aqueduct."

"Right. He's a lawyer. Defends politicians under investigation for corruption."

"Sounds like a lucrative line of work. Did I hear that Reggie Lithgow was in Rome?"

"He was. After university in England he joined the Foreign Office like his father, and Rome was his first assignment. Married an Italian woman and they immediately transferred him to Paraguay. Or maybe it was Uruguay. One of the Guays."

The update went on through another round of beers, and Art removed his tie and put it in his pocket. They exhausted the boys and turned to the girls.

"I suppose you want to start with Lidia, since you two were inseparable that last year. She's here in Rome."

"My guess is that she's married. A beautiful girl like that would not have stayed single long."

Art took a deep breath and nodded slowly. "Actually, she is not married, though there may be a commitment and she seems very happy. We don't see much of her. She works in the Vatican press office."

"Really? That's interesting, and it makes sense. Her father was a newspaper editor and I remember her wanting to study journalism in college. Good for her." Rick was lost in thought for a moment before his friend spoke.

"You must remember Michela, the girl I dated when we were juniors?"

"How could I forget her? She broke her leg on our ski week in Ándalo and the *carabinieri* had to take her down the mountain on a snowcat. She was on crutches for a month afterward and as I recall took full advantage of her celebrity status."

"Right. Well now she lives in Milan and has a travel agency."

"Do you still…?"

"No, I never see her. She's married with three kids." He took another pull from his glass, looked past Rick toward the door, and lowered his voice. "All right, Rick. You do recall Giulia Livingston, don't you?"

"Giulia. Oh, yeah, the politician. Class president. Wore her hair in a ponytail, even though it was totally out of fashion. I think she dated that nerd whose name I don't recall. What's she up to?"

"She just walked in."

Rick groaned and turned around.

Giulia wore jeans and a sweater, both of which complemented her figure, not that any compliments were needed. Her hair was shoulder-length but pushed back over her ear on one side, exposing a pearl earring. The girl who was plain in high school was now anything but, and she knew it. She glanced at the table, noticed Rick, and her eyes went wide with surprise.

"Rick Montoya. Is that really you?"

What do you say when you meet someone you haven't seen in ages, and find that their appearance has changed so much for the better that said person is barely recognizable? If you say they look great, does it imply that previously they did not? Rick was now of the very sharp horns of this dilemma. Be neutral, he decided.

"Giulia, how good to see you,"

They exchanged air kisses and a warm hug, both clinging longer than might be expected under the circumstances. Rick tried to identify her perfume, without success.

She waved at Art. "*Ciao*, Arturo."

"*Ciao*, Giulia." Another hug and more air kisses. "What can I get you?"

"Nothing, I can't stay," she answered, but kept her eyes on Rick as she took the chair next to him, placing a small purse on the table.

"How long has it been, Giulia? Since we graduated?"

"I think so. I heard you moved here. Starting a translating business?"

"I've had a translating business for years back in Albuquerque, so I thought with the Internet I could do it here just as well as there, and I'd like to get into interpreting as well."

"How ya' gonna keep 'em down in New Mexico once they've seen Roma?"

"You can say that again. And what are you doing with your life?" His eyes moved to her left hand. "You're not married yet?"

She reached over and touched his ring finger. "No, and it appears that you are not either." Her hand stayed on his for a few seconds just as Art returned and set a glass in front of her.

Art leaned back in his chair and observed his two classmates. "You two seem to be reuniting well."

Rick didn't appear to have heard the comment. "And what do you do with your time, Giulia?"

The strand of hair got loose, and she carefully pushed it back behind her ear as Rick watched. "I have a tourism business. See the Forum, Rome by night, the Vatican museums, that sort of thing. Bus tours, small groups, VIP tours for one or two people. We do it all."

"Business good?"

"Almost too good. Sometimes I have trouble keeping up with the demand." She checked her watch. "In fact, I really should be leaving. One of my guides just quit and I have to fill in for him. I came in to meet a friend, but she doesn't seem to be here." She got to her feet, followed by Rick and Art. "Rick, it was so good to see you."

"It was wonderful seeing you, Giulia. Do you have a card? Perhaps we could get together and really catch up."

She pulled one from her purse, handed it to him, and took

one of his. After more hugs she hurried out the door, watched by the two men.

"That was fast," said Rick as he lowered himself into his chair.

"She's changed a bit since high school, hasn't she?"

"You could say that. But still very intense." He took a longer drink of the beer and inclined his head toward his friend. "Art, she didn't just drop in here by chance. This was all arranged, wasn't it?"

"Of course it was. You're already thinking like an Italian. Welcome back to Italy."

Chapter Four

The next morning, Rick was almost back to his normal early-rising schedule. Perhaps by the following day he would be up at dawn and do his run before breakfast. When he walked into the kitchen he found a note from his uncle saying that he could come to his office to brief him on what he'd found in the count's notes the previous afternoon. Though worded informally, it had the tone of an order, and next to it was Piero's business card with the address. Rick tucked it into his pants pocket, picked up the house keys, and left the apartment. He would have breakfast on the way.

At Piazza del Populo he took the left fork and started down Via del Babuino, reminding him of the count's project to cover the streets of downtown Rome. This one was named for one of the city's talking statues, where Romans for centuries had pasted anti-establishment notes as a form of anonymous protest. When he was almost to Piazza di Spagna the reclining figure of the *babuino* appeared, a few sticky notes attached to his torso. Rick didn't stop to read them, but continued until the street opened into the square, already filling with tourists taking pictures of the Spanish Steps. Just before the steps he walked into a pedestrian alley between the buildings, marked as a metro stop, and at the end of it into a tunnel. Rather than descend to the train tracks, he walked up the ramp to the left. There a series of ramps, escalators, and moving sidewalks carried him under the buildings, under the Villa Borghese park, and eventually returned him to the sunlight at the top of Via Veneto.

When he reached the sidewalk at the top of the escalator he stopped to look around. It was a section of Rome he knew well, having lived in a third-floor apartment on one of the side streets when he was in high school. It was an area of the city developed in the late nineteenth century, after Italy had finally been united and Rome became the capital of the new nation. Housing was needed for all the new government workers, politicians, and hangers-on, so apartment blocks had sprung up in place of villas and gardens. Would it have changed much since he lived there? Essentially, it would not. Businesses came and went—a shoe store becomes a jeweler, a restaurant gets new owners, a bank becomes a shoe store—but the basic commercial character of the neighborhood stays the same. The restaurants and *caffes* along Via Veneto were still there, their tables on the sidewalk next to the street, as were the large newspaper kiosks and trees shading all the sidewalk activity. Close your eyes and it's *la dolce vita* from the 1950s.

He eschewed the fancy coffee places on Via Veneto and turned left on Via Sardegna, remembering that all the cross streets in this section of town were named for regions of Italy. His breakfast destination was Lotti, a combination coffee bar, bakery, and in summer, *gelateria*. When he'd lived a few blocks away, his mother often sent him there, the only place in the neighborhood that sold fresh milk on Sundays. The aroma of fresh-baked *cornetti* and brewed coffee hit his senses as soon as he walked in the door. Most of the regulars were long gone, already at their desks in offices nearby, but a few were still standing at the bar in various stages of wakefulness. Rick paid the woman sitting at the cash register and was given a tiny slip. Using a small paper napkin, he picked up an almond *cornetto* from the bakery side before crossing over to the bar and ordering his *cappuccino*, leaving the slip under a euro coin. Three minutes later, alert after a jolt of caffeine, he was back on the street and walking the final two blocks to the police station, a yellow fascist-era structure squeezed among nineteenth-century architecture. He identified himself to the sergeant on duty and received a pass along with directions to Commissario Fontana's office.

Uncle Piero was at his desk talking on the phone when Rick pushed through the door left slightly ajar. The policeman waved his nephew toward a chair in front of the desk. Rick looked around a room which was bare of anything but the essentials needed to carry on police business. A meeting table with six chairs stood in one corner, two leather chairs sat in the other with a small table between them. On a wall next to the table stretched a large street map of the city, its surface perforated with tiny holes where pins had been stuck. There was no other decoration on the walls save the required photograph of the President of the Republic behind Piero's desk chair, flanked by the flags of Italy and the *Polizia dello Stato*. No filing cabinets; they would be somewhere else in the building. Rick saw no case displaying professional awards or photographs of the *commissario* with notable people, though Piero had been given plenty of both over the years. It was not his style, and such knickknacks could detract from the cold efficiency of the room.

Piero closed his conversation and put the phone in its cradle. "*Buon giorno*, Riccardo. Did you have breakfast?"

"I just stopped at Lotti. It hasn't changed."

"Thankfully." He leaned back in his chair and crossed his legs, exposing a bit of argyle sock. "I talked to Aunt Filomena this morning and told her you're very interested in taking the apartment. She is so pleased to have a relative living there that she has given you a rental rate that is way below the market. If I weren't already well located I would be tempted to take it myself. She will call the *portinaio* and tell him to let you in when you show up." He tore a sheet off a notepad and passed it to Rick. "Here's the address."

"I'll go see it when I leave here." Rick looked at the paper and put it in his pocket. "I didn't think finding a place to live would be so easy. I will send Filomena a box of chocolates."

"Don't send her chocolates, she lives in Perugia. Flowers would be better. Now tell me what you found from reading the count's journals, or whatever they are."

Rick pulled the notes from his jacket pocket and unfolded them on his lap. "I doubt if much will be helpful in finding out who killed him, but I found it all quite interesting, especially relating to the city of Rome. As the countess likely told you, her husband was working on a book about the streets of the *centro storico*, but from the material I read, it would have been a long time before he could have started writing it. What I saw were notes on his research, if that's the word for what he was doing."

"Could you get an idea of how he organized this research?"

"I know what you're getting at, Uncle. I had the same thought. Like what streets he had been working on at the time of his demise?"

"Precisely."

"Well, at first I thought he might be doing it alphabetically, since that would be the logical order for a book. Start with Via Acquasparta, let's say, and then go through other A streets in the area before moving on to the Bs. But I concluded he was doing it by sections, like marking off a grid and going from one street to another. That would make more sense, especially since streets in this city change names at every corner. Also it avoided his walking back and forth. I shuffled through the folders and found a city map, hoping it would be marked to show where he'd been, but unfortunately not. Still, as I read the notes I used the map to locate streets that he was writing about and found that, yes, he had been working on streets in the same small area. I can point them out."

Rick got to his feet and walked to the map on the wall. He pointed to a congested area of downtown Rome that nestled inside a double bend of the Tiber. "It was this section."

"Rione Ponte," said Piero, referring to one of the traditional divisions of the city. "Around the antiques shops on Via dei Coronari."

"Just south of that, Uncle. Between Via dei Coronari and Corso Vittorio Emanuele. As I remember from walking them, the streets there are as narrow and crooked as any part of town."

"You remember correctly. There was a murder down there a couple years ago, and when we had to close down the streets to examine the crime scene, traffic was stopped all the way from Piazza Navona to the river. What kind of information was in his notes?"

"Almost everything was information from people on the street. He asked them how the street had changed in the time they had lived or worked on it. He was meticulous about writing down the names of the people, even if they didn't give him much information. It was obvious that he always looked for the oldest person on each street, the one with the longest memory. If he found pensioners who had lived there all their lives, he hit the jackpot, and that happened on a couple streets. One woman went over every storefront on the street and was able to name each of the businesses that had been in it during her lifetime. A fruit vendor, then a bicycle repair shop, then a tobacco shop, then a florist, that kind of thing. The count had three pages of notes on what she told him."

"The man must have had a gift for getting people to open up to him."

"Or she just liked to talk.

"Did he put dates on his notes, I hope?"

"He did. Part of his British attention to detail, or fastidious-ness. So I know which streets he was working on just before he was murdered."

"Now we could be getting somewhere." Piero made a tent with his figures and placed his chin on it in thought. "We've got the streets where he spent the time just before his death, and even the names of the people he talked to. It might be a good idea for you to go down there and talk to them."

"Me?"

"Well, you're the one who has read the count's notes and knows what they told him. You are the logical person to talk to those people."

"But I'm not a policeman."

"That's all right. Sergeant Lamponi is, and she'll go with you."

It was not good news for Rick, as much as the idea of poking around in a murder investigation appealed to him. Carmella would continue to bend his ear about her personal problems. But it appeared that the *commissario* had made up his mind.

Piero picked up his desk phone and pressed a button. "Is Lamponi around? Good, send her to my office." He put down the phone and turned back to Rick as he opened a file on his desk. "This is the Count Zimbardi file, and at this point it doesn't have much except the initial crime scene reports, the autopsy, the bus ticket from his pocket, and the statements from the people who found the body as well as the first policemen on the scene. Perhaps what you find out will beef it up." He held his open hand a few inches above the file to show how much more could be filled in.

Piero was about to close the folder when Rick stopped him. "Is that the bus ticket?" The policeman nodded and passed over the plastic envelope. Rick held it up and studied both sides of the ticket inside. The time stamp was slightly blurred, but not enough to make it illegible. He passed it back as they heard a knock on the door.

"You wanted to see me, Commissario?" She peered in and noticed Rick, but waited for her superior to reply.

"Sergeant, you remember my nephew?"

Rick got to his feet and shook hands with the new arrival. No sweatshirt, jeans, and sneakers this time; she was smartly dressed in a well-pressed blue uniform with black shoes. It was as if this was the twin of the person who had picked Rick up at Fiumicino.

"*Salve*, Carmella."

"*Ciao*, Riccardo. You appear more rested than when I saw you last." She looked at Piero, perhaps wondering if she had been called in only to greet Rick.

"Sergeant, Riccardo is helping on the Zimbardi murder case. He's translated some materials that the count wrote in English, and they give clues to where the man spent his last days. The count was working on a project about the history of streets, and he was interviewing people who lived and worked on those streets. I want you to go talk to those people."

"Yes, Sir."

"And Riccardo will go with you. He has all the notes on what the people told the count."

Was she resentful that he would be tagging along? Rick watched for a reaction from Carmella and couldn't detect any. He pulled out his notes, walked to the map, and pointed. "The count's most recent entries had him in this part of the city. Specifically, on these streets. His notes were dated, but he may have written them a day or two after he visited the locations. From the way they were written I sense that he took informal notes when he was talking to people and later sat down at home and cleaned them up. So, what I read were not first drafts."

"Still," said Piero, "he was in the general area just before he was killed, even if you don't know exactly which streets."

"I'm quite sure which street it was where he spent those last few days, Uncle."

"So go down and see what you can find out. Sergeant, you're working on the Palmeri case, aren't you?"

"Yes, but we'll be arresting him this afternoon."

"Good. Tomorrow morning?" The *commissario* looked from one face to another.

"Yes, Sir," said Rick and Carmella in unison.

Fifteen minutes later Rick was on Via Buoncompagni waiting for a bus to take him down the hill into the flat center of the city where the apartment was located. The time and place of the next morning's rendezvous with Carmella had been set, and he hoped that by then, after reading more of the count's notes, they would have people to seek out. He mulled over the meeting with his uncle. It was almost as if the man was looking for a way to get him into police work through the side door, just as he had suspected. Wouldn't Mamma love that, her son following in the footsteps of her brother? Not really.

The bus he took roared down the street, veering left sharply to get through a yellow light and onto Via Veneto, forcing all the passengers to grab seats, poles, or each other to keep from falling over. As it passed the American Embassy, Rick worked his way through the crowd to punch his ticket on the boxed machine attached to one of the upright poles. The passengers around him gazed out through the dirty windows or talked on cell phones. The bus made more stops for people getting on and off, but by the time it turned onto the Corso, the city's longest and straightest street, it was almost full and Rick had been squeezed toward the front. Just as well, he was getting close to his stop. He was staring out at those walking along the sidewalk, going almost as fast as the bus, when he felt a nudge near his waist. When it happened again he turned to see a short man working his way toward the door. Rick reached down and realized his wallet was missing. Another rookie mistake. The busiest bus route in the city, he should have been more vigilant.

"Hey!" he called out instinctively in English.

The man kept going toward the door but dropped the wallet on the floor of the bus. In a split second he was out on the street, timing his caper perfectly for when the doors of the bus opened. A gray-haired woman picked up the wallet and passed it to Rick who was trying to get to the door.

"You should be more careful, young man," she said in Italian. "These thieves are everywhere. Haven't you ever been on a bus before?" The way she talked, it was Rick's fault. She looked down, noticed his cowboy boots, and her expression changed from scolding to derision. "Ah, a tourist," she said to people around them, as if that explained everything. "No wonder."

Rick kept his mouth shut. No use making the situation more embarrassing by responding in Italian. Thankfully, his stop was coming up and he squeezed his way forward under the shaking heads of the Roman strap-hangers. First learning that he would be working with Carmella and now this. If those were the worst things to happen to him this day, he was fortunate. He stepped onto the street and started walking toward the apartment when his cell phone rang. Not a number he was familiar with, but then he was in a new city now. He pressed the button and put it to his ear.

"Montoya."

"Reek! I need your help!"

Rick looked at the phone in his hand and wished it wasn't his. The words had been spoken in Spanish, with a *porteño* accent he remembered all too well. How the hell did Juan Alberto, the crazy Argentine, get my number? Does he know I'm in Rome? Good God, is *he* in Rome?

Perhaps things can get worse after all.

• ● ● ● •

Rick was still recovering from his conversation with Juan Alberto Sanguinetti when he pushed open the door to a bar just off Piazza Navona. It was early for a second coffee, but he needed something to help sort out what his old friend had said. Rick mentally put quotation marks around the word *friend* as he recalled those times, years earlier, on the campus of the University of New Mexico. They had met not on campus during class hours but one night in a bar on Central Avenue, which would be expected since Juan Alberto didn't spend much time in class. That evening the Argentine was with three women, one of whom knew Rick, and she had waved him over to their table. Introductions were made, and Rick not only met Juan Alberto, but the two other ladies, one of whom he ended up dating, something Juan Alberto took credit for during the rest of the semester. In Juan Alberto's opinion, said introduction—analogous to removing a thorn from Rick's paw—entitled him to seek Rick's help whenever needed, which turned out to be with some frequency.

This one-sided relationship ended only when Juan Alberto's academic luck ran out. Even with the hefty out-of-state tuition that Juan Alberto's father was sending from Buenos Aires, the university could not justify keeping someone on the books who did not understand that it was an institution of higher learning. Unfortunately for Juan Alberto, a letter to this effect was sent to his parents, squashing his plan to stay on in Albuquerque and use the tuition money to buy a part ownership of a massage parlor. Reluctantly he was driven to the airport by his *buen amigo* Rick Montoya to board a plane for the southern hemisphere. After walking him through the check-in process—Juan Alberto had never truly mastered the English language—Rick assumed he was seeing the last of Juan Alberto Sanguinetti.

Now he found that his assumption was incorrect.

He ordered a double espresso.

The convoluted tale that Juan Alberto had given over the phone was all too typical of schemes he had been involved in back in New Mexico. The Argentine, it appeared, had not changed, except perhaps for the worse. He told Rick that in Buenos Aires he had talked a local wine producer into sending him to Rome to get the exclusive contract from the Vatican to buy Argentine wines. The pope was a local guy, after all, and he would certainly want to serve his home wines for official entertaining. Neither Juan Alberto nor his employers knew that popes do not do any official entertaining, but that was not the only problem with Juan Alberto's scheme. He sold himself as having connections to the pope's Argentine family, but those connections were less than flimsy. They were nonexistent. He also claimed to be fluent in Italian. His name was Sanguinetti, what could be more Italian? Unfortunately, his Italian was even worse than his English, and it was his great-grandfather who had been born in the Old Country. Juan Alberto figured that he could waltz into the Vatican, flash some of his Latin charm, and land a contract with ease. Instead, he found that the Curia was impenetrable. After several attempts to get a *pie* in the *puerta,* Juan Alberto decided to call his old buddy Rick Montoya. A female acquaintance from his days in New Mexico had mentioned in an e-mail that Rick was moving to Rome. Unfortunately, Rick's cell phone number had remained the same from his college days.

As he stirred double sugar into his double coffee, Rick cursed the FCC for allowing him to keep his number when he had changed plans a few years earlier. Then he cursed the girl who had tipped off Juan Alberto he was moving to Rome. When he was finished cursing, and had finished half his coffee, he returned to Juan Alberto's problem. Could he be of any help? Who did he know in the Vatican? The answer hit him about the same second as the caffeine, both serving to widen his eyes.

Lidia.

Art said that she worked in the Vatican press office. It would be great to see her again, and since Art said she wasn't married, it would be an easy way to say hello without complications. Art had hinted she was in some kind of relationship, so he would tread carefully. Asking for help on behalf of Juan Alberto would be a good way to do it, so he wouldn't look so obvious. And who knows, she might even suggest someone to at least talk to Juan Alberto, thereby allowing Rick to slip off the hook. I did that favor for you, Juan Alberto, so good luck and *hasta luego.* He drained his cup, walked happily out to the street, and started in the direction of his new abode.

Five minutes later he was pressing the bell on a massive set of wooden doors. The building was old, Rick guessed seventeenth century, but it could have been older. The doors—really gates—were large enough to allow vehicles to enter, carriages when it was built and now cars. That meant that there was room inside for parking, though Rick long ago decided that he would not be getting a car himself. He would walk or use public transportation to get around Rome. As if wanting to confirm his decision, the traffic roared so loudly behind him that he wondered if the *portiere* would be able to hear his ring. Exhaust from the buses hovered with him against the door, like it was also trying to get off the street. He was ready to push the bell again when a tiny door opened well below eye level. A face, or part of one, looked warily out through it.

"Yes?"

It felt like getting into a speakeasy or exclusive private club. Should his uncle have given him the password? He bent over and spoke through the opening. "I am Riccardo Montoya, here to see my aunt's apartment."

"Anybody with you?" asked the face.

"Just me."

The hole snapped shut and Rick heard a click. A person-sized door, cut into one of the gates, swung open with a creak and Rick stepped through it into the courtyard. The *portiere* appeared from behind the door as it swung shut. The face Rick had seen through the opening was the front of a round head, attached to an equally round body. The entire figure, dressed in blue overalls, came up to Rick's chin. The courtyard was large enough for a horse and carriage to make a U-turn, but now it held four cars parked along the walls. The thick gates, and the building itself, lowered the traffic noise by dozens of decibels, and the air was noticeably clearer. Above them was the open sky, at the moment beginning to cloud up. Below it, windows looked down on the courtyard on all four sides and he wondered if his great aunt's apartment was one of those facing the street. He hoped not.

As Rick looked up, the other man surveyed him with squinted eyes, but they widened when they got to Rick's cowboy boots.

"The *signora* said you were an American. Are you a cowboy?"

A curious thing to ask. Rick had been on horses a few times at his uncles' northern New Mexico ranches. Surely that was enough to call himself a cowboy. "You might say that. I come from New Mexico, where Billy the Kid was shot by Pat Garrett. And what is your name?"

The cowboy connection made such a strong impression that the man was at a loss for words. Finally he found his voice. "I, uh, am Giorgio." He stood frozen in his place until Rick extended his hand.

"My pleasure, Giorgio. Can we go to the apartment now?"

"Oh, yes, of course." He hurried off toward the rear of the courtyard with Rick following behind him taking one step for each of Giorgio's two. They stopped at a dutch door where the small man opened the top part and reached around to retrieve a key off a set of hooks. It was the typical Italian *portiere* hovel, with a wood desk, beat-up sofa facing a tiny TV set, and tools hanging on the wall as well as spread across the desk. Rick could not help noticing that the walls were covered with movie photos, all of them westerns and mostly Sergio Leone spaghetti westerns. Clint Eastwood, with his trademark wrinkled stogie, had top billing. Did Giorgio know that the series had been filmed mostly in Europe? One thing for sure, Rick had an important ally in the building even before moving in, and he had his cowboy boots to thank for it.

They walked to an elevator and took it to the top of three floors where they stepped into a tiny hallway with two doors. Giorgio fumbled with the key, unlocked one of the doors, and led the way with a polite *"faccio strada?"* Rick followed him into semi-darkness. The *portiere* switched on a bare ceiling light and hurried to each of the windows, opening them and then pushing its set of hinged shutters. They banged against the outside wall and light streamed into the room, which was a combination living and dining area. Dark brown beams that looked like they could have been original ran across the ceiling, but in Italy one never knew what was old and what was new. The floor was gray tile that clicked under Rick's cowboy boots, making him glad that he was on the top floor and not the apartment underneath.

He had not thought to ask his uncle about furnishings, and was pleasantly surprised to find a few pieces of furniture which didn't look all that bad. Certainly good enough for a start. Under the ceiling lamp sat a round wood dining table with four chairs, and on the other side of the small room were two chairs and a matching sofa, with a floor lamp between them. He walked to the windows and found that one side looked down on the courtyard while the other looked over the tiled roof of the lower building next door. Other taller buildings, including some church domes, were visible in the distance.

"The kitchen is here," said Giorgio, pointing his arm back in the direction of the door. It was a small, galley layout, what one of Rick's more colorful American aunts would have called a one-butt kitchen. No dishwasher, as expected, but instead the typical European drying rack over the sink. Under one section of the counter was a small refrigerator, also typical since Italians tended to shop daily. A stove was wedged next to it, one that could barely fit a medium-sized chicken, topped by two burners. All in all, perfect for Rick's needs.

"The bedroom and bathroom are this way." Giorgio gestured with almost a bow. The bedroom furnishings consisted of a bed and an armoire which took up almost all the floor space. Next to it was a bathroom with, to Rick's relief, a shower in the corner. He never took baths. The final surprise was a small, bare room overlooking the courtyard, that Rick decided would be his office. There was just enough space for a desk.

"The building has WiFi," said Giorgio, as if reading Rick's mind.

"Thank you, Giorgio. I'll be moving in as soon as I can buy sheets and towels."

• ● ● ● •

"You are Signor Montoya?" The door today had been opened by the countess herself, who looked Rick up and down as if he was dressed in overalls. The gatekeeper to the building must have called ahead, so who else would be ringing her doorbell? And this had to be the countess, looking like someone sent from Central Casting for the part: gray head, owlish face, a thin string of pearls, reading glasses hanging from a gold chain, knit dress, and sensible shoes.

"Yes, Countess. My pleasure." He extended his hand, which was taken with a tinge of reluctance. "I should be able to finish reading your husband's notes today," he said. "And I can make my report to Commissario Fontana."

She stepped back to allow him to enter, then closed the door. "What have you found so far?" She crossed her arms across her chest and squinted at Rick, like he was the plumber who had come to fix a clogged drain. She probably treated all tradesmen the same way. Was she regretting her decision to tell the police about the count's journals? Or was she naturally cranky?

"There was considerable information about where the count had been in the days before he died. Whether that has any relevance to the investigation is something the *commissario* will have to evaluate." He was sounding like a bureaucrat.

She closed her eyes for a moment, shook her head, and gestured toward to hall. "Well, have at it. You know the way up to the count's study. You can let yourself out when you're finished." She turned and walked off.

Rick went down the hallway and climbed the stairs into the study. It was as he had left it, down to the folders on the desk which held strips of paper marking where he had left off. After giving the globe a spin he pulled off his jacket, settled into the chair, and went to work. The previous day he had read through all the street notes, so today he started with the journal. It was really a diary, but that word brought the image of a young girl writing in her pink bedroom. Gentlemen like the count wrote journals, not diaries, but the purpose was the same, if not the content. Count Zimbardi composed in a stilted first-person style, like something a nineteenth-century British chronicler would have written, heavy on impressions and flowery descriptions. It matched the handwriting, also something from a previous era. The journal was different from the notes he had taken from his interviews with people on the streets, which were detailed but factual, but Rick found each interesting in its own way. The journal covered more than the notes about the street research, as would be expected, including mention of what appeared to be frequent evenings at Il Tuffo, the bar that Gonzalo, the butler, had said was a favorite hangout for the count.

Lady luck was sitting on my shoulder this evening. I surprised even myself with my prowess, but it was assisted by the plethora of fortunate card combinations that frequently were sent my way by the dealer. A round of drinks was expected after such success, and I did not disappoint my companions.

So the count had a good night. The bar, as Rick had found after getting the address from Gonzalo, was in the general neighborhood of the streets research. Significant? Probably not. Rick turned the pages of the journal, reading the count's observations on what he had seen, read, and eaten during each day. Most of it was mundane, making him wonder why the count would consider it important enough to put to paper. Who did he think would read this stuff? Perhaps that question wasn't important; keeping a journal was simply something nobility did, even obscure Roman nobility. As he got closer to the fateful day, Rick found himself skimming, but two weeks before the count's demise, an entry jumped out.

This project has brought me the utmost satisfaction, but today I am most disturbed. It was certainly expected, when I began this journey into the past, that examples of Roman skullduggery would emerge from my research. But my assumption was that anything I unearthed of that nature would be relatively benign or from decades past. If my suspicions are correct, that does not, in one instance at least, appear to be the case.

Bingo. Rick copied it into his notes and read on, but was disappointed to find nothing more referencing the count's suspicions. Perhaps, after tantalizing his future reader—if indeed he expected someone to read the journal someday—the man didn't want to write more until he had reached a conclusion himself. Rick went back to the notes and tried to pinpoint what streets the count had been prowling the week of his journal entry, and narrowed it down to two. Then he went back to the journal and re-read entries for the weeks previous to the mention of the skullduggery. In doing so he saw a name that he hadn't noticed before. The count had lunched with someone named Girolamo, and Rick had focused on the descriptions of the food and wine when he'd read it the first time. Who was Girolamo?

He leaned back in the chair, which was surprisingly comfortable, and clasped his hands behind his head. Outside the small window he could see one wispy cloud floating over the ruins in the direction of the Campidoglio and Rome's city hall. He had finished reading the count's notes and journal, and now had a sense of the man that he would try to describe to his uncle. Snobbish? Certainly, but in contrast, he enjoyed his game of cards in what had to be a neighborhood bar where the clientele would not be composed of nobility. The interest in history was stereotypically *noblesse oblige*, but he could have done worse things with his time. If he talked the way he wrote, his speech would have been affected, and undoubtedly include a British upper-class accent when he spoke English. The image Rick conjured up of Count Umberto Zimbardi was a man of hefty girth who wore vests and oxblood oxfords with his tweed suits, and was thinning on top. He looked around the study to see if there were any photographs of the deceased to see if he had guessed correctly, but found only framed pictures of ships and that one pigeon.

He was going to press the butler button but stopped himself, getting up from the desk after arranging the papers neatly on its surface. Folding his notes and putting them in his pocket, he walked to the stairs and descended to the hallway below. He was almost to the doorway when he heard the voice of Countess Zimbardi. She had heard his boots on the uncarpeted hallway floor.

"Have you finished, young man? It certainly took you long enough."

Rick looked into the living room but did not enter. She was sitting in a chair that must have been her regular reading place, since a floor lamp stood next to it and an open book, spine up, lay on the table under it. She eyed him over the half-glasses. There was no invitation to sit down, or even to enter the room. He stood at the doorway and noticed that she was dressed differently than when he arrived. The knit dress had been replaced by an almost florescent silk skirt and dark blouse, and in place of the sensible shoes were a pair with heels that were anything but sensible for walking around the city. A blush of pink highlighted her cheeks, along with a lipstick color more appropriate for a young princess than an aging countess. The woman had somewhere to go and Rick was keeping her from it.

"Yes, Countess, I've gone through all the notes from his project and also his journal."

"Well?"

"Nothing jumped out to me as significant, but I will tell Commissario Fontana what I've read and he will decide. Perhaps the most important information concerns where the count was doing his research in those final weeks. It was in the Ponte section of the city."

"Which is nowhere near where he was killed."

"That may be, but I'm sure the police will want to check every possibility."

She made a circular motion with her hand. "Yes, like they have done already. Well, you go and report to your policeman. As if it will help." She picked up her book and adjusted her glasses as if he had disappeared.

Rick started toward the door but turned after one step. "Countess, in your husband's journal he mentions someone named Girolamo. Can you tell me who he is? The *commissario* will ask."

The question got her attention. She closed the book and placed it on her lap while giving Rick a stony stare. "I don't see how Girolamo could be of interest to him," she said quickly. After adjusting the hem of her skirt to cover her knee, she took a breath and spoke more deliberately. "Girolamo Syms-Mulford was the count's closest friend. They knew each other since they were in school together in England. He is a very distinguished historian. I don't think he would be of any help in the case."

That would be for Piero to decide, Rick thought. "Thank you, Countess." He waited for a reply, and when none came, he walked to the door and let himself out, glad he was done with Countess Zimbardi.

When he crossed Via Arenula a few minutes later he was still thinking about the countess' reaction to the mention of Girolamo Syms-Mulford. From the name alone he could guess that the man was of dual nationality, just like the count. A distinguished historian, she had said. Perhaps Girolamo shared the count's interest in the history of Roman streets and the friends had talked about it. He stopped in front of the faded frescoes of Palazzo Spada and pulled out his cell phone. The number was answered on the third ring.

"Good afternoon, Riccardo. I hope you are calling to tell me about some dramatic revelation gleaned from your afternoon reading of the count's papers."

"No smoking gun, Zio, not even a warm one. But there may be someone to interview who might shed light on the count's final days." He told Piero about Girolamo Syms-Mulford, had to repeat the name twice and then spell it out so his uncle could write it down.

"I'll run the name, but I agree that it is someone to talk to. Since the man may be more British than Italian, you should be the one to do the interview."

"Me?" It was a question he had been asking frequently.

"Why not? I'm busy with another case, and I suspect he's not the kind of person who would open up to Sergeant Lamponi. You can gain his confidence by speaking English."

His uncle had a point about Carmella. A moped sped by Rick with a high whine, so he waited to reply. "I'd be glad to do it."

"*Va bene*. When we locate him we'll call ahead to say a police representative will be doing the interview."

This was getting interesting. He was becoming a cop without being a cop. "I was thinking about something else, Zio. I'm close to the bar where the count used to play cards. This might be a good time to drop in. Some of the men he knew might be there at this hour."

There was no immediate reply and Rick thought he might have gone too far. Just when it was getting interesting. Finally his uncle spoke.

"Sorry, someone stuck his head in the door. Yes, that sounds like a good idea."

"How can I get them to talk, since I'm not with the police?"

"You'll figure something out."

Chapter Five

The Bar Il Tuffo was squeezed between two ancient buildings a few blocks from where the count had been doing his research. The street was typical of downtown Rome, luxurious residences on the upper floors, seedy businesses at the ground level, and a general aura of decadence. It was just what the rich residents preferred—keep opulence inside the walls. Darkness had set in, and Rick could see the highly decorated ceilings of the higher floors where curtains had not yet been drawn. Like all streets in the downtown, this one had no sidewalk, and he walked down the center, moving aside for the occasional passing car. The pavement had begun to wear down in spots, exposing rectangular bricks that had been put down centuries earlier to cover older stone. Rome was a city of layers.

It was also a city of small, stuffy bars where working people had their coffee in the morning and male pensioners gathered in the afternoons and evenings to gossip and play cards. It occurred to Rick that there could be a municipal ordinance that required such an establishment when a neighborhood reached a specified number of inhabitants. Il Tuffo certainly fit the criteria. The windows were small and looked like they hadn't been washed in months. The glass door was plastered with announcements of concerts, art exhibits, and other events taking place in the area, most of them already past. Rick pushed it open and entered. There could not have been a more obvious contrast to the opulent residence of Count Zimbardi.

Smoking had been banned in such places for years, but one would not guess it after seeing the dingy walls and ceiling. The single room was the size of the count's study, though larger in cubic feet, thanks to high ceilings. Cobwebs hanging from two fans indicated they had not been used, or cleaned, in some time. A plain wood bar ran the length of the wall on Rick's left, and on the right were four tables. By most measures for such institutions, the place was packed. Two tables of the four lining the right side of the long room were full, and several men stood at the bar. The men at the tables displayed graying or pink heads, a good sign that he might encounter the count's cronies. Those at the bar were younger, but not by much. Everyone was dressed in drab browns and blacks, clothing that was in style decades earlier, though for their generation it was still in fashion.

The sole sartorial exception was one guy at the bar who looked like he'd just stepped off the stage of a vaudeville revue. He sported light gray slacks, a red blazer, and a pink tie that looked even brighter than it was thanks to a contrasting black shirt. Complementing the outfit was a pair of wrap-around sunglasses, hardly a necessity in the dim atmosphere of the establishment. Rick looked at the man in amazement before thinking that he looked vaguely familiar. The man looked at Rick and gave him a slight bow.

"Signor Montoya, what brings you to Il Tuffo?"

"Gonzalo?"

Another bow. "It is I."

"But you look…different."

Gonzalo spread his hands in an Italian gesture typically translated as "What can I say?"

"What can I say?" he said. "It's my day off, and after dressing in that black butler suit all week, I always need a bit of a change."

"Okay." Rick was unable to come up with anything more profound.

"Are you simply in need of a coffee, Signor Montoya, or is there something more to your appearance here?" Rick could not see his eyes, thanks to the dark glasses, but the edges of his mouth turned up slightly, indicating some level of mirth.

"Well, I—"

"You are working with the police. I assume that's why you've turned up in Il Tuffo. Am I wrong?"

"You are correct, Gonzalo. This place could be a trove of useful insights into the behavior of the count, so when you told me about it I decided to drop by. Your presence here is an extra bonus, since we don't get to chat at the *palazzo*. Can I buy you something to drink?"

He signaled to the woman behind the bar, who lumbered over to them. Rick wondered if she got her job so that the wives of the pensioners would not have an excuse to nag at their husbands for spending too much time at Il Tuffo. She wiped her hands on a dirty rag as she waited for the order.

"Thank you, Signor Montoya, I'll just have another *arranciata*. I don't drink alcohol."

Rick ordered Gonzalo's orange drink and an espresso for himself.

"I must ask you about the count. Do you have any thoughts about why he was killed?"

Gonzalo poured the rest of his drink from can to glass. "I've thought a great deal about that, Signor Montoya, and have come to no firm conclusion. The circumstances of his death were strange, to say the least."

Another can of orange soda arrived along with Rick's coffee.

"In what way?"

"Why was he on that bridge at that time of night? It was very peculiar behavior for the count. He went out by himself frequently, mainly to play cards with his friends." He glanced at one of the two tables. "But why he was crossing Tiburina Island that night is to me a mystery."

Rick looked at the bottles behind the bar as he took his first, and last, sip of coffee, and a thought occurred to him. "Did the count ever…?"

"He didn't hate wine, if that's what you're getting at. Nor did he turn down the occasional spirit. Despite his ties with England, he liked Jack Daniels bourbon, from your part of the world, Signor Montoya."

Rick was tempted to point out that Jack Daniels was in fact not a bourbon but a sour mash whiskey, the error being a pet peeve of his, but he let it go in the interest of keeping Gonzalo on his side in the investigation. The man could be very helpful, no matter how he dressed.

Rick turned his attention back to the card tables. "Do you think any of these men knew the count?"

"I'm sure of it. Let me introduce you." He looked down at Rick's cowboy boots. "I'll make up something to give you cover."

Gonzalo took his glass, still half full, and walked with Rick to the tables. There was a lull in the action, the players studying their cards and emitting noncommittal grunts. The butler coughed to get their attention. It worked for three of the men, who looked up with wary curiosity.

"Looking sharp tonight, Gonzalo."

The comment elicited chuckles from the others, but Gonzalo ignored it.

"*Signori*, I present to you Signor Montoya, a distant relative of Count Zimbardi, visiting from America."

Both tables went silent and Rick wondered if this had been a good idea to pose as a relative. The count could have left them all with a bad taste in their collective mouths, a parting insult or debt unpaid. "I'll cover the pot tomorrow," he might have said, and then ended up on the bridge that night, leaving his card-playing cronies in the lurch. They stared at Rick with solemn faces and he started planning his escape route. The door wasn't that far, and given their ages, he knew he was quicker than any of them.

The one who had commented on Gonzalo's attire got to his feet, walked to Rick, and wrapped him in a warm hug. One by one the others rose and did the same, each mumbling something during the embrace. "One of the greats." "We still miss him." "A true gentleman." On it went until they had all offered condolences. Then, abandoning their cards, they silently pulled chairs up to the table for Rick and Gonzalo to join them.

"They're waiting for you to buy a round," Gonzalo whispered in Rick's ear when they'd sat down. "It's what they miss most about the count."

Rick dutifully waved his finger in a circle at the barmaid who had been watching the scene. She gave him a toothy grin and started pouring.

"We didn't know the count had any relatives in America," said the man sitting close to Rick. He was studying Rick's footwear.

"Maybe he doesn't speak Italian, Tino," said another.

"I do speak Italian," Rick responded, eliciting murmurs of approval from the group. "I was hoping you could tell me more about the count. Did he come here often?"

The tray arrived and its small glasses were distributed to the gathering. Wishes of good health followed, and the first man, who seemed to have an unstated leadership role in the group, answered.

"The count was a regular, all right. Not every night, of course, but you could find him here most of the time. Which didn't speak well of the countess." He chuckled and then realized what he'd said. "I didn't mean any disrespect to her, of course."

"None taken," Rick assured. "He liked playing cards, it appeared."

A man whose few strands of gray hair were combed carefully over his bald spot spoke, his voice creaky. "The count didn't just like cards, he loved them. Gambling was his passion, and not just with cards."

"So I understand," Rick said, hoping that the acknowledgement would encourage them to open up about the subject. It did.

Comb-over turned to the group. "Do you remember that time when he bet Sandro that the next person to walk into the bar would order a *grappa*?" They nodded in unison, lost in the sweet nostalgia of the memory.

They all started taking turns telling Rick about the count.

"Many days he was the last one to leave. Gilda had to throw him out." Everyone looked at the barmaid, who was busy moving dirt around on the counter.

"They should have set up a cot for him in the back room."

"When he wasn't here, he was at the track."

The de facto leader held up his hand. "*Ragazzi*, we shouldn't be recounting such things about the count to his relative, distant as he might be."

Gonzalo stepped in. "It's quite all right, Signor Montoya is aware that the count was a colorful character, aren't you, Signor Montoya?" The butler had apparently decided to jump into the game with both feet.

"Yes, Gonzalo, certainly. I'd like to hear about him, warts and all."

One of the men, who had been quiet up to then, cleared his throat. Three of the others, who were about to make a contribution, stopped in deference and waited for him to speak. Whereas the others wore jackets and sweaters, and went tie-less, this gentleman had a suit and tie, though in contrast to Gonzalo, the colors were subdued. His hair had left him years earlier, and his squinted eyes were barely visible through thick glasses. When he finally spoke he sounded like someone on the TV true crime shows, whose face is blocked out and voice electronically modified to hide his identity. Everyone leaned closer.

"Signor Montoya," the man began, "Count Zimbardi was a man of many facets, a man who lived different lives at the same time. He was of noble blood, and did not try to hide that fact, not that he could if he'd wanted to. He was the count and that was that. But he wore his nobility with a certain reluctance. I thought he wished he could shed it, like changing out of a tuxedo into something more casual, but keeping the formal wear hung in the closet for when needed. Here he insisted we call him Umberto, didn't he?"

The others at the table nodded, but kept silent. Rick noticed that the drinks were getting low, and hoped that the protocol didn't require another round. The man took a drink from his glass and continued.

"It is true that the count enjoyed a wager of any type. Alas, it cannot be said that he was skilled in games of chance; he was always certain that the next wager, unlike the last, would bring the expected good fortune. It was a trait which earned him many friends, and not only here at Il Tuffo. But he had other interests, as you may know. History was his passion."

Smiles and nods from the audience around the two tables.

"So he did have his serious side," the man continued. "While he never talked about it directly, there were hints that he was a music lover. One night, after several rounds from Gilda, he mentioned a harp teacher. We found it curious that he would be taking harp lessons, but why not? It was just before he was found dead. Ironic, isn't it?"

At first Rick didn't understand the irony, but when several of the group looked heavenward, he got it.

"So, in many ways, the count was a complicated man, Signor Montoya, though that could perhaps be said of any of us. He had his failings, but who can claim not to have failed many times in the journey that is life? No, what is more important are a man's qualities. The count's were numerous, and it is those that we will always remember. He was descended from a long line of Roman nobility, something that would have ruined many lesser men. So he was Count Zimbardi, and it is by that title that most people in Rome will remember him. But to those around this table,

Signor Montoya, to those of us who called him a friend, that man was simply…Umberto."

There was not a dry eye in the room. Even Gilda was wiping back tears with her rag.

Rick heaved a sigh and ordered another round.

• ● ● ● •

Rick and Gonzalo stood at the corner just down from Il Tuffo, unbothered by automobile traffic since the street was too narrow for it. A gaggle of young tourists speaking some Scandinavian language shuffled past them, looking for one of the main streets, which this one wasn't. One of them spotted Gonzalo's out-fit and said something to the others, eliciting some laughing. Fortunately, Gonzalo didn't notice.

"That was not the count that I had pictured when I read his journal, Gonzalo. Betting on horses? He had mentioned the card games, but I had no idea that he was such a serious gambler. And harp lessons? What was that about?"

The butler, as he had throughout the session in the bar, remained unperturbed. Rick decided that perturbation was something for-eign to the butlering profession, even when a butler was on his day off.

"Often people are not what they seem, Signor Montoya," he said, brushing something from his red jacket to support his point. "The count was a complicated man. I was aware of his penchant for making the occasional wager, including that he frequented the race track, though I believe he kept that activity from the countess. I recall that the person with whom he placed his bets showed up at the bar one evening. A most unsavory fellow named Rospo." He shook his head, about the most emotion he had shown all evening. "The harp lessons? I recall overhearing him mention to the countess that he was considering taking music lessons, but didn't realize he had decided to follow through. It was one evening after dinner. He was sipping his bourbon and reading *Il*

Giornale, and she was watching a *telenovela*. When he told her, she laughed, saying music lessons would be foolish at his age."

That sounded like the countess, Rick thought. "What was his reaction?"

"I believe he said 'It's now or never, *cara*.' He always called her *cara*."

A gust of wind blew around the corner like a New Mexico dust devil, swirling dirt and paper scraps around their legs before moving down the street in search of others to annoy. Gonzalo brushed himself off.

"I must be on my way, Signor Montoya. It was a pleasure to see you. Do you think something you heard tonight may be of some help to the police in finding who was responsible for Count Zimbardi's death?"

"I hope so, Gonzalo. I'll report it to the *commissario* in charge of the case, the one who sent me to do the translation of the count's papers. By the way, I read something today about someone named Girolamo Syms-Mulford. Does that name mean anything to you?"

"Yes. Signor Syms-Mulford called frequently. Since I usually answered the phone I know his voice, but I never saw the man at the Zimbardi residence. He was at the count's funeral, but I was not introduced to him."

A butler would not be introduced to any of the Zimbardis' circle of wealthy friends, even at a funeral. Rick extended his hand. "Gonzalo, my thanks for helping me with the group in there. Let's hope that it is helpful to the police."

"I certainly hope it is." He shook Rick's hand, turned, and walked away.

Rick pulled out his phone to see if he'd missed any calls, noticing the hour. It agreed with what his stomach was telling him, that it was dinnertime. A nice bowl of pasta and a glass of wine was just what he needed, and he could digest what he'd heard from the card players along with the food. But where? He was close to the river, so he decided to cross it at the Ponte Sant' Angelo and walk into the Borgo, a grid of streets between the castle and the Vatican, where he was sure to find a simple *trattoria*. After a few turns from one small street to another, he toyed with the idea of asking directions, but was saved from the humiliation when he heard the roar of traffic along the Lungotevere. He followed the noise and went from a narrow alley with no cars to a three-lane street teeming with them. He ran across just as the light was about to change, speeding up the last few feet as the drivers began revving their engines. He stopped to catch his breath and looked at the Sant' Angelo bridge, its five arches—massive and delicate at the same time—supporting a pedestrian passageway guarded by Bernini's angels. To the right the former mausoleum of the emperor Hadrian, transformed over the centuries into the pope's fortress and now, like so many of the city's landmarks, a museum. Everything was lit from below, including the giant dome of Saint Peter's looming in the distance.

It all reminded Rick why he had moved back to Rome, and also that he was a long way from Albuquerque.

He crossed the bridge, glancing down at the river running darkly and silently below. On the other side, in the shadow of the castle, the street had been widened into a virtual *piazza*. A large tourist bus was parked on the Tiber side, its engine humming in neutral, and he could see the guide standing inside next to the driver, gesturing at the castle. Moving closer, he could see the people in the seats looking out the windows as the man talked. Suddenly the door of the bus opened and he heard a voice.

"Hey, cowboy."

Giulia stepped out of the bus while the guide continued his presentation, and Rick watched her descent, again marveling at the change from high school.

"*Ciao*, Giulia. Another chance encounter, like in the pub?"

"I'm good, but I'm not that good, Rick. Do you always wear cowboy boots now? I hadn't noticed them yesterday."

"I noticed what *you* were wearing."

"And if I'd known I was going to run into you again, I would not have been in uniform." She had on a white blouse under a blue jacket that matched her skirt. A name tag on her lapel included the name of the company: Livingston Tours S.A.

"I've always been attracted to women in uniform."

She saluted, then took his arm and walked him toward the wall overlooking the river. Her thumb jerked back toward the bus. "He'll be talking for a while about the castle so we have time to chat. And, fortunately, it looks like he's going to work out. I came along to see how he was doing. I like to keep an eye on my guides, since they are the face of the business."

"This is the replacement you were talking about last night?"

"No, no, that job is still open. It's a daytime tour guide I need, for the main city monuments. " She was still holding his arm. "You know, Rick, I was thinking after I saw you last night—"

"I've been thinking as well."

"Really? Would you want to fill in for that guide? Just until I get someone permanent."

Rick sighed. They were clearly thinking of different things. Did she really want him to work as a tour guide? Is that why she appeared in the pub? Giulia had not changed from her high school persona—all business, all the time. What a waste.

"Let me think about it some more. I've got all sorts of things going at the moment. Finding an apartment, making contacts for my translation business, getting my papers, settling in. You know how it is."

She turned when she heard the bus driver tap on the horn. "Of course, I understand. We still have to get together to catch up. You have my card."

"Yes, we'll have to do that."

"Got to go, the tour is on a strict schedule." She gave him a peck on the cheek and ran to the bus door. Taking the front seat, she looked out the window at Rick standing on the sidewalk. He looked taller than she'd remembered, and his shoulders seemed broader. His hair was longer and more fashionable than in high school. And those cowboy boots definitely added flair. Yes, the years had improved Rick Montoya.

"Everything all right, Giulia?" asked the driver.

She watched Rick wave as the bus started toward the Vatican.

"Everything's fine. Except I'm an idiot."

Rick pushed open the door to be immediately overcome by the odor of stale beer and fried food. After his encounter with Giulia he'd decided that his appetite wasn't what he thought it was, so a beer and some pub fare would be enough. He'd crossed back over the river, managed to find his way to O'Shea's, but now his nose was telling him that it might not have been the right decision. Too late. Art was sitting at one of the tables, spotted Rick, and waved him over. He was dressed in his same post-work attire: dark suit, white shirt, striped tie loosened at the knot.

"Don't you have a home?"

Art pointed to the closest screen. "And miss this baseball game? No score in the bottom of the eighth. Very exciting."

Rick took a seat at the table. "I don't remember you following baseball."

"I've taken up our national pastime recently. To keep ties with my native country outside the football season. I'm finding more to the game than I thought. Strategy."

Rick got Guido's eye and pointed to Art's beer. The bartender nodded and pulled a glass off the shelf.

"I always thought it was a guy trying to hit a ball with a piece of wood." The beer arrived and he took a sip. "I just ran into Giulia."

"Another chance encounter?"

"This time it really was by chance." He told Art about the conversation in the shadow of the castle.

"Ouch. The woman is clueless about the important things in life. I guess that's why she's successful in business. Reminds me of my boss, though Giulia is much better looking than my boss." Art waved his hand as if brushing away the thought. "But enough about that topic, what else is happening in the life of Riccardo Montoya since I saw you last night?"

"I was almost pickpocketed on the bus, and some old lady accused me of being a tourist."

"The two incidents were related, I trust?"

Rick nodded and took a longer drink of the beer. It should have curbed his appetite but it had the opposite effect. He looked around to see if the night's menu was written on a board somewhere. It wasn't.

"She must have spotted your cowboy boots," Art said. "They're not in fashion here yet."

"Correct. Also today, my uncle roped me into helping him with an investigation."

"Really? The cop picks some rube, who almost gets mugged on the bus, to help him solve a crime? Sounds like nepotism run amok, even for this town."

"It actually made sense. At least initially, when he asked me to translate some journals written by the victim. Now he wants me to start interviewing people. But I have to say, I'm fascinated by it."

"Was the victim pickpocketed on a bus?"

"No, murdered. On the Ponte Fabrizio."

Art squinted as he delved into his memory bank. "I think I saw that on the TV crime news. A couple weeks ago, wasn't it? Some big shot."

"A count."

"An accountant? Then he must have been a big shot."

"No, Art, a count. As in nobility."

"Aha. Well, I don't know any noble accountants. Ignoble is the term that comes to mind when describing my profession. So who did him in?"

"That's what my uncle is trying to figure out. Listen, Art, let's move from the crime pages to the real estate section for some upbeat news. I looked at an apartment today, owned by a distant relative, and it's perfect. Near Piazza Navona, one bedroom, not too noisy, view of the rooftops. I'll probably move in a day or two."

"The cop will be glad to be rid of you." Art had apparently decided that "the cop" was the appropriate way to refer to Rick's uncle. "Can't say I blame him. What cop wants some hayseed tourist who can't keep from getting pickpocketed living under the same roof, relative or not? It's a bad reflection on him."

Rick looked up as a loud group burst through the door. He guessed Australians, from their accents, and regulars, since Guido immediately began pulling cans of Fosters from the refrigerator behind the bar. "Rattle your dags, Guido," one of them called out as they tromped to a table in the far corner and took it over like they owned it. Art didn't notice the commotion. He was glued to the screen, where the game had moved into the top of the ninth, still scoreless.

Rick glanced up and then back at his friend. "Let me ask you something, Art. I found out today that the count was taking harp lessons."

"So you think he had some premonition about dying?"

"We'll likely never know that, but what I need to find out is where to track down his teacher. How can I get a list of harp teachers in Rome? There couldn't be that many."

Art extended both his hands, pointing two index fingers at Rick. "You, my friend, are in luck." He shifted to turn the fingers toward a nearby table. A man a few years their junior was scribbling on large sheets of paper and neglecting his glass of red wine. He wore a sweater that was too heavy for the season, and sported round glasses with bright red rims. Behind the glasses, and below a disheveled head of hair, was a face that belonged in a Botticelli painting.

"Al Firestone," said Art, with a touch of awe in his voice.

"Am I supposed to know who he is?"

"Of course not." Art leaned forward in a conspiratorial manner. "Al is in Rome on a music scholarship, he studies at the conservatory."

"So he may know about harp teachers."

"Perhaps, but his renown here at the bar is for his technique with the Italian ladies. Even though he's been here six months, he doesn't speak much Italian. But since he knows his music, he uses musical phrases when he meets Italian girls. Because musical terminology is really Italian, it works. Of course his good looks don't hurt." Art shrugged.

"I don't get it."

"Here's an example," Art's brow furrowed in thought as he tried to think of one. "A girl walks up to him and says, '*Ciao, come stai?*' Al gives her his forlorn look and answers, '*Allegro, ma non troppo.*' The lady's heart melts, and proceeds to comfort him. He asks her if she'd be interested in a bit of *capriccio andante*. One thing leads to another, and before you know it they're back at his apartment where he gives her a glass of wine and suggests an *opera affetuosa*. That leads to a *scherzo adagio*, which before you know it culminates in a *crescendo fortissimo*."

"Bring down the curtain," Rick said. "I don't need to hear about an encore. What I need is a lead on harp teachers."

Art picked up his glass. "Let's ask."

When they reached the other table, Al Firestone looked up. "What's going on, Art?" He shuffled the papers, which were musical scores, and pushed his pen to one side. Rick and Art took seats.

"Al, this is my old friend Rick Montoya who just moved back to Rome."

The two shook hands. "My pleasure, Rick. What brings you back?"

"Seeking my fortune. I'm a translator and interpreter and

thought Rome is a good place to work. Art tells me you are the pub's resident musician."

Al's glasses slipped down his nose and he pushed them back. "I suppose so."

They were interrupted by a woman who walked up and put her hand on Al's shoulder. "*Ci vediamo domani*, Al?" Her voice was like warm honey.

Al looked up at her, but no words came out. Art leaned toward him. "She wants to know if she'll be seeing you tomorrow."

Al's face brightened. "*Si, si. Dalle due alle tre.*"

"*Ciao*, Al." She moved off, her languid stroll studied by the three men who remained silent until she disappeared out the door.

"Between two and three," Rick finally said. "Your Italian is pretty good, Al, even though you didn't understand her question."

"He always uses that line, Rick. *Falstaff*, isn't it, Al?"

"Yeah. Act two. One of my favorite Verdi operas, and the more famous of only two comedies the maestro composed. But Arrigo Boito wrote the libretto, so I guess I have to credit him. Where are you coming from in the States, Rick?"

"New Mexico. Albuquerque."

"Been there," said Al, noticing his wine. He took a small sip. "I auditioned for a violin chair in the New Mexico Symphony when I got out of Oberlin. Didn't get the job, it went to some relative of the governor."

"That sounds like New Mexico," said Rick. "Sorry your experience there was negative."

"Not at all. The violinist who won the chair invited me out to dinner. Hotter than I was used to, that's for sure."

"Do you remember the restaurant he took you to?"

"A she, actually. Some French place. I don't remember the name."

"French? When you said it was hot, I assumed it was Mexican food."

"I wasn't referring to the meal."

Rick and Art exchanged looks.

"Tell me something, Al," said Rick. "I have a friend who is thinking of studying harp. Art thought you might know of some harp teachers."

Al rubbed his chin, which looked like it had never grown enough beard to be shaved. "I only know of one, she's at the conservatory. Her name is Angelini."

"Good name for a harp teacher," said Art, chuckling.

"Why is that?" Al asked.

Rick went on before Art could answer. "How would my friend get in touch with her?"

"She's only at the conservatory a few days a week, like most of the teachers, but she probably has a studio somewhere. None of them can live on what the conservatory pays, so they perform when they can and give private lessons. Call the conservatory to get her contact info." He glanced at his scores and looked back at the two visitors. The implication was clear.

"We'll let you get back to your work, Al," said Art. He and Rick stood, glasses in hand.

"Nice to meet you, Rick. Hope your friend enjoys the harp."

"I'm sure he will. Thanks for the help, Al. Good to meet you as well."

They returned to their original table.

"I see what you mean about him," said Rick. "I'll tell my uncle about Signora Angelini. He'll probably want to interview her. Another beer?" Art nodded and Rick caught Guido's eye, signaling another round. "Did I tell you about the Argentine wine merchant?"

"Another one of your bad jokes?"

"I wish it were." He told Art about Juan Alberto Sanguinetti, and by the time he was finished his friend was laughing as if it really were a joke.

"I've got to meet this guy."

"Take my word for it, you don't want to. But I was thinking, who do I know at the Vatican that could at least give me a name that I could pass to Juan Alberto to get him off my back?"

Art's face lit up. "Lidia."

"Exactly. You said she works at the Vatican press office. Maybe she knows who buys the wine. There must be a cafeteria for the Curia, or a restaurant, or something. The Swiss Guards must have a mess hall. Is there a commissary?"

"Lidia will know everything. I'd bet on it."

Chapter Six

Standing at the bar the next morning, cocooned by the sounds and smells of caffeine, Rick tried to organize his thoughts on what he had learned the day before. Once again Rick and Piero had missed each other the previous night and that morning, even though they were living in the same apartment. A note left in the kitchen said the *commissario* would be waiting in the *questura* for a full briefing. A half cup of the strong coffee jolted Rick's brain enough to solve the first problem of the morning: What is an Italian word for "skullduggery?" The harp lessons and tidbits about gambling seemed minor compared to that one ominous notation in the count's journal. What shenanigans could the man have discovered? Was it the reason for his demise? Rick chewed on those questions as he chewed his chocolate *cornetto*. It had been kept warm in the glass case, so it tasted like it had just emerged from the oven. He toyed with the idea of having another, and a second coffee to go with it, but decided instead to head for his uncle's office.

And well that he did. When Rick walked into the police station, Carmella was standing at the front desk talking with the duty officer. She noticed him and gestured toward the large clock on the wall before jerking a thumb toward Piero's office.

"*Buon giorno*," she said as they walked down the corridor. Apparently, he was beyond needing a pass to wander the building.

"*Buon giorno*, Carmella."

That was the extent of their conversation before reaching the *commissario's* office. Piero wore a tailored suit, lightweight wool for the chill which still hung in the spring morning air. He greeted Rick, and waved him and Carmella toward the two chairs in front of his desk. His manner was businesslike, as Rick expected in the presence of an underling.

Piero leaned back in his chair. "Tell us what you found yesterday."

Rick told them. His notes were in his pocket but he didn't find the need to pull them out. He went over the main points of what he read in the count's journal, including the mention of the Englishman, Syms-Mulford, and described the countess' reaction when he asked her about the man. He recounted his visit to the card players. Then he told them of Signora Angelini, the harp teacher suggested by Al Firestone.

Piero's first words were about the count's journal. "The man saw something that disturbed him. We must find out what that was. Tell me exactly what he wrote."

Rick now pulled out his notes and found the lines, translating them carefully.

Piero rubbed his chin in thought. "It sounds like it was more than someone not giving him a proper receipt," referring to a common method used by stores and restaurants to avoid paying sales tax. "Let's hope you and Sergeant Lamponi can find out what it was when you interview people on that street. I'll track down the harp teacher. I've asked them downstairs to check on this Britisher who was a friend of the count. What was the name again?"

Rick checked his notes. "Girolamo Syms-Mulford."

"Yes, now I remember. With a name like that he should be easy for them to find." He tapped his pen on the pad. "The count's gambling also raises possible motives, and makes me wonder if he had some debts."

Carmella held up her hand. "I've worked on those cases before, Sir. It could have been someone urging him to pay up and the warning went bad."

"Have you heard of this guy, Rospo?" Rick asked her.

She nodded. "I know him, but he doesn't strike me as the kind who would get violent. We can talk to him. I know where he's found most days."

Piero leaned forward and put his hands on the desk. "You can go see him after you poke around the count's last street, which is likely where he saw something that bothered him. Riccardo, you can brief me on the two meetings at lunch." He nodded at the policewoman and she stood up, knowing from experience when the *commissario* was finished.

"I'll meet you in front with the car, Riccardo."

Before Rick could answer, she was out the door.

"Did you visit the apartment yesterday?" Piero was into the next topic.

"Yes. Yes, I did. It's perfect. I'll move in tomorrow, if that's all right with you."

"Might as well, with our schedules, I never see you anyway. Don't tell your mother yet. She thinks that by staying with me I'm keeping a careful eye on you."

"*In loco parentis.*"

"Exactly. My sister thinks you're still a child."

"She always will, Zio."

• • ● ● •

When Rick got out to the street, Carmella was in the driver's seat of the police car, its engine revving slowly. Inside, he looked in vain for a seat belt. Apparently police didn't use them, perhaps better to leap quickly to the aid of the citizenry. The tires screeched as she took off up the street.

"Riccardo, you're not married, are you?"

The question took him by surprise. "No, I'm not."

She shifted into second and turned the corner while the tires complained loudly. She'd have little tread on them if she always drove like this.

"If you ever do, don't have children."

Rick was afraid to ask what recent event in Carmella's life had prompted such advice, so he said nothing, and she was comfortable with his silence. The only noise during the rest of the trip came from outside the car.

Twenty minutes later, after fighting their way through the traffic of downtown Rome, Rick and Carmella were close to their destination. Even with a police car it was difficult to maneuver through the streets, and impossible to get close to Via Anacleto. When she spotted an empty spot near Campo de' Fiori, she grabbed it. It wasn't a full parking space, but large enough to squeeze in at an angle. Without *Polizia* printed on the side, the car would be a prime candidate for a ticket. As they stepped to the pavement Rick noticed that Carmella's parking job was earning stares from the foreign tourists and indifference from the locals.

"It's down here," she said to Rick, pointing to a street so narrow that he wondered if they would have to walk single file. Buildings on both sides were barely tall enough to block direct sunlight from reaching the cobblestone pavement, except perhaps at midday in the summer. They walked the length of the street, about fifty meters, to the corner where a rectangular stone plaque on the wall marked the beginning of Via Anacleto II. Rick made a mental note to find out who this Anacleto guy was. From the Roman numeral after his name, he had to be a pope, but it wasn't one he recognized.

Carmella stopped and surveyed the street, about half the length of the one they had just walked. "Let's walk down to the next corner, then work our way back and see who we can find to talk to. You brought along your notes on who the count interviewed?"

Rick froze. He was back in high school and had forgotten his homework. "I left them with my uncle for his file. But I think I can remember."

She shook her head but said nothing.

They were far enough from the guidebook sites that the businesses on the street catered strictly to locals. No restaurants, not a single souvenir shop, not even a shoe store. As such, no tourists and, at the moment, almost no one of any type. The buildings were the same height as the others in this part of town, two and three stories, with the same gray or yellowed facades. Doors to the residences on the upper floors were squeezed between the businesses at street level. Like all the streets in downtown Rome, there was no sidewalk, but since parking was prohibited, it didn't matter. Rough cobblestone, sometimes chipped, made walking the street tricky without flat soles, though Rick managed in his cowboy boots. The windows of the first business they passed were so dirty that they couldn't see inside, but the thump-thump of a machine and a small sign told them it was a print shop. Directly across the street were the padlocked doors of a garage. After the printer was another garage, but its metal shutter was rolled up above the doorway to reveal a man in greasy overalls working on a Vespa. Three mopeds were parked on the street in front, and Rick could see wheels and other parts hanging from the walls inside.

Across from the mechanic, in a space barely large enough to hold three customers, a glass counter displayed square trays of pizza. Below it ran a row of soft drink cans. The mechanic and the printers did not have far to go to buy their pizza by the slice, if they weren't turned off by the smells coming from the kitchen behind the counter. The next business on that side of the street sported only a boarded facade, with no indication of what had been there at one time. They were almost to the corner, and since street names in Rome often last for only one block, to the end of Via Anacleto itself. On the last section of the *pizzeria* side of the street sat what in the Bronx might be called a bodega, a store selling a wide variety of food in cans and boxes, as well as meats and cheeses, bread and milk. Across from it was another storefront business, this one a furniture restorer who could be seen through the glass door. The strong odor of linseed oil overpowered what little aroma remained in the air from the pizza slices.

Carmella jerked her thumb toward the man behind the glass. "We'll start with this guy. Do you remember anything in the count's notes about him?"

Rick had an idea to get him off the hook. "You know, Carmella, it would be better if you don't know what the count had written. Then you have a fresh view of each person, without any preconceived ideas you might have gotten through the eyes of the count. I can read you the notes later."

She thought about that a moment. "Maybe you're right."

It worked. Rick smiled as he opened the door to let her go in. The space, dimly lit by a few bulbs hanging from the ceiling, was made even murkier by the furniture cluttering the one room, each piece a darker brown than the next. The floor was spotted with brown, the ceiling had a brownish hue, and the apron of the man, like his hands, was covered with brown stains. He looked at Carmella's uniform and rubbed his hands on the apron. Enough light hit his face to show a stubby beard, though it could have been stain rubbed off from his hands.

The man only stared, so Carmella started the conversation. "I am Sergeant Lamponi, this is Lieutenant Montoya. We are investigating a homicide."

Rick covered his surprise at being called a lieutenant, and kept his eyes on the restorer. In TV cop shows a murderer often betrayed nervousness when first confronted by the police. This guy's face didn't betray anything.

"The old count? I saw something on the news, with his picture. I wondered why he hadn't shown up here in a few days to do more snooping. Who killed him?"

Rick, being the lieutenant, thought he should be saying something. "That's what we're investigating, Signor…?"

"Avellone. You got any leads?"

"We'll ask the questions, Signor Avellone." Not sure what to say next, he turned to Carmella, who fortunately took the cue.

"What kind of snooping did the count do?"

The man again rubbed his hands on the apron. It was a toss-up as to which was more stained. "He said he was interested in the history of the street, so he asked about what I remembered from the time I've been here, what business was at this address in the past, that kind of thing. I played along. You never know when someone might want an old piece of furniture refurbished, and he obviously had money. I get a lot of rich people in here with furniture they've had sitting around for a while and they get the idea that it might be worth something. So they pay me to make it look like new. I don't tell them that doing that decreases the value."

"When was the last time you saw him?" Carmella asked.

"I remember seeing the news of the murder and thinking that he'd just been snooping here a couple days before. I saw him on the street that day, but he didn't come in." He pointed his dirty chin toward the door. "He always spent more time with Pina, so that wasn't unusual." The half smile on his face exposed yellow teeth.

"Pina?"

"She owns the store across the street."

Carmella pulled a card from her jacket and passed it to Avellone. "If you remember anything that might help with the investigation, call me."

The man squinted at the card, which was unreadable, given the lack of light.

When Rick and Carmella stepped back on the street they didn't have far to go for their next stop. The sign above the door read Alimentare Giuseppina, and they could see Pina herself through the glass. The long apron not only didn't cover her curves, it somehow accentuated them.

"Perhaps our count was interested in more than street history," said Carmella as she marched to the door.

Rick followed behind, and once again he was introduced as Lieutenant Montoya. He was immediately surrounded by pleasant smells and tried not to allow them to distract him from his newly assigned duties as a police officer. It was not easy, since the cheeses and cold cuts were battling it out to see who would dominate the airways. The prosciutto and mortadella hanging from hooks were putting up a good fight, but thanks to a feisty caciocavallo and an especially pungent gorgonzola, the cheeses were winning. Rick felt a twinge of hunger.

Pina blinked back tears when she heard the reason for their visit. "A wonderful gentleman, Umberto. You would never have taken him for a member of the Roman nobility, not that I've had much contact with Roman nobility, but you get what I mean. Loved making jokes. Always something nice to say." She found a tissue somewhere in her apron and touched it to her eyes.

It all seemed genuine to Rick, and he crossed her off the suspect list, not that he had one yet. "When did you see him last?"

Pina took a moment to compose herself. "When I saw the news on TV I realized we had talked only the day before he was killed. It was quite a shock, I don't mind telling you. They had a very nice picture of him on the newscast, and then showed the bridge where he was found. I used to walk across that bridge when I was a child, since I had an aunt who lived in Trastevere. She died a few years ago. Broke her hip, then got pneumonia and never recovered. Same thing happened to my grandmother. There's something about breaking a hip that—"

Carmella broke in. "Did he seem any different from normal that last day you talked? Preoccupied? Nervous?"

She thought about it. "Not really. He said he was finishing up his research and would be moving on to another street. But he promised he'd be back to say hello when he was in the neighborhood. He would have, too. Very thoughtful, Umberto was."

She had returned the tissue to her pocket, but now it reappeared. "Here I am talking about him in the past tense."

"Were you able to help him with his project?" Rick asked.

"A little," she said with a sniff. "I grew up here, so I told Umberto what I could about the street." She pointed upward. "Still live on the second floor in the apartment I inherited from my father. He ran the store until he died."

Probably broke his hip, Rick thought. "Are many apartments on the street lived in by people like you, who have been here all their lives? That was the count's interest, we understand."

She thought before answering. "Avellone, across the street, he bought the business from someone else, and he's been here for only about twenty years. Signor Leopoldo, who fixes *motorini*, he's been on the street even less time, maybe a decade. He's from somewhere in the south." The way she said it, south sounded like another country. "Ahmed, the pizza guy, is from North Africa, so I don't think he was much help to Umberto. Which leaves the Stampelli family. Three generations and they've always lived above their print shop. Eugenio, the *nonno*, must have filled Umberto's ear since he likes to tell stories. It drives Ludovico crazy. Ludovico is his son, who's about my age, and he's always complaining to me about his father living in the past. Silvio, the kid, just tunes out. Earphones." She put her hands over her ears in case they didn't understand.

As she had done across the street, Carmella handed Pina a card and asked her to call if she recalled anything that might help with the case. The woman placed the card on the counter next to a display of anchovy jars and promised she would.

"Men are pigs," Carmella said to Rick when they were back on the pavement. "I hope you won't take that personally, Riccardo."

"Of course not. But what caused you to make such an observation?"

"The count didn't spend his time with Pina because she was good at slicing mortadella. Did you notice what she said about him being so generous? Even a kid like you should know what that means. And she has the apartment above the shop." She rested her case with a deep, cackling laugh.

Rick tried to come up with a rejoinder to demonstrate that he was a man of the world. "That takes her off the suspect list," was the best he could muster.

They crossed the street again and went two doors down to the place that sold pizza by the slice. Ahmed was putting out the first tray of the day in hopes of luring someone in for a mid-morning snack, but given the amount of foot traffic on the street, it appeared that his hopes would come to naught. He was dressed in a tee-shirt covered by a white apron, already spotted with tomato sauce. The shop had no doors or windows. It had once been a garage—or a storage area before the era of cars—and was protected by a rolling metal shutter that now hid itself above the doorway.

Ahmed looked up at the two people approaching his shop. A toothy smile that contrasted with his dark skin disappeared when he noticed Carmella's police uniform. He caught himself and re-flashed the smile. "Would you like a slice? Fresh out of the oven, it is, very tasty. Just the thing to hold you until lunchtime."

"Not today, Ahmed." Using his first name clearly rattled him, which was Carmella's intention. "We are investigating a murder and need to ask you some questions."

Rick studied the man's face and thought he detected relief. If Ahmed was potentially in trouble with the authorities, it wasn't for homicide.

"Someone I know? I mean, knew?"

"Count Zimbardi," said Rick. "He was doing research on this street, talking with people. He must have spoken with you."

"This I do not recall."

Carmella reached in her pocket and took out a photograph. "This is the guy," she said, passing it to Ahmed.

He stared at the photo and rubbed his chin. "Yes, I remember this man. He came in twice and bought pizza. No anchovies. He made a point of asking for his slices without anchovies. It was not a problem, I never put anchovies on my pizza. Too expensive."

"He didn't ask you anything? About the street?" Carmella was ready to move to the next store.

"About the street? Why would he ask me about the street? I am not understanding."

"I think we can take that as a no," Rick said to Carmella.

She nodded. "Thank you for your help, Ahmed. We'll be back when we're ready for pizza without anchovies." She was out in the street before he could reply.

"That was useless," she said to Rick as they stood in the middle of the street. A Fiat Cinquecento appeared and they moved aside to let it pass. It was the closest Via Anacleto would get to gridlock. "Let's see if our *motorino* mechanic can be more helpful. What did she say his name is?"

"Leopoldo, I think."

"Right."

The shop was about as wide as Ahmed's place, but unlike the *pizzeria* it was open all the way to the back of the building, forming a deep, dimly lit cave. Leopoldo was the cave man, and he filled the part with long hair and a scraggly beard. But instead of animal skins, he wore overalls with a dirty tee-shirt under the bib. He was working on a small engine that sat on a wood bench against the wall. Sensing immediately that Carmella and Rick were not there to get their moped repaired, his expression was a scowl, though Rick guessed it was his normal face, even for customers.

"Signor Leopoldo?" He nodded and sized up his visitors in silence. "We need to ask you some questions," Carmella continued. "We are investigating the death of Count Zimbardi, and we understand he spent some time on this street in the weeks before he died. Did he talk to you?"

"I didn't kill him."

"We didn't say you did." Rick took on his role as the lieutenant. "Do you remember when you saw him last?" It was the question Carmella had used with the others, so he felt comfortable posing it.

"A couple weeks ago. He asked me how long I'd been here, and when I told him he didn't seem that interested in what I had to say. I'm from Basilicata and I'm not a count." He wiped his hand across his nose, leaving a greasy mark.

"Did he seem at all agitated when you saw him last?" Rick was getting into the rhythm of the questioning routine. He looked at Carmella who gave him a bored sigh.

"Nah. He asked me a few more questions, about working on the street. He wanted to know what was in the space before I started renting it."

"And?"

"The people who lived upstairs used it for storage and as a garage." He pointed upward. "When they sold the apartment and moved to Rieti, they decided to keep this and rent it out. I was looking for a larger space and I took it."

Larger? Did you work out of a closet before renting this place? Rick suppressed the desire to ask that question, instead turning to Carmella. She took the cue.

"If you think of anything that might shed some light on the count's murder, this is my number."

Leopoldo studied her card before slipping it into one of his pockets and nodding in silence. Carmella inclined her head toward the street and led the way out. They looked up and down, but the only traffic, foot or vehicle, was a man in brown working clothes who entered Pina's mini-mart.

"One more and then we are off to see Rospo, the bookie. I hope this one gives us something, otherwise it will be a bust. Do you remember the names of the men in this print shop?"

"Three generations of Stampatelli. Eugenio is the grandfather, his son Ludovico, and Silvio the kid."

"You've got a good memory. Does that come with being a translator?"

"I never thought of it that way, Carmella. Perhaps you're right."

"My son has a very selective memory, and it's always what serves him. He's just like his father."

"You mentioned that once." He gestured toward the door of their last stop on the street. "Shall we go in?"

She stepped to the door and opened it. After breathing the odors of varnish, salami, pizza, and gasoline, they were now bathed in the smell of ink, which after the gasoline had a certain sweetness. It took a moment for their eyes to adjust again to the light, or lack of it, after being outside. Once they focused, forms began to appear. A press filled the rear space from floor to ceiling. It looked like several metal drums had been stacked sideways and connected by gears, and it emitted a steady thump every second. As they looked closer they could see paper shooting out from under the lowest drum into a basket, as well as someone standing next to it watching the basket fill. It had to be the grandson, whom Rick guessed to be around eighteen. The boy wore blue jeans and a Rolling Stones tee-shirt, and his hair grew down over his neck. Two smaller presses were silent, and against one entire wall was a long table stacked with paper. A man, this one certainly the grandfather, was putting the paper in brown cardboard boxes under a row of neon lamps that gave the room its eerie light. He was a large man, dressed in brown overalls over a neatly pressed work shirt. After the mechanics shop and the furniture restorer, the place looked like a hospital operating room. There was no sign of Ludovico, the middle generation.

The boy noticed them first and removed his earbuds. "Nonno," he called out, but then frowned and shook his head. "He wears earplugs," he said under his breath to the two visitors, and walked over to his grandfather.

A tap on the shoulder got the old man's attention. He looked at the boy and then saw Rick and Carmella. As he walked to them, he reached into his ears and pulled out pieces of spongy material from each. "I use these to keep my hearing sharp," he said to them. "It's as good now as when I started working here almost seventy years ago."

"Prevention is the best medicine," said Rick.

"What?"

"I said prevention... I said my name is Montoya, and this is

Sergeant Lamponi." Rick spoke louder, wondering if turning off the press would ruin the print run. "We'd like to ask you some questions. You are Signor Stampatelli?"

The man's normal posture was bent, but he leaned forward even more. He was someone who took authority seriously, and Carmella's uniform symbolized authority. "Stampatelli, Eugenio, at your service, Officer. This is my grandson, Silvio. He is the fourth generation of Stampatelli printers; the business was started by my father before the war. My son, Ludovico, is out at the moment."

The last sentence may have been said with either annoyance or nervousness, Rick couldn't be sure which. The boy watched as his grandfather spoke, occasionally checking on the sheets still popping from under the printing drums.

"We are investigating the death of Count Zimbardi," Carmella said. "And we understand he was talking to people on this street just before he died."

"Are you talking to everyone on the street?" He suddenly turned to his grandson. "Silvio, turn off that printer, they can't hear what I'm saying."

The boy complied, and then walked back and stood next to his grandfather.

Rick tried to think why that would be the first question out of the man, and decided it was just nosiness. "Yes, Sir, yours is the last stop. Do you remember the last time you saw Count Zimbardi?"

Eugenio stroked his chin. "It was about two weeks ago. I remember reading in the papers about the murder and thinking that he had been here the day before, in the morning. We had had a long conversation about the printing business. He was going to write a book about the history of the street. Did you know that?"

"Yes, we did," replied Carmella. "Did he seem different from the previous times that you talked? I assume there were other times."

"Oh, yes, many other times. I was the best source for the

street's history of anyone. I started working here when I was younger than Silvio, just after the war. That last day I saw the count I told him about my father fooling the Nazis."

"Really?" said Rick. His history curiosity was piqued, and it was obvious that the elder Stampatelli would not mind telling the story again. The grandson, however, managed to contain his enthusiasm.

"Nonno, the police aren't interested in that old story." His grandson's plea was to no avail. When the old man started to talk, the boy gritted his teeth in frustration.

"It was late in the war, after Mussolini had been removed from office by the king who then fled south to join the Americans. The Germans took over the city and there was no pretense anymore about we Italians being their allies. The Nazis were the occupying army and ran Rome from their command post on Via Veneto. Many collaborated with the Germans, but many others resisted, each in their own way. For my father it was printing."

Rick was fascinated. Even Carmella was intrigued. Silvio groaned and disappeared behind the presses. Eugenio continued.

"Everything was controlled, as you can imagine. You needed a form filled out and stamped by the proper authorities to do anything. What was the name of that movie with Humphrey Bogart?"

The question took Rick by surprise. He thought of the *African Queen*, since Bogart and Hepburn were fighting the Germans in that one. Then it hit him. "*Casablanca?*"

"Right. You remember that it all centered around the papers to get the guy on the plane to Portugal?"

"The letters of transit," said Carmella. Rick was impressed.

"That's right," said Stampatelli, pointing a finger at her. "That was just the kind of document that my father printed, right here in this shop. Fake, of course, but they were such good copies the Nazis never caught on." He paused to let it sink in.

"How about printing money?" Carmella asked. "He could have used it to finance the resistance."

"Much too difficult. Special kind of paper, unique watermark, just the right ink colors. No, he stuck with documents, in black and white. Not that they were that easy to counterfeit, mind you."

"I'm sure they weren't," said Rick. "Was that the kind of story the count was looking for?"

"It certainly was. He wrote down a lot when I told him my stories."

Carmella's voice showed annoyance. "You didn't say yet whether the count appeared any different the last time you spoke. Was he agitated? Disturbed? You may have been the last person on the street to speak with him."

Grandfather Stampatelli closed his eyes tightly as he tried to remember. When he opened them again he said: "Now that you mention it, he did appear preoccupied with something. Let's see, Silvio was sweeping up and I was telling the count about my father's work during the war, when my son came in. The count said he had to get to an appointment and left. It was not like him."

"Was it something your son said?"

"I don't think Ludovico had said anything."

The boy reappeared from behind the machinery. "I remember that day, Nonno, but I don't think he acted strange at all. He just had to go somewhere."

Carmella's mood changed from annoyance to impatience, though there was little difference between the two. "We also have to be somewhere else." She pulled out a card and handed it to the grandfather. "If you think of anything else, I can be reached at this number. When do you think your son will be here so we can interview him?"

"He should be here now, I think he's making a delivery. Do you know when he'll be back, Silvio?" But the boy had again disappeared behind the large printing press. The old man shrugged and smiled weakly.

Rick and Carmella thanked him and walked back out to the street. In the distance the man who had gone into Pina's mini-mart came back out, glanced down the street at them, and walked in the opposite direction.

"See that guy, Riccardo? I'll bet you my week's pay that he's the missing Ludovico Stampatelli. He's dressed the same as his father, and if he was making a delivery, I'm guessing it was to Pina. Except Pina doesn't need any printing work. Did I mention that men are pigs?"

"I believe you did, Carmella."

She made a sound something between a chuckle and a harrumph. "Enough of our count's street meanderings, we're off to see his bookie Rospo. I think you'll find him interesting."

Back in the car it seemed for an instant that the traffic had lightened up, but it was a cruel illusion, serving only to bring them out to Corso Vittorio Emanuele, which looked like a parking lot. Carmella turned sharply and looked out of the rear window, then jerked the car into reverse. "Get out the lollipop; it's in the glove box."

Rick wasn't sure what she meant, but dutifully opened the glove box where there was a round red piece of cardboard, like a bull's eye, on the end of a stick. It was what the police used to direct traffic. Carmella had managed to turn them around completely so that they were facing the opposite direction. It was the wrong way on a one-way street.

"Put down your window and wave it." She pressed a button somewhere and the car's siren came to life, bouncing its wail off the surrounding buildings. Five exciting minutes later they were driving past the Circus Maximus and stopping at a traffic light in front of the FAO building. It was the first red light that Carmella had decided to give its due. They turned left and drove along the side of the Palatine Hill toward the Colosseum, passing rows of buses waiting for their tourists to return. At the end of the line Carmella made a sharp U-turn and stopped behind the last bus in line.

"I thought we were going to the track," said Rick, happy to

put his feet on solid ground. He looked down at his hands and saw that the blood was returning to his knuckles.

"Rospo should be here today. He works a couple jobs."

Just ahead was the Arch of Constantine, and beyond it the Colosseum. Even periodic restoration and cleaning could not detract from the ancient aura of the two structures. The arch looked like the decorative entrance to a castle, left standing after someone had made off with the rest of the structure. To the right the immense bulk of the Flavian Amphitheater loomed confidently over its smaller neighbor. Despite missing walls, and craterlike holes in its facade, the Colosseum was the city's top dog, and it knew it.

It was a perfect morning, even by Rome standards, and the tourists were taking advantage of the weather. Rick remembered living in the city in his youth, when nationalities were easily spotted by their dress, and shoes were the easiest giveaway. Not anymore. Markets were worldwide and the same styles caught on as quickly in Tokyo as in Bucharest. Sneakers were everywhere, along with tee-shirts and cargo shorts, not to mention baseball caps. Only by getting close enough to hear what language was being spoken could one make a sure guess of the country of origin. Carmella's uniform, however, stood out.

Rick had thought that his first visit to the Colosseum after moving back to Rome would be with someone visiting from America, but here he was, only a few days after his arrival, striding toward it. This guy Rospo must work as a guide or ticket-taker, but that didn't make sense. Those must be city government jobs, and he surely wouldn't be working as a bookie on the side. Then again, it was Italy.

As they got closer to the Colosseum entrance the crowds got heavier, as did the number of vendors selling everything from tee-shirts to models of the Leaning Tower of Pisa. To one side a crew of men, dressed up as gladiators and Roman legionnaires, brandished martial implements and posed with tourist for as much of a fee as they could squeeze out of them. Today most of those posing with them were young Japanese women who giggled while their friends, armed with real cameras rather than phones, took the pictures. What did these guys do when it got cold? Those hairy legs could get mighty chilled with just sandals and a skimpy skirt covering them. Rick would have to come back in January to see if they were still there. As he pondered this he was poked by Carmella.

"There he is." She then called out. "Rospo!"

Rick turned to see a short legionnaire brandishing an even shorter sword. His breastplate glistened in the sun and his shoulders were covered with a scarlet cape. The only aspect that detracted from the martial image was a helmet plume needing a coating of hair wax to keep it upright. The legionnaire was smoking a cigarette, apparently oblivious that tobacco first crossed the ocean well after the Roman Empire fell. At least he wasn't wearing a wristwatch.

The legionnaire swore, but in Italian, not Latin. "Carmella? Just what I need on a good day, a cop breaking my *coglioni.*" He stubbed out the cigarette, careful not to burn his exposed toes. "Whatever you want, can we make it quick? I'm losing money every minute I'm not posing with tourists. And let me tell you, on a day like this it's like having a permit to print money." He sheathed the sword.

"It will be quick if you cooperate, Rospo. This is Lieutenant Montoya. We're investigating the murder of Count Zimbardi."

That got his attention. The man was used to dealing with the police, but clearly not on homicide cases. He did his best to maintain his composure. "Sure, Carmella, what can I tell you? You know me, I'm always anxious to help the cops. "

Rick decided it was time for him to step in. "Count Umberto Zimbardi. You had some business dealings with him at the track?"

"The count? Did I ever. One of my best customers, and such a gentleman. But down to earth, mind you. If he hadn't dressed in those tailored suits you would have thought he was just one of the regulars. Of course he had to have tailored suits, since he couldn't fit into anything off the rack." He shrugged, and his red cape slipped slightly.

"What about his betting habits?"

"It was a habit, all right. I've never met anyone who was into wagering more than the count, and there is no small number of addicted gamblers at the Ippodromo, I can assure you. It's what keeps the place afloat. It was fun to be with him when the race started. He actually believed every time the horses left the gate that his was going to finish first, and would be in shock when it didn't. But the shock wore off fast, and there he was again at the rail, positive that this one, this time, was going to do it."

"And sometimes he was right."

"Well, sure. Even a blind squirrel occasionally finds a nut."

"How about payment?" asked Carmella. "Did you ever have a problem?"

Nino shook his head. "I always deal in cash. If he was borrowing to get cash to pay me, it was with somebody else, and I never heard anything about him being a deadbeat. Word of that kind of thing gets around pretty fast. You don't want to deal with those kind of people or you could get caught in the crossfire, if you get my drift."

"*Ciao*, Rospo," said a voice like honey. It belonged to a voluptuous woman with sandals, flowing hair, and a toga slit to the thigh. She winked at Rick as she passed.

"*Ciao*, Calpurnia." Rospo watched her before he turned back to Rick. "She makes as much as the rest of us put together. What guy wouldn't want to have his picture taken with her? And does she milk it. Beyond reproach, my ass."

Carmella gave Rick a look which said that they weren't going to get much more out of Signor Rospo. She turned back to the legionnaire. "When was the last time you saw the count?" It was said like she was going through the motions.

Rospo reached inside his breastplate and pulled out a

smartphone. "I can tell you exactly, I keep all my appointments on this. If I lost it I'd be totally screwed." They waited while he made various taps with his thumbs. "Here it is, sixteen days ago, at eleven in the morning. We met for coffee. If I remember right…here it is." He looked up from the screen. "I always make notes on this whenever I have a meeting. It's a dynamite app, keeps track of everything." His eyes went back to the phone. "Yes, I was correct. There was someone else there, named Syms-Mulford, spoke with a British accent."

"You wrote all this down in your phone?" Rick asked.

"Networking. It's how I get new clients. This other guy didn't seem like the type to need my services, but you never know." He stole a glance at a group of tourists posing with a gladiator holding a sword and a net, the competition. "Listen, I don't want to be rude, but I really have to get back to work."

"Just one more thing," said Carmella. "Do you remember if the count seemed any different that morning? Upset? Nervous?"

"Well, none of his horses had come in the previous day, so I didn't have any money for him, but that was normal. He gave me a list of his bets for that afternoon." Rospo again consulted his phone. "None of them paid off, according to my records. Just as well, or I'd have had to take his winnings to his widow."

"Sure you would have, Rospo," said Carmella, her words accompanied by an eye roll. "If you think of anything else, you know how to reach me."

Rospo returned his phone to inside the breastplate, pulled out his sword, and melted back into the crowd of tourists.

Five minutes later Rick and Carmella were in the car and returning to the police station.

"Did you get that, Riccardo? That Rospo met the count the morning of the day he was murdered? And he was with Syms-Mulford. This could be important."

"I suppose." Rick stared out the window at the traffic.

"You somewhere else, Riccardo? I'll bet you're thinking about meeting with this guy Syms-Mulford. Don't worry, you'll do just fine."

In fact he wasn't thinking about meeting the count's friend at all. His thoughts were on his next stop: the Vatican press office to see Lidia.

Carmella let him out at the Vittorio Emanuelle Bridge. She had offered to take him all the way to St. Peter's Square, but he insisted that he could make his way on foot from the river. It would give him time to compose his thoughts about what he would say to Lidia, assuming she was in the office that day. He probably should have called ahead, but he'd thought that surprising her would be fun. When Carmella pressed him about where he was going, he merely said that he was meeting an old high school friend. That was all she needed to know.

He crossed the river and worked his way through the traffic to Via della Conciliazione, at six decades old, one of the newest streets in the city, as well as one of the widest. It had been built to commemorate the end of decades of bad feelings between church and state when Mussolini signed the Lateran Pact and the pope finally recognized Italy as a nation. Rick was sure that very few of the tourists who now walked along its sidewalk toward St. Peter's Basilica knew the history. For them it was just a wide street with a great view of the cathedral facade and a few fascist-style buildings. As it got closer to the cathedral, souvenir shops began to appear, but unlike most of Rome their wares were religious, from posters of the pope to small models of St. Peter's Basilica.

Most of the postcards displayed on the sidewalk racks were split between portaits of the pontiff, interior scenes of the basilica, and the ceiling of the Sistine Chapel. Apparently, there were tourists who still sent postcards to friends and family back home, but the practice had to be fading thanks to cell phones that could send photos instantly. Rick remembered vacation trips as a kid when his mother always made a point of sending postcards from every stop. He thought then that it was a way for her to make them envious of the Montoyas' exotic travels, but later concluded it was simply an Italian thing. Or a bit of both. He squinted at the dome of St. Peter in the distance.

Lidia. How long had it been? It had to have been that tearful goodbye the summer after graduation. He was off to his father's alma mater, the University of New Mexico, and she to a small Catholic college in the Midwest. They had exchanged e-mails for a while but after a year the messages became infrequent and eventually trailed off to nothing. Rick was heavily involved in college social life and he assumed that she was as well. As attractive as she was, Lidia would have had no problem finding male companionship. Rick had put her out of his mind and concentrated on the ladies he met at UNM, of whom there were many. After graduation he had stayed in New Mexico, working at various jobs until starting his translation business, but through those years he never got very serious about any of his girlfriends. The idea of marriage—or even a long-term relationship—had not entered his mind. Would it be a similar story with Lidia?

The end of the street emptied into a small plaza before spreading into the much wider St. Peter's Square at the unmarked border between Italy and Vatican City. On both sides of the street sat identical stone buildings, each extending out over the sidewalk, and the one on the right held the Vatican Press Office. Rick looked at himself in the glass of the window, straightened his collar, and opened the door. His eyes were drawn to a larger-than-life-size picture of the pope that covered one wall. The pontiff was leaning over to pat the head of a child who looked up at him with wide eyes. In the center of the room a woman sat at a desk behind a computer. She looked up when Rick entered and flashed him a smile touched with piety—that's the way he interpreted it. But it was the Vatican, after all, so perhaps it was part of their training.

"May I help you?" she said in English. She must have noticed his cowboy boots.

He walked to the desk. "Is Lidia Williams in? I was told she works here." He stayed with English.

The pleasant smile turned to a frown, but one of incomprehension rather than annoyance. "I don't think I know any Lidia Williams. But I'm relatively new here, let me check." She picked up the phone on her desk and punched in a number. When the person on the other end of the line answered, she switched to Italian and made the inquiry. Rick could not hear what she was told, but she looked up at Rick and the smile returned, but wider. She pointed to an open doorway. "You'll find her in the third office on the right, down that hallway."

"Thank you," said Rick. He could almost feel her smile on his back as he went where he was told. The third door on the right was marked with a sign that said "Seminars and Special Events." The door was slightly ajar and he tapped lightly.

"*Avanti.*"

The voice was the same. He pushed open the door and saw Lidia sitting behind a desk, her eyes on the screen of a computer. In profile she had lost none of her beauty—if anything it had been enhanced by the years. She hit a button to save her work and turned to the doorway. Her mouth dropped open.

"Oh, my Lord, it's Rick Montoya. How wonderful to see you." She got up from the chair.

He stared for a few seconds until he finally found words.

"Lidia… you've changed."

"I'm still the same, Rick. Only now I'm called Sister Teresa."

Chapter Seven

Rick suggested they go somewhere in the neighborhood for a coffee, and Sister Teresa politely declined. He was unfamiliar with the protocols of sisterhood, but sensed that nuns didn't go alone to bars with men who aren't family. Instead, the two of them sat at a Formica table in what was the lunchroom at the Vatican Press Office, sipping bad coffee from a machine in the corner. Two other employees, one the receptionist who had greeted Rick when he came in, were at another table eating lunches they'd heated in the office microwave. Except for two posters of the pope, both from foreign trips, the walls were bare. There were no windows. Rick leaned back in his chair and Sister Teresa sat primly, her hands on her cup.

"Thank you for asking, Rick. I get that question a lot from old friends and the answer is yes, I am truly happy. I have never once regretted my decision. I can assure you that I'm at total peace with myself, not that my feelings are important in the scheme of things." She glanced at the poster near their table, then back at Rick. "How is your family, Rick? I remember your parents fondly. And your sister, where is she now?"

"Anna is happily married in Albuquerque with two sons, much to the delight of my mother. She and dad are now in Brazil, where he was posted earlier this year. You remember that I have an Uncle Piero?"

"I think I do. A policeman somewhere in the south?"

"Right. He's now in Rome and I'm staying with him until I can move into an apartment I'll be renting from a distant relative. Near Piazza Navona."

"Nice," said Sister Teresa. "Please give them all my regards."

"I will do that. And your folks?"

"They are well. Dad's paper dragged him back to the home office in Boston a couple years ago, but they have kept the apartment here and visit every few months. As you remember, my mother has lots of family here, so she can't stay away for long."

Rick was slowly getting used to the fact that his beautiful old flame was a nun. She wore no makeup, but she never had in high school. She didn't need it then and didn't need it now. The habit covered her body, but it didn't appear that she'd put on any weight. She'd never eaten much when they were on dates, and likely her eating habits hadn't changed. There was a difference in her, however, and as she spoke he tried to put his finger on it. Serenity? Yes, that was it.

"Tell me about your work here." He couldn't bring himself to call her Sister Teresa.

She sipped her coffee before responding. "Anything that doesn't fall naturally into the job description of someone else is given to me, so it's different almost every day. Last week some Bolivians brought in their prize llama to be blessed by the pope."

"Really? So you arranged it?"

"No. Popes don't do that sort of thing, so I got them a cardinal. They went away happy. We get a lot of people who want to give the pope gifts, which can be tricky. One time, if you can believe it, some American college coach gave him a football helmet during the weekly audience. The Holy Father had no idea what it was, and security was afraid it contained a bomb."

Rick was unable to picture the pope wearing a football helmet. "The poor guy was trying to improve his record. I wonder if it worked. It sounds like you do some fascinating things here."

She shrugged. "It can be. But I'll tell you a secret, Rick." She looked at the other table, where her two colleagues were eating, and then lowered her voice. "I've put in my application for a transfer."

"A better job here in the Vatican?"

"No. Missionary work. It's what I've always wanted to do. Rick, I think it's my true calling. I just have to convince the bureaucracy that it is."

"What do your parents think of your plans?"

"I haven't told them, but I'm sure they'll be horrified. They think their daughter working in the Vatican Press Office is very cool. But I didn't take the vows to be cool." Her face showed a determination he didn't remember from high school. Perhaps Lidia had changed more than the way she dressed. "But you haven't told me about your work."

"I was doing translating back in Albuquerque, working out of a home office, and realized that with the Internet I could do it anywhere. So why not Rome? I'm hoping to get into interpreting jobs as well."

"I'm sure you'll be a great success." She looked at the large clock on the wall. "Rick, I've got to get back to my office."

As they got to their feet, Rick reluctantly decided that he had to bring up the other subject. "Before you go, can I ask your advice on something?"

"Of course."

"I have an Argentine friend who is here in Rome representing a wine producer in his country. He would love to sell wine in Vatican City, but has no idea of how to start. Any ideas?" It was the abbreviated version of Juan Alberto's dilemma, omitting the fact that the guy was here under false pretenses, was somewhat of a sleaze, and couldn't be trusted. Lidia—Sister Teresa—didn't require details, busy as she was.

"They do drink wine here. Give me your friend's name and cell phone, and I'll see what I can find out."

Rick quickly pulled out a card and passed it to her. "It might be easier just to call me."

A few minutes later Rick was outside trying to shake off the image of Lidia in a nun's habit. It wasn't the full costume, long and black with her face framed in white wings. Instead she wore plain gray, ankle length and a head cover of the same color. But the total effect was the same—she was a nun. He reminded himself what she'd said about being very happy, which was the most important, and he believed her. Despite that, he couldn't help getting an empty feeling about the encounter. There was no reason for it, so he tried to shake it off and return to the other issues at hand, mainly the murder of the count. He was anxious to know if his uncle had tracked down Syms-Mulford and set up an interview. There was something about the man's relationship with the late count that intrigued Rick, as much as the name itself.

There were mundane practical issues as well, the foremost being moving into his apartment. He needed to shop for towels and sheets, and knew just the store where to do it, relatively close to his new address. A church bell rang, marking midday, and reminding him that he was supposed to meet his uncle for lunch. He looked across St. Peter's Square at the facade of the basilica, the arms of Bernini's colonnade beckoning him toward it. The square was dotted with groups of tourists, expected any day regardless of the weather, and certainly on a sunny morning like this.

Living in Rome was like living in a museum, and it was a shame not to take advantage of it. Otherwise he might as well have stayed in Albuquerque. He stepped off the curb and started toward the basilica just as his phone rang. He checked the number and reluctantly answered in Spanish.

"*Si*, Juan Alberto."

"*Reek*, I was wondering if you have been able to find a way to help your old friend."

Rick shook his head. "I am working on it, Juan Alberto, just now, as a matter of fact. But nothing firm yet. You'll be the first one to know. And what about you? This is your responsibility, or did you forget that?"

"I am quite aware of that, Reek. As we speak I am waiting for someone here in the Vatican so that I can send something positive back to my bosses in Buenos Aires."

Perhaps Rick had spoken too harshly. "That sounds excellent, Juan Alberto. Someone in the Curia?" He looked over at the group of medieval buildings that dominated one side of the square. "I've always wondered where the offices are located."

"I am not precisely inside the Vatican, Reek. In fact I am in St. Peter's Square."

Rick had been walking as he talked, and now stopped. He looked around the vast square and in the distance spotted Juan Alberto, dressed in a dark suit, standing near a group of Japanese tourists. Rick held the phone away from his ear and looked at the time on its face. Against his better instincts—which were to put off meeting with Juan Alberto as long as possible—but giving in to curiosity, he starting walking in his direction. "Stay put, Juan Alberto, I'll be right there." He hung up and the Argentine looked around, a puzzled frown on his face. Juan Alberto appeared the same, with perhaps a few more pounds added to his lank frame. Same slicked-back hair, same clean-shaven face. Same arrogant air that went along with his passport. Like so many natives of Buenos Aires, Juan Alberto considered himself a European who, by some cruel and inexplicable twist of fate, happened to have been born in South America.

Juan Alberto was looking up at the obelisk when Rick approached. "*Huevón*."

Juan Alberto spun around. "*Reek!*" The two exchanged spine-crushing *abrazos*, as required of two Latino men who had not seen each other in years. "You look great, my friend. Who would have thought that these two old *amigos* would reunite here in Italy?"

"Technically speaking, we aren't in Italy, but your point is well taken." Rick pointed to his friend's suit. "You have an appointment and I don't want to keep you, but I happened to be close by so I had to come over."

Juan Alberto looked around and then back at Rick. "He should be here any moment. Ah, I think I see him coming now."

Rick followed his friend's eyes and saw a small man walking toward them carrying something under his arm that appeared to be a large piece of cardboard. The guy wore a tattered suit with a thin tie, and hanging from his other arm was a camera. He was searching the crowd as he walked. Juan Alberto waved and the man nodded and waddled toward them, grasping the cardboard. He looked at Rick's cowboy boots.

"I don't suppose you speak Italian either."

"In fact I do," Rick replied.

"Well, tell your Spanish friend here I don't normally work out in the sun since I don't want the pope to fade. I'll expect a good tip."

"Juan Alberto, the guy said something about the pope fading. What is he—?"

Rick stopped when the man turned the cardboard over and set it up on the stone pavement, braced by two sticks. It was a life-size photograph of the pontiff.

Juan Alberto grinned. "I saw this guy yesterday out on the street, Reek, and had a brilliant idea."

"I don't think I want to ask."

Juan Alberto stepped next to the pope. "I thought that taking the picture in front of St. Peter's would add veracity to the photograph. My boss was expecting me to see the pope, so it makes sense that I would get a photo, no?"

"Absolutely. And the pope is often found in St. Peter's Square greeting visiting wine salesmen."

The short man stood with his camera. "Are you two done chatting? The sun's pretty bright."

Juan Alberto didn't understand the words but somehow got the point. He walked next to the pope and tried putting his arm over the white cardboard shoulder. Rick shook his head and wagged a finger. Juan Alberto took his hand down and looked at the camera with a serious face. Rick gave him a thumbs-up as the camera snapped. Then they both looked over the shoulder of the cameraman as he showed them the photos.

"That will be perfect," said Juan Alberto. "Reek, all I have are fifty euro notes. Could you spare something smaller so I can tip this guy?"

• • ● • •

Piero's lunch spot was Giggetto, a restaurant in the heart of Rome's Jewish quarter, the Ghetto. It was still early when Rick left Juan Alberto, and the weather was perfect, so he decided to walk rather than take a taxi. He crossed the Tiber and made his way to the Via Giulia, one of the straightest in Rome, built by Pope Julius II who gave it his name. As he walked, he dragged his mind away from Lidia and thought of another Giulia, again marveling at how she had changed for the better. She was still the same person, programmed for success, but at least the exterior made it more pleasant to be around her. And what was wrong with being a success in business? That's what he was trying to do, wasn't it? Maybe he should give her a call, especially since Lidia was now very much out of the picture.

Piero was sitting at a table reading the menu when Rick walked through the door. To Rick's great surprise, his uncle's suit jacket was hanging behind him on the chair back. Informality gone rampant. The shirt was perfectly tailored, its sleeves just the right fit between baggy and too tight, and the spread collar held the knot of a solid blue tie. It would all be covered by the napkin once the food arrived.

"Hope I'm not late." Rick took the chair across from his uncle.

"Not at all. I've ordered wine, a Velletri Rosso, so we'll have to have something that goes with red. Which should not be a problem here. Did you eat in the Ghetto often when you lived here?"

"A few times. I had a Jewish classmate who lived down here. She said her family had been in this area of Rome since the forties."

"Not very long."

"Not the nineteen forties, Zio, just the forties. The first century."

"Ah. So you are familiar with the food?"

"Absolutely. Her mother made wonderful *carciofi alla giudia*."

"That is a specialty here."

The waiter arrived with mineral water and the wine, and Piero ordered the Jerusalem artichokes for both of them, along with *supplì al telefono*, another fried specialty. He poured wine into their glasses, they toasted each other, and took their first sips. The room was about half full, mostly with what looked like local businessmen, though few of them wore jackets or ties. Perhaps that was what had convinced Piero to go casual.

"I saw Sergeant Lamponi just before I came here and she told me about your meetings this morning, but I'd like to hear about them from you. You went first to the street where Count Zimbardi spent his last days, if I remember correctly."

"At least part of his last days. He saw various people, including Rospo the bookie and Syms-Mulford, as we found out later from Rospo. So the man was busy. But let me go over each of the people we saw."

Piero took another drink of wine and sat back to listen. Rick described the street in the order he and Carmella had walked it: Signor Avellone the furniture restorer, Pina in the *salumaio*, Ahmed the pizza maker, Leopoldo who fixed mopeds, and finally two of the three generations of Stampatelli in the print shop. By the time he finished they were well into the flat, crisp artichokes and crunchy, round *supplì* which had arrived at the same time as Ahmed. Rick cut one of the rice balls in half and the cheese inside it stretched into the strings that gave the dish its nickname.

"Sergeant Lamponi told me of her suspicions that male villainy may have been at play," said Piero when Rick finished. He popped the last crunchy piece of his artichoke into his mouth while awaiting Rick's reply.

"She does have a penchant for suspecting such things, but in this case she could be correct. The count's interest in Pina may well have been for more than her memories of living on the street. And the middle Stampatelli could also have been in a relationship with the lovely Pina, which the arrival of the rich count on the scene threatened. If that's what happened, it puts Ludovico Stampatelli on a list of suspects."

"You will have to go back and talk with Ludovico. And what about the bookie? Did you get anything from him?"

The waiter appeared to take away their plates and inquire as to what would be next. Rick did not hesitate, ordering *melanzane alla parmigiana*, while Piero opted for *funghi porcini*.

Rick took another sip of the *vino rosso*. "An interesting fellow, our man Rospo. The way he talked was right on character for a bookie. Like in a movie. Mind you, it was difficult to picture him as such, he being dressed in what was essentially a short skirt. But he was helpful in getting more of a picture of the count, whom he described as a good customer who paid his bets and was addicted to gambling. It coincided with what I'd heard from the card players at the bar. More important was that Rospo saw the count that last day. By itself that's not much, but he mentioned that Count Zimbardi was with his good friend Girolamo Syms-Mulford. So we can add Syms-Mulford to the list of people who saw the count on the day of his murder."

"Which makes your interview with him more important. I set it up for late this afternoon, by the way. He will meet you at his office."

"Office?"

"He works part-time at some institute for historical studies near the Circus Maximus. I was told he spends his time writing and doing research. This city is filled with little groups that study arcane issues and think they are contributing to the betterment of mankind. I haven't seen much improvement as a result of their efforts, but what do I know? I'm only a cynical policeman."

"Did you run a check on him?"

"Dual citizenship with Great Britain, as you would expect, but essentially he's clean." He studied the bottle and appeared to be on the verge of ordering another. Instead he changed topics. "You're still planning on moving into the apartment tomorrow, Riccardo?"

"Yes, I thought I would. When I leave here I'm going to buy sheets for the bed and towels for the bathroom, and drop them off. Tomorrow morning I'll leave and let you get back to a normal home life."

"Such as it is." Piero shook his head. "Did you know that I almost got married five years ago?"

Rick had his wineglass at his lips, but he brought it down slowly to the table. Rick's mother always said that his uncle was not one to share details of his personal life, which made the comment a stunner. When Rick had been in high school in Rome, Piero was working somewhere in the south, and the Montoyas didn't see him often. When they did, the policeman was anything but forthcoming about things personal. Rick's mother complained about Piero's need for privacy, saying it wasn't very Italian. Indeed, when he started working on translations, Rick found that there is no word in Italian for "privacy." In the phone call when he told his mother of his plans for moving to Rome, she didn't even ask him to find out what was going on with her brother's life outside the office. For her it was a lost cause.

So Rick was jolted by the peripety of his uncle's question.

"No, Zio, I didn't."

Piero studied his wineglass. "She was a doctor—still is, of course. I met her when I was working on an especially complicated case in Sicily, and she had been called in to help the medical examiner. We started seeing each other, frequently. After solving that case I went through a slow period at the office, almost no criminal activity. It doesn't happen often, but when it does, we police find it a mixed blessing; boredom, but also the chance to relax and enjoy life outside the office. She came to think that that was the way it always was in police work, and I didn't have the heart to tell her it wasn't. We talked about moving in together and even marriage. I knew that we were in the eye of the hurricane, its wall about to bear down on me, and that's exactly what happened. All hell broke loose, a series of mob murders that were part of a power struggle between the families. I went for days, weeks, without seeing her, and she caught on to what a policeman's life is really like. She concluded that it wasn't for her." He took a long swig of wine. "Can't say that I blamed her."

Rick didn't know how to respond. The Italian in him said that Piero was opening up to him for a reason, perhaps expecting Rick to respond in kind when the opportunity arose. Or he just wanted to show that he trusted his nephew. Certainly this revelation would not be shared with Rick's mother, and Piero sensed that. More likely the man had simply come to a stage in his life when he needed someone outside the office to talk to about things. That was what Anna had said back in Albuquerque, but she had been referring to his work. Personal stuff was not what Rick expected.

Fortunately, the second courses arrived and were placed in front of them. Eggplant parmesan was one of Rick's favorites, and this one looked especially inviting. Straight from the broiler, it was in a round metal dish with handles, and the edges were crusted with burnt cheese, a sure sign of the real thing. He told himself to wait before digging in. Like with pizza just out of the oven, the combination of tomato and cheese on *melanzane alla parmigiana* was a recipe for a burned mouth. Caution was required, but the smells and look of the dish silently urged him to dig in. Piero's *porcini* mushrooms were less menacing but equally inviting. Rather than grilled, these came out of the oven looking like two steaks sprinkled with parsley and wafting an aroma of garlic. Wishes of *buon appetito* were exchanged.

"What is your feeling about this case so far, Riccardo?"

Rick was relieved his uncle had changed the subject; the previous one was making him uncomfortable. If the man wished to return to his private life at a later time, he was ready to listen, but he wouldn't probe. Rick concluded he must be more of a Montoya than a Fontana when it came to being nosy, though his mother would never characterize innocent interest in a relative's life as being nosy.

"The most logical scenario is still a mugging gone bad, Uncle, but since reading the count's papers and talking with people he knew, I cannot help thinking that there is more to it. He clearly had discovered something he didn't like, but what was it and who was doing it? I keep thinking that it has to be connected to the people he saw on the last days, but logic tells me it could have nothing to do with them." He carefully sliced a piece of eggplant.

"I like the way your mind works, Riccardo. Perhaps your meeting with this man Syms-Mulford will get us some answers. Also, I have tracked down the harp teacher, so you and Sergeant Lamponi can go see her tomorrow. Is that *melanzane* to your liking?"

"Yes, it's excellent." He took a drink from his glass of mineral water, sloshing it around on the top of his mouth where the blistered skin was starting to peel off.

Rick didn't have to wait long for the door to the courtyard to open, which was fortunate since he was weighted down with heavy shopping bags.

The *portiere* had beamed when he saw Rick's face through

the hole in the door. "Mister Montoya. Let me help you with the bags."

So now it was mister. "That's all right, Giorgio, I've got them. If you could just give me the key, I'll be fine." He started walking back to the elevator, with Giorgio scurrying ahead of him. They came together again at the elevator door, where Rick had put down his burdens and pressed the button. He took the key from the man's hand. "I can handle it from here, thank you."

"Are you sure there is nothing else I can help with?"

"If there is, I'll call down. That phone I saw in the kitchen rings in your room?"

"Yes, Mister Montoya." He couldn't keep his eyes off Rick's cowboy boots.

Once in the apartment Rick put down his shopping bags and stepped into the living room. Giorgio must have come up and opened the shutters and windows to air out the place, since light streamed in from both sides of the room. After taking one step, he froze.

Two unblinking eyes looked straight at Rick.

The intruder was sitting in the chair nearest the open window on the right side. He must have come across the rooftops, climbed in, and was deciding what to do next. Rick interrupted his thought, and now the two exchanged stares without speaking. Finally Rick broke the impasse.

"If you were looking for valuables, you came to the wrong apartment. As you can see it's almost deserted." Still the intruder remained silent and didn't move…perhaps deciding if he could make a leap for the open window and escape. Rick continued, his voice calm. "Or were you looking for something else? Maybe a place to sleep? Or perhaps something to eat."

The last word elicited a reaction, and it was the one Rick expected.

"Meow."

"Is that all you have to say for yourself? You break into my apartment and you can't even apologize? Wait a minute; have you been in here before? You look like you think you own the place." He walked to the chair and stroked the cat under the chin where a collar hung loosely from the neck. While continuing to scratch with his right hand, Rick turned the collar and read what was on the metal disc hanging from it: *Fellini*, and below it a phone number. "Classy name."

Fellini didn't appear to hear, being completely immersed in the scratching session. Rick pulled out his cell phone and punched in the number. It rang three times before a woman answered.

"Who is this?" Annoyance dripped from the words, spoken with a Roman accent.

Rick chuckled. "You don't know me, but Fellini has broken into my apartment and is holding me hostage." Not entirely untrue; when Rick had stopped the neck-scratching the cat had pawed him until he resumed it.

"I don't need any practical jokes today, thank you very much. Who is this?"

"This is Riccardo. Fellini came through my window, and—"

"He does that." The words were clipped and impatient, making it impossible to guess the age of the speaker. "Just push him back out and he'll find his way home. You must be new in the *quartiere* or you'd know that."

"Excuse me for being new. And thank you for the warm welcome to the neighborhood."

The sarcasm was wasted. "Look, I'm busy with customers. Fellini can take care of himself. Good afternoon." She hung up.

"Your mistress is one tough cookie," said Rick to the cat in English. Accustomed to being addressed in Italian, Fellini tilted his head at Rick, stared for a few moments, and decided it was time for a bath. Rick took his bags into the bedroom and made the bed. When he returned the cat was gone.

• • ● • •

The institute where Girolamo Syms-Mulford occupied an office was located in a house at the edge of the Aventine, the southernmost of the city's famous hills and the most tranquil. It overlooked the Circus Maximus, recognizable by its oval shape but now just an immense open field of dirt and occasional patches of grass. For the World Cup, and other big events, the city government set up a huge screen at one end, for the entertainment of the masses. It was not as good as chariot races, but given the municipal budget it was the best they could do to keep alive the Roman tradition of bread and circuses. The institute's building had once been a luxurious residence, and like so many such buildings around Rome, it had been turned into offices. Tall trees, classic Roman pines, surrounded the structure and gave it an aura of stability. Rick estimated that it had been built in the nineteen twenties, though the imposing fence and a guard house were much more recent. At the moment no one was guarding, and he pushed the buzzer at the gate, which immediately clicked open. Not very tight security. The path meandered around the trees to the front door, which was ajar. He pushed it open and found himself in what had been an elegant residential hallway, but now was bare except for a table that held pamphlets of the institute.

"Can I help you?"

The voice was from an open door to one side. Rick walked to it and saw a woman sitting at a desk in a room that must have been a vestibule when a family had resided there. With the desk, her chair, and a small bookcase, it was cramped. Rick stood at the doorway. "Signor Syms-Mulford? I have an appointment."

"Halfway up the stairs, first door on the left."

Rick thanked her, started up a circular stairway, and came to a small landing. The door, slightly open, was on the left, just as she had said. Rick knocked.

"Come in," said a stately voice speaking English.

Rick pushed open the door as a gentleman—most certainly a gentleman—rose from behind a large, wooden desk. His ample frame was covered by a tweed suit seeing its last use of the season before the arrival of warmer weather. The head of hair was the most impressive feature of Syms-Mulford. Thick, full, and white, it sent the signal that, come what may, it would be there for the duration. The man came around the desk and shook Rick's hand with a firm grip.

"Mister Montoya, I trust. The commissioner told me that you speak English, so I didn't see the need to use Italian." He glanced down at Rick's boots. "I do trust you'll understand the Queen's English."

"If not, you can translate it into Italian."

"Quite, quite. Do sit down. Coffee?" He motioned Rick toward one of two leather chairs.

The office was not spacious, but considerably larger than that of the woman downstairs. It had an excellent view of the Circus Maximus, such as it was, but more impressively of the south side of the Palatine Hill, the most exclusive address in the city two millennia ago. Bookshelves lined the other walls but Rick couldn't read the titles. Probably all history; wasn't that what the man studied? He turned down the offer of coffee.

"Thank you for meeting with me, Mr. Syms-Mumlford."

The man took on a serious look as he settled into the other chair, and Rick expected a question. "It is my duty to help the authorities. But I am puzzled by your presence. Obviously, an American, but one, I trust, who is fluent in Italian."

"I am fluent, yes. The police call on me in certain situations." Rick moved his hand in the air.

A conspiratorial smile spread across Syms-Mulford's mouth. "Ah, I see. Hush, hush, and all that. I had a dear friend at Her Majesty's embassy here who was often involved in delicate situations. At least that's the way he described his work."

"I do translations."

Syms-Mulford smiled conspiratorially. "Of course you do. Well, I certainly won't press you about what you are engaged in."

"Thank you, Sir. But what is important right now is getting to the bottom of Count Zimbardi's death."

"Hear, hear."

"You had know the count for a long time?"

"Indeed, I had. I lived in Florence as a child until I was sent off to school in England. The Italians thought it barbaric that I would be dispatched to another country at so young an age, but the Syms-Mulfords had been doing it for generations. Umberto and I found ourselves at the same school, and immediately discovered that we were both half Italian and had grown up in Italy. We became thick as thieves, the two of us, speaking Italian when we needed to keep secrets." He grunted. "Got into trouble with that trick on several occasions, I dare say. We kept in touch after the university, and when I moved to Rome the friendship was fortified."

Rick moved his eyes across the shelves and back to his host. "You are a historian?"

"I suppose that is one way to describe my work. I am a student of Vatican history, but specifically the eleventh to the fifteenth centuries, from Gregory the Seventh to the arrival of Martin Luther on the scene. If you know anything about the period, Mister Montoya, you know that it was one which gave us some of the more colorful popes, if I may characterize them in that manner."

Rick remembered something. "Perhaps you can tell me who Anacleto was."

A puzzled look on Syms-Mulford's face changed quickly to a smile. "Ah, Anacleto, of course. The name of the street where Umberto was doing his…research. I suppose you've been to it?"

Rick deflected the question with his own. "I was curious as to the origin of the name. A pope?"

"No, at least not in the *Annuario Pontificio*, which is the official Vatican position. Anacleto was an anti-pope, one of dozens throughout church history, but his anti-papacy was

especially messy, even by the standards of the time. It began when Honorius the Second died, and a group of mostly younger cardinals immediately got together and elected Gregorio Papareschi as his successor. Papareschi took the papal name Innocent the Second. The vote outraged Cardinal Pietro Pierleoni's supporters, who promptly elected him pope. That was Anacleto. Both men were consecrated as pope the same day, but in different churches. Ironically, given his eventual anti-pope designation, Anacleto's ceremony took place in St. Peter's, since his Roman family had control of it. What followed was a schism that lasted about eight years, during which Innocent traveled around Europe garnering support for his papacy, but it was really only when Anacleto died that the dust-up ended."

He crooked his head at Rick. "Was that more than you really wanted to know about this fellow Anacleto, Mister Montoya?"

Rick was impressed. The guy really knew his stuff, and imparted it with the aura of a true academic. The upper-class British accent helped greatly, of course.

"Not at all, that was fascinating. So you were aware of the count's hobby and its connection with the street of that name."

"Indeed, I was. Umberto frequently recounted his daily adventures to me. His project was not exactly the type of research that I normally engage in, mind you. I'm more into poring over ancient documents. But such efforts as his can have their place, I suppose."

How could he ask about skullduggery without revealing that he had read it in the count's papers? Rick asked: "What kind of adventures did the count tell you about?"

Syms-Mulford folded one leg over the other, revealing a gray silk sock. "Perhaps that was the wrong word to characterize his interviews. I don't recall exactly, but there was one source, a woman, I believe, who knew a great deal about the street."

That would be Pina. "Do you recall anything specific he said about her, or the others on the street? We can't help speculating

that his death had a connection with someone on the street."

"Assuming it was not just random violence? Such things do happen in the city." He took a pensive breath. "I assume you are asking if there was any kind of conflict with someone on the street. Well, certainly not with this woman; the way he described it, he had a good relationship with her. The others on the street?" He shook his head. "I don't recall anything that would suggest a problem, and I think he would have said something."

"When did you see the count last?" Rick knew the answer, if Rospo was to be believed.

"It was the very day of the evening he was killed. We met for coffee at a bar where he used to play cards. Not the most elegant of establishments, but he enjoyed going there."

That would be Il Tuffo, so the stories matched. "How did he seem that day? Different from other meetings?"

The question took Syms-Mulford out of his previously reserved demeanor, and he coughed, which Rick took to be a stalling device. "Umberto was not quite himself, which I took to be connected somehow to his bookie. The man was leaving just as I arrived. Perhaps he brought Umberto news that his horses had not performed well. I trust the police are aware of my friend's gambling habit."

"Yes," Rick answered simply. No need to tell him that the count's bar buddies and Rospo had been interviewed. "You didn't ask him what was bothering him?"

"I had tried scolding him about the gambling in the past, and it never did any good. I was not about to push him on it again."

"Do you know where he went after you saw him?"

"To Via Anacleto. But you probably already knew that."

Rick didn't want to answer, so he just nodded. "Thank you for your time. I must let you get back to your work." He got to his feet, followed by Syms-Mulford.

"I am always willing to help the authorities," he said with a conspiratorial smile. "Especially when they are involved in delicate situations, like my embassy friend."

"Mr. Syms-Mulford, I am really only—"

"Of course, of course. I understand." He drew an imaginary zipper across his lips.

• • ● • •

Rick took a long pull on his beer, a local lager that Art had recommended. The TV on the wall near them had a basketball game, but since neither team was recognizable, it wasn't even clear in what country it was being played. Half the players sported heavy beards. The usual odor of stale beer mixed with fried foods floated through the pub's air, somehow dimming the already faint light coming from randomly placed fixtures. From Guido's perspective it was a plus: it kept the electric bill down as well as making it difficult for his patrons to notice the dust.

At one of the tables sat Rick and Art Verardo, glasses of beer before them. Art wore his usual accountant's uniform; Rick had on jeans and a lightweight sweater.

"Why didn't you tell me she was a nun?"

"And spoil your fun? I couldn't do that." Art chuckled and took a drink from his glass. "And you know, Rick, what they say about kissing a nun."

"I do, and that joke will never be the same for me after seeing Sister Teresa." He sighed a profound sigh. "I feel guilty asking her for help with the crazy Argentine."

"Nonsense, that's just the kind of thing she does, if I remember correctly. Tell me something; is she still strikingly good looking, despite a total lack of makeup?"

Rick could only nod and stare at his beer glass. A cheer went up from a corner of the pub from a group of men watching the basketball game, but they were too far from Rick and Art's table to hear what language they were speaking, or if English, with what kind of accent. Most had beards.

"Rick, my friend, you seem despondent, and Guido doesn't allow

despondency here. If you don't snap out of it he'll give us the bum's rush. There is no reason for you to be down in the dumps, despite the small detail of your beautiful ex-girlfriend taking vows. You are not to blame—at least I hope you aren't. But consider this: you're now living in Rome, Italy. Think of that: Rome, Italy, the Eternal City. There are people who would kill to be living here, and…"

He held up his hand. "Wait, that reminds me, how is your count's murder investigation going? Is the perpetrator in custody, so that the Roman public can once again walk the streets in safety, knowing the rogue is behind bars? Has this wicked fiend finally been—"

"Enough, Art. The answer is no, but we're working on it."

"Your reply does not instill confidence. Have you interrogated the harp teacher yet?"

"No, but we talked to the people on the street where the count spent his last day." Rick told him of the count's street history project and the people he and Carmella had interviewed on Via Anacleto. Art focused immediately on Pina, the *salumaio*.

"So, this Count Zimbardi could have been interested in more than her salami."

"Leave it to your perverse mind to go right to that detail. I also talked this afternoon with the count's dearest friend, another Anglo-Italian."

"We get a few of those here to watch British football."

As if on cue, shouts exploded from the corner.

"Art, this is not the kind of place Girolamo Syms-Mulford would frequent, I can assure you."

"Too classy for him?"

"You could say that."

"Who's too classy?" It was a feminine voice, causing Rick and Art to look up from their drinks and see Giulia standing behind their table. They both got to their feet and exchanged kisses with the new arrival. She was not in her business uniform, but instead wore a colorful sweater and slacks, both fitting nicely.

"You're looking quite fetching tonight, my dear." Art held the chair out for her. "What would you like to drink?"

"Thank you, Art. A glass of red wine would be nice."

"Guido's house plonk? Coming right up." He got up and walked to the bar.

"How are you settling in, Rick?" She pushed her hair on one side behind the ear, exposing a dangly earring.

"I'm moving into an apartment tomorrow. And keeping busy otherwise. Did you find someone to be your tour guide?"

He hadn't meant the question to embarrass her, but it appeared to have that effect. "Oh, that, I'll work it out. I should not have bothered you, with moving in and all. Where's the apartment?"

"Near Piazza Navona. It's owned by a distant relative who lives in Perugia."

"I've just recruited someone to start a branch in Perugia. It gets a lot of tourists. But there I go talking business again."

The glass of red wine was placed in front of her. "You always talk business." Art sat back in his seat. No one said anything for a full minute after she tapped her glass to theirs. Finally Art broke the silence.

"Rick saw Lidia."

"Oh, really? How did that go, Rick?"

Rick gave Art an annoyed look before answering. "Well, since our friend here had not informed me of Lidia's new, uh, vocation, I was naturally taken aback. But it turned out fine, and we had a very pleasant conversation."

Giulia smiled. "You weren't disappointed?"

"Why would I be disappointed?"

"This conversation is turning awkward," said Art, "and it is my fault for bringing up Lidia. Why don't we talk about something else? Like your business, Giulia? Did you find the guide you needed?"

"Rick just asked me that. No, but my problem now is something else."

"There are always problems when you are running your own business," said Art. "It's why I have preferred not to branch out on my own. My boss has the problems, leaving me to simply crunch numbers all day."

Rick tried to be a bit more diplomatic. Perhaps some of his father's skills had rubbed off on him. "Since I'm starting my own business I wouldn't mind hearing about yours, Giulia."

She smiled, seemed about to take his hand, but didn't. "Thank you, Rick. Well, it's this: we get requests from tour operators from South America and Spain for guided tours of the city in Spanish. If I had someone…" She held up her hands defensively. "Not you, Rick. I know you speak Spanish but I wasn't thinking of you. Honestly."

"I believe you, Giulia." He looked at Art and then back at her. "By coincidence, I just might know someone who could at least temporarily fill the bill. Do they have to know Rome well or do you tell them what they're supposed to say?"

"Each one of my tours is programmed ahead of time. The material is written out and the guide, at least for the new guides, merely have to read what is prepared for them. Of course it's in English."

"This guy knows enough English so he could probably work with that."

"Rick," said Art, "you're not thinking of—?"

"I'm not sure if he'd be willing," Rick interrupted, "but he's temporarily in Rome and may have some time on his hands. If he does, I'll ask him to give you a call." He looked at Art, who was rubbing his head like he'd suddenly developed a headache.

Art picked up the two empty beer glasses. "I'll get us a couple more."

"I think it's my turn to buy, Art."

"No, Rick, I embezzled enough at the office today to cover this easily." He got up and walked to the bar, leaving Rick and Giulia to themselves.

"When are we going to get together, Rick? I mean just the two of us. Are you free for dinner the day after tomorrow?"

Was she asking him out? He was the virtually unemployed new arrival and she the successful businesswoman, so what was the protocol here? He'd figure it out later.

"I am definitely free, Giulia, and I'd enjoy that."

Chapter Eight

Moving day.

After breakfast Rick had bade farewell to his uncle, bundled his suitcases into a taxi, and used his new keys to get himself into the courtyard and apartment. Giorgio was nowhere to be found; it was either his day off or he was conveniently somewhere else in the building so he wouldn't have to help. Rick managed to get everything into and off the elevator, and pushed it into the apartment. The windows were shut, as he'd left them, but the outside shutters were open to let in light. He looked out over the rooftops and wondered if Fellini had shown up to be annoyed at finding himself shut out. He opened one of the windows, just in case, and wrestled the suitcases into the bedroom. He'd made the bed on his last visit, and now opened one of the suitcases on it.

After everything was in its place he walked back through the living room and dining nook to the kitchen. It was sparsely furnished, but had all the basics he needed, starting with a pot large enough to cook pasta. On the shelves next to a set of plates he saw the standard espresso pot, good to have, though he planned to have his breakfast on the street. He would start the next morning trying out the neighborhood bars to decide which would become his regular stop. Everyone made good *cappuccini*, so the issue was the baked goods. They had to have warm, fresh *cornetti*.

He looked in the refrigerator, and it contained a single bottle of mineral water. Time to stock it, and the shelves, beginning with something for lunch. He picked up the keys that he'd left on the small dining table and went out the door.

The building had a rear exit, bringing him out to a crowded little *piazza*, its quiet a contrast with the din of the front of the building. Parked cars filled the space at strange angles, their squat forms contrasting with a tall, stone Corinthian column in the middle. Even in Rome, it looked out of place. Rick walked through the square to a narrow street and began searching for a deli. He knew that in this city there was always a *salumaio* nearby, and he was not disappointed. He spotted one, and as he got closer, the smell of fresh cheese and meats attacked his nostrils. He pushed open the door and found himself in an establishment which could be anywhere in Italy. Fresh pasta lay in baskets in the window, cans and jars lined the shelves on two sides, and directly ahead was a display case with delicacies of all types, from prepared dishes ready for the oven to any number of cheeses and desserts.

He had found his *salumaio*. Adding to the store's draw, as if convenience and variety were not enough, was the very attractive woman behind the counter who was now waiting on a customer. She glanced at him and smiled as she dealt with an elderly man's sliced prosciutto, asking how many *etti* he needed. Rick watched the transaction, and immediately had the sense that he'd met the woman before. There was something about her manner. But where? He guessed she was about his age, so he could have known her when he'd lived in Rome as a kid. No, too long ago. At the pub or sitting near him in a restaurant? No, he would have remembered that. The man took his sack and change, and walked toward the door. She looked at Rick.

"What may I get you today?"

He had been so mesmerized by her looks that he hadn't thought about what he needed. Why hadn't he made a list?

But he could always come back; it's not like he had to get into the car and drive to the supermarket, like in Albuquerque. She waited, and the smile was starting to turn down, but only slightly. Amused? Or bemused?

"Orange juice?"

She pointed to the shelf to his right. "Regular and blood orange, take your pick."

He pulled one carton off and put it on the counter. "*Rosette.* Two." He pointed to rolls in the bread bin behind her. "And then some mortadella. One *etto* should do it." He was into it now, thinking lunch.

"If you're going to make two sandwiches," she said as she wrapped the rolls, "I'd suggest at least two *etti*," she said, "or you'll both go hungry."

"It's just me," Rick said while thinking: was she probing? Don't flatter yourself, Montoya. "*Va bene, due etti.*"

"Mayonnaise?" She sliced the mortadella. "It's over there." She pointed to another shelf and Rick picked off a tube and added it to his pile.

"That *insalata russa* looks tempting." He pointed to a pan of diced potatoes, peas, and carrots in a thick dressing, topped with clear aspic. It was one of Rick's favorites that he hadn't eaten since his last time in Italy. "About this much." He put his thumbs and fingers together, and she spooned out that size into a plastic container."

"*Vino?*" She pointed to the opposite shelf.

"Good idea." He thought about what should go with his sandwiches and couldn't decide. He certainly didn't want to make another rookie mistake in front of her.

"That *bianco* on the end should be perfect." Was she was reading his mind?

"I was just going to pick that one." He took the bottle of white from the shelf. "I think that should do it."

She nodded and added up the items while he watched her tap

the keys. Nothing on the ring finger. She hit total, tore off the paper, and handed it to Rick before putting his items in a plastic bag. Rick paid her, said thank you, and turned to leave. After one step he stopped.

"What day are you closed?"

"All day Sunday, and Monday in the morning. If you forgot something, I'm here until seven."

Rick swallowed hard, thanked her again, and left the store. All the way back to his apartment he tried to remember where he'd seen her before. Nothing came to him and he decided it was just wishful thinking. He also decided he wasn't that hungry, so made one sandwich and put it on a plate with the half the salad. Should he open the bottle of wine? No, it wasn't cold, and he needed all his senses for his afternoon meeting with Carmella at the music conservatory to interview Signora Angelini. Instead, he opened the mineral water, poured some in a glass, and carried everything to the dining table. As he sat down he noticed a gray face staring at him through the window glass. Or was it staring at the sandwich?

"Sorry, Fellini, I've got nothing for you."

The next time he went food shopping he would pick something up for the poor guy.

Rome's most famous music academy was located on a quiet side street near the Spanish Steps, far enough away from the shops that most tourists seen wandering down the street were lost. Rick knew he was on the right one when he spotted Carmella's police car parked in the distance. Further confirmation came from the deep tones of a violin bouncing off the buildings, though when he got closer he realized it was a cello. Carmella was talking on her cell phone as he approached, waving her free hand. As he got closer her voice drowned out the cello.

"Well, do what you want. You should be old enough by now to make your own decisions, even though you've never made a good one in your life. But unlike the last time, don't expect me to bail you out when it doesn't work. Even if you don't learn from your mistakes, I learn from mine." She noticed Rick approaching and lowered her voice. "I have to go. *Ciao, figlio. Baci.*"

Talking with her son had not put Carmella in a good mood. He could tell by the scowl on her face, and hoped it wouldn't transfer to him. "*Salve*, Carmella."

He needn't have worried, she went directly to business. "*Salve*, Riccardo. I've been thinking about this Angelini woman we're going to interview. There is no way that the count would have started taking harp lessons at his age, there has to be something more to it. You know what I'm expecting here?"

Given the sergeant's propensity to think the worst of the opposite sex, he knew exactly what she was expecting here. "No, Carmella, what are you expecting?"

"Monkey business. The count wasn't just plucking her harp."

"But that's what you said with the woman who runs the *salumaio*."

Carmella threw him a malicious smile. "So he couldn't be stringing along two women?"

Rick was rescued from having to reply by his ringing phone. He fished it out of his pocket while Carmella waited impatiently.

"Montoya... oh, *ciao* Lidia, I mean Teresa...that's very kind of you...tomorrow morning an appointment with him?...of course, I'll make it work. My Argentine friend will be very appreciative... wait, let me get something to write it down." He squeezed the phone between his ear and shoulder and made an "I need something to write with" gesture to Carmella. She pulled a pen and pad from her jacket pocket and passed it to him. "Okay, go ahead... got it. I can't thank you enough, Lidia...I mean Teresa. Sorry, I can't get used to it...bye." He tore off the sheet and passed the pad and pen back to the policewoman. "That was an old high school friend. She's helping me with something."

"An old friend, and you can't remember if her name is Lidia or Teresa?"

"It's a long story. Let's go, Signora Angelini is expecting us."

They walked up a few steps and entered the conservatory. It had been all stone on the outside, giving it a feeling of permanence that was typical of buildings in the neighborhood, but inside it was wood and more wood, starting with creaking floors. A long hallway extended straight ahead to a tall window in the distance. Lights dangled at precise intervals from cords attached to the high ceiling, spreading a dim light on the floor in front of doors on both sides of the corridor. Behind one of the doors was the invisible cellist, now playing minor chords, like background music in a suspense movie.

"Can I help you?" The voice came from a window squeezed between bulletin boards crammed with notices competing for space. It came from a man dressed in a blue suit with the musical logo on the breast pocket. He looked up at them from over a copy of *La Gazzetta dello Sport*.

"We have an appointment with Signora Angelini," said Carmella.

"Third door to the right." His eyes dropped back to the paper.

As Rick and Carmella started down the middle of the hall, he wondered if the floor would hold them, since its well-worn boards not only groaned but bent slightly under their weight. Rick moved to one side. When they reached the door, Carmella rapped loudly.

"*Avanti.*"

Signora Angelini was not what Rick expected, especially after Carmella's theory about why the count was taking lessons. He was unable to estimate a true age, which, he decided, was just what the woman intended. Bright red hair, bordering on orange, was piled on top of her head like a lacquered beehive. The makeup was so heavy it looked like she had forgotten to take off one layer before applying another, and the same could be said of the bright red lipstick. It was a look. But as striking as she was above the neck, it was her arms that drew Rick's attention. Years, or more likely decades earlier, Signora Angelini must have become enamored with tattoos, since her arms were now covered with ink of different colors. Had she once had an affair with a tattoo artist? Unfortunately, she was now paying the price for a bad decision earlier in her life, though it was impossible for him to ascertain how much earlier. Each of the designs had a musical theme, but now the harps, angels, and musical notes were faded by time and blurred from wrinkles, some to the point of being unidentifiable. Back in New Mexico Rick had wondered what some of his tattooed friends would look like after the passage of time. Now he knew. To her credit, Signora Angelini must have come to terms with the inking and made the decision not to be ashamed of it. Her sleeveless blouse was the confirmation.

"Who's he? They told me I would be visited by a policewoman. I expected only one."

"This is Lieutenant Montoya, Signora. He is also working on the case."

Signora Angelini was not happy with the explanation, but waved them both to folding chairs. The room was without frills. Except for an ornate harp next to her, and a stack of metal music stands in one corner, it held only the row of chairs. The walls were bare, one florescent light hung from the high ceiling, and a single window looked out onto a brick wall. As they took their seats, the distant cello shifted to a slightly less ominous theme, giving Rick hope that something would come out of the interview. He worked hard to keep himself from staring at the woman's arms.

"Thank you for taking the time to speak with us." Rick hoped it would soften the woman's mood. It did not.

"Get it over with. What do you want to know?"

"When did you last see the count?" It was the standard question, and Rick decided to get it out of the way so that his supposed authority was established before Carmella took over.

"He had a regular lesson here about a week before he was killed. I remember my son calling me when he heard the news of the murder. I had told him I was giving Count Zimbardi lessons, so he knew I'd want to know."

"How did he appear that day?" Carmella asked. "Normal? Agitated?"

"My son?"

"No, the count."

"Him? Normal. As bad as ever."

Rick jumped on the reply. "Bad? In what way?"

"He wasn't a very good student, if I might understate. I don't expect all my students to become concert-quality musicians, but the count was essentially tone deaf. He tried, but it was no use. So much determination with so little talent, it was sad, really."

"But you kept trying to teach him."

She held out her arms with the palms up, exposing some tattoos that Rick hadn't seen before, but with a continuation of the musical theme. "That's what I do. I teach, they pay me. It puts food on the table."

"Do you know what made the count decide to learn to play the harp?"

Signora Angelini didn't hesitate with her answer. "'She's Leaving Home.' It was his favorite."

Carmella nodded.

"I don't understand," said Rick.

"Song by the Beatles," said Carmella. "It has harp in the backup."

Unlike Rick, Signora Angelini did not appear surprised by Carmella's mastery of Beatles discography. She continued. "I could see immediately that he would never learn to play, but who am I to be telling him that? And he paid up front for a month of weekly lessons."

"So he'd only been taking lessons for four weeks when he was killed?" Rick asked.

"He'd just paid me for the second month." She noticed the look on Carmella's face and added; "It was nonrefundable."

"How did the count find you?" Carmella asked. "Yellow Pages?"

"Do they still have Yellow Pages? No, he got my name from my son."

"How did he meet your son?"

"He came into his shop one day. My son restores furniture."

Later Rick and Carmella stood on the street in front of the conservatory. The cello music had stopped, replaced by an accordion, its chords back to minor. Carmella leaned against her patrol car, her arms folded across her chest.

"So now Avellone, the furniture restorer, is connected to the harp teacher," she said. "It all goes back to the street. Something happened on that damned street. You have to get back there and talk to those people again."

"Me?"

"I've got another case I'm working on that's coming to conclusion. Lots of paperwork to fill out on it or the judges will toss it out. Tomorrow's my day off so I have to get it done. Why don't you go over and poke around Via Anacleto this afternoon? I'd be curious to know why Avellone didn't mention that his mother was giving the count harp lessons."

Rick was curious too, but didn't want to feel like he was being ordered around by Carmella. "I'll see if I can fit it into my schedule. I have to meet with a friend this afternoon."

Carmella opened the door to the car. "I hope you'll get the name straight before you go."

Rick let the comment go. He was getting used to her sarcasm. "Do you still think the count was doing more with Signora Angelini than plucking the harp?"

"Kid, you still don't want to get it, do you? Did you see those tattoos?" Shaking her head, she got in, started the engine, and drove off at twice the speed allowed for the narrow street.

Rick could not understand why the tattoos confirmed the

monkey business, but was afraid to ask. He pulled out his phone and punched in Juan Alberto's number. From the encounter at St. Peter's Square with the Argentine, he was sure they guy was running low on cash. In New Mexico, Juan Alberto had always been low on cash, and now he was probably spending his money from the wine company like he spent his college allowance—loosely and quickly. This job with Giulia's bus tours would be just the thing to tide him over.

"*Hola,* Reek." There were voices in the background. Was he at a bar at this hour?

"*Hola*, Juan Alberto. I have a couple things. First, I got an appointment for you tomorrow morning at ten with a certain Father Galeazzo, at the Vatican. He should be the guy who can make a decision on wine purchases. Write down this address."

"Wait a moment, let me get something to write with." His voice became muffled, like he was putting his hand over the phone. "*Mijita*, can you give me a pen and paper?" was what Rick thought he heard, spoken in Spanish. A moment later he was back and took down the information. "This is excellent, Reek. I will meet you there at ten."

"What do you mean meet me? This is your appointment."

"I cannot do this alone, Reek. What if this Galeazzo does not speak Spanish? No, no, you must be there with me. It is what good friends do, no?"

Rick rubbed his eyes. "Sure, Juan Alberto, I'll be there. Oh, and there's another thing. I have an American friend who runs a tourism business and wants to expand into dealing with groups from South America. She needs a Spanish-speaker, at least temporarily, and I thought of you. I'll give you her number."

There was hesitation from Juan Alberto. "I don't know, Reek. I'm pretty busy."

Busy with what? Chasing women? "She'll pay you, of course."

"Well, since you are my good friend, Reek, I will call her as a favor to you."

• ● **●** ● •

Via Anacleto was nearly as deserted as the previous day when Rick had walked it with Carmella. A scruffy cat was curled up in the doorway of the garage in the middle of the block, catching a bit of sunshine that made its way through the clouds and landed on the paving stones. Two boys with school backpacks clutched greasy squares of Ahmed's pizza and strolled down the middle of the street as they ate. Chugging along past them was the same ancient Fiat 500 he'd seen on the street before, driven by a man so old Rick guessed him to be the original owner.

First stop would be Signor Avellone, who had some explaining to do after they had found out it was his mother who was giving the count harp lessons. Rick pushed open the door and his sense of smell was immediately enveloped by mineral spirits. His vision took longer to adapt to the darkness, and an annoying buzz pushed into his ears. When he finally got all three senses in order, he spotted Avellone passing an electric sander over what appeared to be a small table or bench. The man wore no mask over his face, but perhaps breathing in all the varnish fumes made him immune to the effects of sawdust. He looked up, noticed Rick, and turned off the sander.

"You're back. Where's the sergeant?"

"Working another case. I have some more questions."

Avellone wiped his hands on his apron, mixing dark brown spots with lighter brown dust. "I didn't think you were here to have a dresser refinished. So ask."

"You didn't tell us that your mother was giving the count harp lessons."

"That doesn't sound like a question." When Rick stood silent, Avellone shrugged a forced shrug. "It didn't seem important. I know my mother couldn't have had anything to do with the count's murder, so why mention it?"

"I think that would have been something for the police, I mean us police, to decide." Rick folded his arms over his chest. He'd read somewhere that doing so was a body language way to establish authority, but the man before him didn't appear fazed. "How did the subject of harp lessons come up? I suppose he just asked you out of the blue if you knew a harp teacher?" Rick snickered.

"Yes."

"Really?"

"Well, there was something else."

"Aha, I thought so."

"When he came in that day he saw a harp that I was restoring for one of my mother's students, and he said he had always wanted to learn to play one. Something about the Beatles. So I gave him Mamma's name."

"Oh. Well, you should have said something. Is there anything else that you 'forgot' to tell us yesterday?" Rick made quotation marks in the air with his fingers.

Avellone gave the question some thought and shook his head. "No. If I had, I would have called you. I mean called the sergeant."

Rick ignored the slight, if it was one. The man was inscrutable, staring at Rick and never changing his expression. No other questions came to mind. "Any detail that you might recall, no matter how trivial it might seem to you, could mean something to us. Don't forget that." Rick heard that said so many times on TV that he thought it would be a good exit line. He turned and left.

Once again, there could not be more of a contrast between the atmosphere of Avellone's shop and that of Pina's deli. The former was eerie darkness with a noxious mixture of the chemical and the distilled hovering in the air. Alimentare Giuseppina overwhelmed the senses in a pleasant and almost sensual way, full of brightness and rich *profumi*. He thought of the place near his apartment where he'd shopped that morning, with that lovely young lady behind the counter. He couldn't very well find fault in the count for returning to this place to enjoy the company of a woman. But was the count meeting with Pina as part of his historical research? Sure, Rick.

He was starting to think like Carmella.

Pina, holding court for two women, stood behind the counter wearing the same apron as the day before. One woman clutched the bag with her food, having already paid. The other was ordering items from Pina, who sliced and wrapped as the three talked. Rick could overhear the conversation and it was clearly not about dinner. Someone's son had shamed the family by turning down a good government job, the coveted *posto*, to instead study art at the university. What kind of job can he get with an art degree, assuming he ever finishes? He would have been set for life. How could they let him do that? Rick was glad Carmella wasn't with him, or she might have joined in. At one point Pina noticed Rick and acknowledged him with a stiff smile.

He raised his hand, using a "take your time" gesture that worked in any language. As he waited, he checked out a row of semolina *gnocchi* under the glass counter. They were cut into yellow disks, ready to be put on a baking sheet and slipped into the oven, then garnished with sauce, perhaps tomato. Or maybe gorgonzola. As always happens in a *salumaio*, Rick began thinking about his next meal. Pina's voice interrupted his thoughts.

"You have returned."

He looked up from the display case. "Yes, Signora, with the hope that something else had come to mind since I was here with Sergeant Lamponi."

She wiped her hands on a cloth pulled from below the counter and looked around, as if to be sure no one else would witness their conversation. "I didn't sleep last night, thinking of Umberto. I thought I was over it, but then your visit yesterday brought back all those times he came by here and we…we talked. And laughed. He had quite a sense of humor, Umberto did."

Rick thought it better to let her talk. He sensed there was something coming that could help the investigation. Also, he didn't have any questions in mind to ask her.

"…We had a lot of laughs. He loved to tell me jokes, and some of them were ones I couldn't repeat to you now, if you know what I mean. Not that he wasn't serious about his historical research, mind you. I remember that last day I saw him…" She put her hand to her mouth, took a breath, and regained her composure. "That last day I saw him, he said something about learning from history, and how history repeats itself. That was very profound, don't you think?"

"Yes, indeed it was."

"That's the kind of person he was, profound. Serious. But funny as well. Do you understand what I mean?"

He didn't understand at all. "Of course, Signora. From what you said, it sounds like the count was being reflective that day. Deep thoughts, and all."

She chewed on the observation before replying. "Could be. I don't remember him telling any jokes."

An idea jumped into Rick's head. "Had he been to talk to any other people on the block that day? Before he came to see you?"

"Oh, that I wouldn't know. I don't think he mentioned seeing anyone else. But I could have forgotten. You'll have to ask them."

"I will." So much for that line of questioning.

"Are you closer to finding Umberto's killer?"

"I hope so, Signora."

Rick thanked her and left, though not before taking another glance at the *gnocchi*. Outside, he continued down the block and tried to convince himself that he'd not wasted his time with Pina. What new information had been gleaned? That the count that day had been more reflective than usual? It was thin gruel indeed.

Ahmed was at his post behind the counter, averting his eyes after spotting Rick, who decided it wasn't worth asking the man any questions. A sign on the metal grill of Signor Leopoldo's motorbike repair shop read "*TORNO SUBITO.*" If the mechanic really was coming right back, he would see him after a visit to the print shop, the next door down.

The Stampatelli operation was in full swing, if the thump

thump of the large printing press and the presence of all three generations gave an indication of such. At the long table at one side, grandfather Eugenio was carefully stacking sheets of paper into equal piles. Next to Eugenio, studying what Rick guessed to be a ledger book, was his son. Carmella had been correct; Ludovico Stampatelli was the man they had seen going into Pina's shop the previous day. He wore a black tee-shirt that looked a size too small, but he struck Rick as the type who would buy shirts that size to show off his biceps. A stubble of black beard covered his chin and cheeks, the color matching his thick hair. His hands, like his father's, were stained with ink. Silvio, the youngest of the three, was the first to notice Rick. He was sweeping the floor around the press, and when he saw the visitor a frightened look spread across his face. Quickly he pushed a small pile of paper scraps into a dustpan and emptied them into a bin in the corner, like he would be punished if the place were not neat for the arrival of visitors. The boy's father looked up from his ledger, then the grandpa also noticed the visitor.

"Can I help you?" asked Ludovico Stampatelli.

"He's the policeman who came by yesterday, asking about the count," the old man said to his son. Then to Rick: "Where's your sergeant?"

"She was called away on another case."

Ludovico's facial expression noticeably darkened when Rick changed from potential customer to cop. He stepped forward. "Didn't my father answer all your questions yesterday?"

"I'm talking again to everyone on the block who spoke with the count. It's standard procedure since people often remember things. And you weren't even here yesterday, so you can tell me now what conversations you had with the count."

"The nosy old coot wasn't interested in talking to me. He spent most of his time with Pina, and when he was here, my father told him enough stories to keep him happy. If you ask me, that history thing was just an excuse to poke his nose where it didn't belong."

"Did you see him the day he was killed?"

"What day was that?"

The son jumped in at that point. "It was the anniversary of the founding of Rome, and we went to the Campidoglio Museums in the afternoon since we could get in for free. You were out that morning delivering a print job when the old man was here. Wasn't he, Grampa?"

"I can't remember, Silvio, my brain isn't as sharp as yours."

Frowning, Ludovico stared at his son for a few moments, and then glanced at his father. "I can't remember either, but I didn't see the count at all that week."

Rick tried to think what Carmella or any other real policeman would ask now, but came up empty, reinforcing his belief that he wouldn't make a good cop. He gave the three Stampatellis the standard "call us if you think of anything" line and left. Outside on the street, he checked to see if the mechanic had returned from his break. The sign was still there, so Signor Leopoldo was still about to be right back. Checking the time on his phone, he decided to walk to the Il Tuffo, only a few blocks away, but then, in Rome's *centro storico*, everything is only a few blocks away. It was about lunchtime, so he hoped that the card players were home eating pasta and he could avoid buying them another round. He didn't need to talk to them again. His purpose in going to the bar was to talk with the woman who worked there. What was her name? Ah, yes, Gilda. How could he forget?

The route took him along Via dei Coronari, a narrow street open only to foot traffic and known for its antiques shops. He remembered being dragged down it as a kid by his mother when she was looking for just the right piece of furniture for their apartment. Her tastes had leaned toward the ornate, and there were plenty of establishments that catered to it. What had surprised him then—and he was reminded of it now—was how few people actually entered these antiques stores. He stopped at one and looked through the glass. The unifying theme of the merchandise, if there was one, he guessed to be early nineteenth century. A woman sat at a writing desk, surrounded by lamps, armoires, busts, tapestries, chandeliers, chairs, and shelves filled with all manner of brick-a-brac. Napoleon could have been sitting next to her and fit in perfectly. He shook his head. Who buys this stuff? The only explanation was that the store had a cadre of loyal customers who popped in on occasion or were alerted when some new old piece was acquired. The woman at the desk did not show concern. Boredom perhaps, but concern, definitely not.

He kept walking, and to his left a small *piazza* appeared with a fountain at its edge. Unblocked by buildings, the sun flowed into the square and reflected off its shiny cobblestones. Rick walked to the bowl of the fountain, scooped some cool water from it, and rubbed it over his face. Just beyond him, at the far end of the *piazza*, potted plants gave partial privacy to the tables of a restaurant, most of them with diners sitting under large umbrellas. The scene couldn't have been more Italian, and it hit him that this *hosteria* would be a perfect place for dinner with Giulia the next night. Rick walked to the opening between the plants, read the posted menu, and went inside to make the reservation. Two minutes later he was working his way through a tangle of alleys to Il Tuffo.

The tables were full, but of blue-collar workers lunching on *panini* and white wine rather than pensioners playing cards. Gilda, with the same haggard look and spotted apron, was bringing a plate of sandwiches to one of the tables when he came in. She gave him a puzzled look which turned to a toothy smile of recognition. Rick remembered that his unfamiliarity with euros caused him to leave her a substantial tip on his previous visit. He'd kicked himself at the time, but now was glad for another rookie error.

"Umberto's distant relative, right?"

"That's correct, Signora. Can I have a coffee, please?"

She got right to it, ignoring an order for another wine at one of the tables, and manhandling the stainless steel machine until it extracted the dark liquid into the tiny cup. She whisked it in front of him and pushed the sugar bowl next to it. "When are you returning to America?"

Rick at first didn't understand, but quickly remembered the cover story Gonzalo had concocted for him: the distant relative from America. "Not for several days. I've been talking to people who knew my…who knew the count. You know, forming a picture of the man."

"That's why you came here the other day."

"Exactly. I talked yesterday with one of his…another of his friends. He told me he'd been here the day the count was killed. Do you remember that?" He spooned sugar into his espresso and stirred, waiting for a reply.

"The British guy? Yeah, I remember that well. Rospo was here too, I think."

"Rospo?" Rick played dumb.

She coughed. "An acquaintance of Umberto. I think Rospo left before the British guy arrived, but maybe it was the other way around. I can't be sure."

"I can't help thinking how sad that was, since the British gentleman didn't realize that it would be the last time he'd see the count."

"From the way they were arguing, it might have been the last time even if Umberto had lived. The two were really going at it. I remember thinking how unlike Umberto it was. He was always so easygoing. And kind. And generous." Lost in memories, she stared into the distance and seemed to be misting up.

"What were they arguing about?"

"What? Oh, the argument? I have no idea. They were speaking English."

Rats. "All in English?"

"Well, now that I think of it, there was at least one word of

Italian, but it's the only one I remember. Umberto at one point yelled out '*mascalzone*.'"

Rick pondered that one as Gilda tended to the men at the tables. The count was calling his boyhood friend a rascal? Maybe they were arguing about a mutual acquaintance. Rospo? More likely it would be Syms-Mulford characterizing Rospo as the *mascalzone,* but then again, the count could have been mad at his bookie for something. Rick's only firm conclusion was that he would have to pay another visit to Mister Gerolamo Syms-Mulford.

He remembered his coffee and added sugar to the small cup. "That was the last time you saw the count as well?"

"No, he came back that evening to play cards."

Rick was about to put the cup to his lips, but stopped. This was news. Why hadn't that come up when he met with the card players? Probably because at that time he was pretending to be a relative of the count and not a policeman, so asking such questions didn't occur to him. The men had no reason to volunteer the information, even if they knew the count was with them the night of his murder.

"Did the count appear any different that night from other times?"

"He did seem nervous."

"Really? What do you mean?"

"It was funny, really. Usually I'd call him a taxi, but that night he had it in his head to take a bus. Someone had given him a bus ticket and he was determined to use it, though I don't think he had ever been on a city bus before. He was uncomfortable about it, I could see that."

"Did the other card players know?"

"No, no. In fact he asked me not to tell them. He was embarrassed."

Which probably meant that none of them had given him the ticket. It had to have been someone he'd seen earlier in the day. Rospo? No, more likely someone on Via Anacleto. If the person who gave him the ticket knew where the count lived, they would have known he'd be crossing that bridge after getting off the bus. Rick pondered and finally sipped his coffee. It was cold.

At that moment Gonzalo entered the establishment carrying two large shopping bags which he put down next to the door. Thankfully, he was back to his butler's outfit. He noticed Rick, smiled, and walked over to him. They shook hands.

"Signor Montoya, it is a pleasure to see you again."

"*Altrettanto*, Gonzalo. Are you on your break?"

He inclined his head toward the bags. "The countess' dry cleaning."

"Can I get you something?"

"A coffee, thank you."

Gilda had returned to her place behind the counter and Rick ordered the espresso for Gonzalo and a mineral water for himself. She went to work.

"Is there any news on the case, Signor Montoya? Perhaps the *commissario* has been in touch with the countess, but she has told me nothing. Not that she is required to do so."

Did Rick detect some bitterness in the man? "I'm not privy to all the details, of course, so I don't know if there have been any breaks in the investigation. I'm sure my—the *commissario*, will call her if there are any."

The coffee came and Gonzalo took a sip, without sugar. "Is your role in it finished, after the translations and the encounter with the count's friends here?"

Rick had a gut feeling that the man could be trusted, and also thought that if he let him in on what he knew, it might be reciprocated. "I've assisted in some of the other details. Interviews on the street where the count was doing his research. I've also spoken to the count's harp teacher." He didn't mention that Carmella had conducted most of that interview.

"Ah, the harp lessons. That was indeed puzzling for me, though after so many years I should have been accustomed to Count Zimbardi's capricious whims." He smiled and took another sip of his espresso. "One time a few years ago, after reading that it was one of Queen Elizabeth's hobbies, he decided he would raise pigeons. Apparently, there is a competitive aspect to pigeons, racing them, which also appealed to his penchant for wagering. But before he could get fully into competition the neighbors complained about the cooing on the roof, and the countess made him get rid of them."

"I recall seeing a photograph of one on the count's desk when I was reading his papers."

"That was Samantha, his favorite. It was very painful for him to part with her."

"I can imagine the disappointment."

"Yes, but he moved on. One of the count's finest character traits was not dwelling on disappointment. If I recall correctly, it was after that that he decided to collect plates."

"Plates?"

Gonzalo drained his cup. "There is an Italian association of restaurants that promotes regional and local dishes. When you order that specialty in one of those restaurants you receive a whimsically decorated ceramic plate at the end of the meal. The count's trips throughout Italy were planned around restaurants that were part of the association, so that he could add to his collection. Of course the culinary aspect of the hobby appealed to him as well; the count was a good fork."

Rick recognized the Italian slang term for someone who enjoys eating. "That doesn't seem to me to be that eccentric a hobby."

"The countess found it extremely déclassé. She put her foot down when he wanted to decorate the walls of the dining room with the plates. He ended up hanging them in the hallway outside his study."

"I don't remember seeing any plates hanging there."

"She had me take them down shortly after the count died and give them to Rocco."

"Rocco?"

"The count's driver, who was quite pleased to get them. Apparently, there is a market for such items on eBay."

"Another coffee, Gonzalo?"

"That's very kind of you, Signor Montoya, but I should be on my way."

"There was one other interview I did, which the *commissario* asked me to do in English... Signor Syms-Mulford. You told me that he called the residence often."

The mention of the name darkened Gonzalo's expression. "Yes, the count's closest friend. They were *compagni di scuola* in England, as he likely told you, and he took the count's death very hard. He has been very attentive to the countess since the murder."

"Attentive?"

"Yes. I know that he's called her almost every day to console the widow of his good friend. Very decent of him." He thanked Rick for the coffee and stepped into the street with the countess' dry cleaning.

Chapter Nine

"Take a good look at that man sitting by himself at the table near the window," Piero said. "Study him carefully and then tell me about him based on what you observe."

Rick and his uncle met for dinner at a restaurant close to Rick's apartment. The orders for the first course had been placed, and a bottle of wine, along with one of mineral water and a bread basket, were within reach of both of them on the table.

"Is this a test?"

Piero took a drink of the wine. "No, Riccardo, it is a game. I play it with my fellow policemen and it helps sharpen their observational skills. You have been working for the police now for a few days, so you might want to try it."

"I suppose, since you come here often, that you know the man."

Piero shrugged. "Perhaps."

Rick looked. "He appears to be well dressed, though his suit looks off the rack, not tailored. That would make him comfortable but not wealthy. The suit looks too big for him, which goes along with his gaunt face. Because of that I would guess that he is that rare Italian who is not that interested in food. He eats to live, doesn't live to eat. He is well groomed; hair combed and recently cut. No wedding ring, but that doesn't mean anything in Italy. He's giving more attention to his newspaper than his food. I can't see what paper it is."

"*La Nazione.*"

"Is that a Rome paper?"

"Firenze."

"So he may well be from Tuscany and is reading the news from home. I'm guessing he is a salesman from that region. Since he's drinking a red, probably Chianti, he may well be a wine distributor of some sort. I should go ask him if he's trying to sell wine to the Vatican."

Piero frowned. "I don't understand."

"Just something else I've become involved in since arriving." Rick told his uncle about Juan Alberto Sanguinetti, his old college friend who obviated the need for enemies. Piero found the story amusing.

"Clearly you must help your friend. And you must also tell me about what you have discovered in the case of Count Zimbardi. I'm sure I will be getting another call from the countess before long."

The arrival of their pasta stopped any discussion of less serious matters. The restaurant was the best, or perhaps only, Genovese restaurant in the city, so they had chosen regional specialties. Rick's was *trenette al pesto.* Besides the basil, walnuts, and olive oil, the ribbons of pasta were tossed with green beans and potatoes, making it truly Ligurian. His uncle had ordered another specialty of the Italian Riviera, *pansôti,* stuffed pasta with a creamy walnut sauce. They exchanged wishes of *buon appetito* and, before putting a fork in their own dishes, took tastes of the other's.

"That pesto is excellent," said Piero. "But I have a colleague from Arenzano, just west of Genova, who says that the best basil for pesto grows in pots on the terrace of his grandmother's house overlooking the Ligurian Sea. The saltwater mists that coat the plants are essential for producing the sweetest leaves. He refuses to eat pesto anywhere else."

"Next time I'm in Genoa I'll have to visit his grandmother."

"You've never been?"

"Just driving around it on the autostrada. Lots of tunnels." He pointed his fork. "Your *pansôti* are excellent as well. Does your colleague require walnuts from his grandmother's trees for his?"

"He's never mentioned that. You were going to tell me what you've found in the investigation."

"Yes, of course." Rick took a sip of wine before continuing. Keeping with the region, it was a straw yellow Cinque Terre. "With one possible exception, it all seems to come back to the street where the count was doing his research. Even his music lessons take us there, since his harp teacher is the mother of the man who restores furniture. I can't think of a motive for those two, but I can for the middle generation of the Stampatelli clan, Ludovico, if what Carmella suspects is true."

"Sergeant Lamponi has a very good nose for such things."

"Well, she thinks that Ludovico Stampatelli was in a relationship with Pina, of the *salumaio*, and he was not happy when the count arrived and started spending time in her shop."

"The wealthy nobleman pushing aside the working man. Perhaps some class envy there along with old-fashioned jealousy. That sounds like something the sergeant would pick up on."

"Ludovico seems like a rough character, I wouldn't be surprised if he's been in trouble already."

"Sergeant Lamponi checked his record, along with that of everyone else on the street. All the Stampatellis are clean except for the boy, who was charged with shoplifting, but his case was dismissed. The others on the street have had no brushes with the law, not even parking tickets." He cut his last little pillow of pasta into two pieces and swirled one around in the cream sauce. "You said there was one exception to the people on the street being involved."

Rick had gone to the bread basket for help in getting the last of the pesto sauce. "Yes, that exception is Signor Syms-Mulford.

The woman in the bar told me that on the count's last day, the two of them had an argument there. Raised voices and all that."

"So she must have heard what the argument was about."

"Unfortunately not, Uncle. They were yelling at each other in English for the most part, but she did hear the count use the word *mascalzone*."

"The count called his friend that?"

"Apparently, but we don't know the context. I can't help remembering what the count wrote about suspecting foul play." Rick still had not come up with a good translation of the word skullduggery.

"What would Signor Syms-Mulford have done to cause his old friend to get so agitated?"

Rick took a long pull from his wineglass before replying. "At the risk of starting to sound like Carmella, my suspicion is that Syms-Mulford may have been getting too cozy with the countess."

"You're joking."

"I ran into the Zimbardi butler, and he said that Syms-Mulford has been telephoning the countess regularly since the count's passing."

"A family friend helping her get through the mourning period."

"Perhaps, but I just can't shake the sense that there's more to it."

"Well, you'll have to make another call on the man."

"I was afraid you'd say that." He tapped his forehead. "Zio, I forgot to tell you something else that the woman in the bar told me. The count was there that night playing cards before he got on the bus. She said she was ready to call him a taxi at the end of the evening, as usual, but he said he was going to take the bus. He wasn't used to riding busses, but someone had given him a ticket and he wanted to try it out."

"Someone who may have wanted him on that bus. I don't suppose she said who it was."

"She did not."

"He could have gotten it that day, or had it for a while and finally decided to use it." Piero swirled the wine in his glass. "The countess found it strange that he was on a bus, of course. If she had known who'd given him the ticket, she would have told me."

The two men were silent as they pondered the ticket mystery.

The pasta dishes had been cleared and menus were placed in front of them to decide on the main course. As they studied the choices, the waiter noted that some excellent fish had arrived that very afternoon if they would like to inspect them. Piero agreed that they would, and the man scurried into the kitchen, returning with a large platter on which lay three silver fish. He pressed his finger on the flesh of each to prove the freshness.

"That middle-sized one should be perfect for the two of us, don't you think, Riccardo?" Rick nodded, the waiter returned to the kitchen, and Piero swirled the *vino bianco* in his glass. "Are you completely settled into your apartment? It meets your expectations?"

"Meets and surpasses, Zio. I may need a few more items to stock the larder, but I am feeling quite at home. When the kitchen is up to standard you will have to come over for dinner. It won't be as good as this, but…"

"I will enjoy seeing it, Riccardo, but I don't want you to go to any trouble. Perhaps we can have a glass of wine there before dining somewhere in the neighborhood."

Rick was certain his uncle was worried he'd be served hamburgers and French fries.

"I'm glad the apartment worked out. How about your translating and interpreting? Unfortunately, I have been keeping you busy on this case, but have you had time to make some contacts? What is it you call it? Networking?" He used the word in English.

"*Bravo*, Zio. The answer is not much. I have talked with several of my old friends from the American School, so they know I'm here and they will pass the word to their contacts. But I haven't gotten around to calling anyone else. I did some translation work back in America for some university professors here, so I'll eventually be in touch so they know I'm now in Rome. How long have I been here? I've lost track."

"I think it's five days."

"It's gone fast."

"Not for Countess Zimbardi, I imagine."

The fish returned to the table in style. The waiter set the platter down on one corner of the table, and allowed them to admire its grill marks and take in the smell of lemon and garlic. A younger waiter brought two spoons, a bottle of olive oil, and two plates, and set them next to the platter. The seasoned waiter then went to work armed only with the two spoons. First he removed the head and tail, then the fins, first on one side and then the other. Holding the fish in place with one spoon, he used the other to slice all around the belly, then delicately lifted one side and turned it over, leaving two equal sides, one containing the spine that was then removed. This left identical filets that he drizzled with olive oil and placed on the two plates. "*Buon appetito*," he said as he set the plates before them.

The man had given a virtuoso performance, and Rick was temped to applaud. Instead he picked up his fork and took a bite, finding that the fish surpassed the presentation. It was nothing like the Red Lobster served back in Albuquerque. The waiter had lingered under the pretense of filling their wineglasses, but Rick knew he was really hoping for a compliment. Piero complied.

"*Eccezionale.*"

The waiter smiled and made a short bow. "*Grazie,* Commissario."

Rick watched him leave. "Do you come here often, Zio?"

"On occasion. I had an investigation in the neighborhood a few years ago and it was convenient to come here for lunch. The case involved a body found in a parked car." He cut a small piece of fish and stabbed it with his fork. "We never did solve it, but I was able to consume a good amount of pesto."

Rick noticed that the man at the window table was concentrating on a plain green salad rather than his newspaper. "What about that man, Zio? Are you going to tell me who he is?"

Piero glanced at the table, as if he had forgotten about the game. "Ah, yes. Signor Doria. He owns this restaurant and a few others. Started out as a cook and worked his way up."

"So like I said, no interest in food."

"None whatsoever."

Rick bid Piero good evening on the sidewalk and tried to cross the busy thoroughfare in front of the restaurant. During the day it would have been easy, and relatively safe, because the traffic would be at a standstill. At this time of night there were few cars, and those on the street were not about to stop for some foolish jaywalker. When he was finally able to scurry across, his phone rang. He pulled it from his jacket when he reached the curb but it was not a number he recognized.

"Montoya."

"Rick? This is Sister Teresa. You sound out of breath. Are you all right?"

"Oh, hi, uh, Teresa. I was just dodging a car. Traffic."

"Be careful. Listen, Rick, I'm sorry to call you so late, but I have a problem that you may be able to help with."

"Of course."

"A group of wealthy church contributors from the States is in town and will be having an audience tomorrow morning with the Holy Father. Tomorrow afternoon one couple wants to visit some churches on their own, and asked me to get a guide who speaks English. I know this is kind of last-minute, but—"

"I'll be glad to do it. Where do I meet them, and when?"

"You're a life-saver, Rick. Can you take down this information?"

After finding himself earlier without pen and paper, he was now properly armed. "Go ahead, I'm ready."

"They are Mr. and Mrs. Lambert Field, and they will be waiting for you in the lobby of the Hassler at three o'clock. They already know what they'd like to see. I'll set up a car and driver tomorrow morning."

He had an idea. "Leave that up to me."

"Really? That would help me greatly; this group is very demanding and tomorrow morning I'll be up to my neck in details."

"Glad to help out. And thanks again for getting my friend the appointment with Father Galeazzo."

"I forgot all about it. Hope it works. *Buona sera*, Rick."

"*Buona sera*, Sister." Was he finally getting used to this new name?

He slipped his phone back into his pocket and entered a jumbled grid of dark streets on his way to his apartment. Despite the hour, he passed people on the street who were perfectly comfortable strolling about the city center. Anyone found in downtown Albuquerque at this time of night would be looking for trouble or trying to avoid it. The center of Rome, unlike most American cities, was still essentially residential, and Romans felt safe walking around their neighborhoods. Rick knew well that there were rough sections of the city, but this one, in the historic center, wasn't one of them.

As he turned a corner he realized that he was close to Guido's Pub. With so much on his mind he wasn't ready to go to bed yet, so why not stop in for a nightcap and perhaps run into someone he knew? A few minutes later he pushed open the door and was greeted with the dank odor of Guido's establishment, and the sight of the proprietor himself behind the bar. He stepped in and saw Art sitting at his usual table with a man who looked vaguely familiar. Art spotted Rick and waved him over.

"Rick, my friend, come join us. You remember Pelé, our classmate? Coincidentally, we were just talking about you."

Rick did remember him. Pelé, whose real name was João

Figeroa, was the only Brazilian he'd ever met who not only couldn't play soccer but wasn't at all interested in the game, a distinction that earned him his nickname. Instead of playing sports, he was captain of the school chess team, which, as he often pointed out, had a better win-loss record than the soccer squad. Pelé had been a short, curly-haired kid with glasses in high school, and now he was a short, bald man with glasses. He looked at Rick with wide eyes, made wider by the thick lenses. They shook hands and Rick sat down after waving a beer order to Guido.

"Good to see you, Pelé. You haven't changed a bit."

"You think so, Rick?"

"Absolutely. Do you live in Rome, or just passing through?"

"I'm here with the embassy. Your father was with the American embassy, wasn't he?"

"Right," said Rick.

"And you…you're not working for the embassy?"

"Nope. Starting my own business. Private sector."

Pelé glanced at Art, and took a sip of his beer before excusing himself for the bathroom.

"What was that about, Art?"

"He believes you're with the CIA."

Rick's beer arrived and he took a long pull. "Why would he… wait a minute, did you…?"

"I might have dropped a hint or two to that effect. Remember how much fun we had playing pranks on him in high school? And then you walk in here like it was all planned, so maybe he thinks I'm a spook too. This is getting better and better."

Rick glanced left and right before lowering his voice. "Perhaps I *am* a spy."

"Really?"

"Of course not, *schemo*. Watch it, here he comes."

Pelé took his seat and flashed a tight smile. "So, Rick, what business are you in? If you don't mind me asking."

"Interpreting, translating. I'm a freelancer. Which reminds me, I need to make a call." He pulled out his phone and punched in a number while the two men watched. He held the phone close to his ear so they could hear only his voice, not Carmella's.

"This is Montoya."

"I'm off duty, kid, and tomorrow's my day off. Why are you bothering me?"

"I know that. I have a job for you."

"Driving?"

"That's right, and it should be lucrative."

Pelé's eyes widened, and Art looked up at the ceiling.

"I like the sound of that."

"The Hassler at three o'clock. I'll be there as well."

"Got it."

Rick hung up and turned back to Pelé. "Sorry for the interruption. As I said, I'm freelancing. I'm just getting started, but I'm hoping it pays off. And what do you do at the embassy?"

"I'm an administrative officer." He downed the rest of his beer in one gulp.

"That's all?" Art said. "Come on, Pelé, you can tell us. We were classmates."

"Of course that's all. I'm in charge of building maintenance, the motor pool, that kind of thing."

"I suppose you got the job because you speak Italian."

"That helped, Art. It was—"

He was interrupted by the ring of Rick's cell phone, the Lobo Fight Song. Rick held up his hand. "I'm really sorry, guys. I'd better take it; it could be someone who needs my services."

Pelé looked at Art, who shrugged.

"Montoya."

"Mister Montoya, you know who is calling."

It was Syms-Mulford. Did he think the phone might be tapped?

"Yes, I do indeed."

"I need to speak to you. Tomorrow morning."

"Of course. When and where?"

"At nine o'clock? Somewhere inconspicuous, but in public, if we might."

What is it with this guy? "How about the Pantheon?"

"Perfect, I can melt into the crowd of tourists."

Rick looked at Pelé, who was following the conversation, and said: "Be sure you're not followed."

"Righto." The line went dead.

"Listen guys," said Pelé, "I've got a big day at work tomorrow. We're doing an inventory, so I'd better head for home. Rick it was great seeing you."

"My pleasure, Pelé, I'm sure we'll run into each other here again."

"That will be great. Good night, Art." He got up, walked quickly to the bar to settle his bill, waved again at the two at the table, and made his escape.

"Rick, what was that second phone call?"

"A guy I interviewed in connection with my uncle's investigation of the count's murder. I needed to talk to him again anyway, so this works out perfectly. Oh, and he thinks I'm some kind of secret agent."

"I'm beginning to think that myself."

"I may have embellished the conversation for Pelé's benefit."

"The look on his face was priceless. Let me buy you another beer as a token of my appreciation."

"Not necessary, but I accept. Next time the drinks are on me, since I have my first job tomorrow, thanks to Lidia. That's what the first call was about."

"Lidia? I don't think I know any Lidia. Now if you're talking about Sister—"

"Don't be a wise ass, Art."

While his friend went to the bar for the next round, Rick tried to imagine what Syms-Mulford could want to talk to him about. He hoped it had something to do with the murder of Count Zimbardi, but given the man's fascination with the cloak and dagger, it could be anything.

•• ● ●•

The Pantheon was an appropriate place for Rick to meet a historian, it being one of the most historic buildings in the city. Built by the Emperor Hadrian as a temple honoring all the Roman gods, it had served various purposes over the centuries but was now essentially a tourist attraction. Tombs, including those of the kings of modern Italy and the painter Raphael, should have bestowed a quiet dignity on the circular space, but it was lost among the hordes of tourists in shorts and baseball caps. At any given time half the visitors were looking up at the oculus in the center of the dome, which despite its elegant Latin name was still just a big hole. Tour guides tried to explain the engineering marvel that was the Pantheon, but most of their charges were most fascinated by the hole.

What happens when it rains? The floor gets wet.

Rick walked under the columned portico and through doors tall enough to have been recycled from a medium-sized castle. Despite the relatively early hour, it was starting to fill with tourists, either in groups herded by umbrella-carrying guides, or wandering around on their own. He hadn't been in the Pantheon since high school, and now, as then, it made an impression. By all logic it should have come crashing down the year it was built, but here it was, almost two millennia later, still standing. Those early Romans knew how to build things to last, as long as the barbarians didn't come through and tear them down.

He looked around and didn't spot Syms-Mulford. Could the guy be more Italian than British, and be late? He didn't think so, and ran his eyes along the wall, where wood benches lined the edge of the marble pavement. They stopped on a figure huddled at the end of one of the benches. It was a man wearing a dark coat, snap-brimmed cap, and sunglasses, reading a newspaper. Who comes into the Pantheon and reads a newspaper wearing sunglasses? Rick walked over and sat down next to him. The man kept his eyes on the paper.

"Mr. Syms-Mulford, was it really necessary to meet like this?"

The man kept reading. "My colleagues at the office were getting nosy about you visiting, and I didn't want them to know you were connected to the police. It is not good for a respected historian to be interrogated by the authorities. Tongues wag."

"Your...disguise?"

"One never knows who one will run into, even in at a location like this. I assumed you would be accustomed to such precautions."

A pair of Eastern European tourists came up and stood close to them, their backs to the wall, to get a better view of the hole. They were too close for Syms-Mulford, who buried his nose in the newspaper until they walked off.

Rick leaned his back against the wall and checked out the hole. "And what is it you wanted to talk to me about?"

"At my office, you never asked me where I was on the night of the murder. You were supposed to have asked me that."

The meeting had been amusing, but now the man was starting to annoy Rick. "Could it have occurred to you that I might have already known where you were that night?"

Syms-Mulford looked at Rick for the first time, then quickly returned his eyes to the newspaper. "So you know."

"I didn't say that."

"But you are still supposed to ask me, aren't you?"

"Okay, where were you, Mr. Syms-Mulford, the night of the count's death?"

"Before I answer, let me state emphatically, that my uppermost concern is shielding Countess Zimbardi from more stress. She has gone through so much already with the death of Umberto, she does not need any further agitation added to the grieving process."

Rick found the declaration fascinating. He wasn't sure what was behind it, but had a good idea. It confirmed his theory about Syms-Mulford and the countess. "I understand your concern. Now, where were you that night?"

"I hope you do indeed understand, Mr. Montoya. In that regard, I would assume than none of our conversation will get back to the countess. None of it concerns her."

A lot of concerns going on here, Rick thought. "You can be assured that I will relay your concerns to the higher authorities in the case."

The statement appeared to satisfy Syms-Mulford. He took a very deep breath and continued. "I was with someone that night."

Rick waited for more, and when none came, he asked: "Who was it?"

"You must understand that I cannot say. It would be terribly embarrassing for…that person."

"A woman?"

"I believe our conversation is arriving at its conclusion, Mr. Montoya." He folded the newspaper.

"Mr. Syms-Mulford, I don't understand. If we at the police were not focusing on where you were that night, why did you feel you had to bring it up to me?"

"I was sure the issue would come up eventually, and I wanted to be the one to volunteer it to you, rather than have it wrung out of me in some windowless basement room at the *questura*." With that he got to his feet, adjusted his sunglasses and hat, and strode into the sunlight.

Rick watched him leave and tried to compute what he'd heard. The guy was with some woman the night Count Zimbardi was murdered. That brought up two possibilities. One: he wasn't with anyone that night and in fact did in the count himself. Two: he was with someone but it would embarrass her, and him, if it came to light. In both scenarios, Syms-Mulford was counting on the police to look the other way, since it involved affairs of the heart. "We are all men of the world, aren't we?" he was saying. But if he was with some woman the night of the murder, who would it be? Again, two possibilities. The obvious one was that it was the countess herself, and that would be embarrassing indeed, fooling around on the very evening when her husband meets his fate. But what if it was some other woman? That would be most embarrassing to Syms-Mulford assuming—and it was still an assumption—that the rascal was also having an affair with the countess. For all these sets and subsets, one thing was certain: it was in the man's interest to keep the countess in the dark.

Rick pulled out his phone, checked the time, and decided he should be on his way. He didn't want to be late for his appointment with Father Galeazzo and Juan Alberto, and assured himself that he had plenty of time. He walked out the door, between the columns, and into the *piazza* in front of the Pantheon. A fountain sat at its center, but there were so many tourists sitting on surrounding steps or milling about that it was not to be seen. Instead, the obelisk at its center seemed to rise from the middle of the crowd. He turned and walked along the side of the Pantheon to another square, this one a bit less overrun with tourists. It was faced by the Santa Maria Sopra Minerva church, built on top of a pagan temple to the goddess Minerva. Romans loved whimsy, and the Egyptian obelisk in this *piazza* sat on the back of a marble elephant. When Rick was a kid he always wanted to come here to see the elephant with the trunk curled around the side. As he looked up at the animal he realized that this could be one of the best things about moving to Rome. Now he could come look at Bernini's elephant whenever he wanted.

He took a few turns around it and walked out to a main street to catch a taxi. Traffic wasn't too busy, but it took a full ten minutes before an empty one appeared and Rick jumped in, giving the address.

"That's near the Vatican, isn't it?"

"I've never been there, but I assume it is."

"Not a good time of day to try to get across the river."

"That might be," answered Rick, "but that's where I have to go."

The driver shrugged and they pulled into a line of cars. A moment later all vehicular movement stopped. Not stopped completely, but enough so that the driver never got out of first gear. Ten minutes passed and they came to an intersection where one or two cars were able to get through with each green light. They speeded up somewhat after the turn, but still the maximum gear was second. Rick looked out and watched an old man with a cane passing them on the sidewalk.

The driver rolled down his window and craned his neck out to get a better view of what was ahead. "You really want to go there?" He settled back in the seat.

"What would have given you that idea? Damn, you've seen through my ruse—I really want to go to the airport."

"You don't have to be like that."

They didn't talk the rest of the way, and Rick got to his appointment five minutes late.

The building was a warehouse. A man dressed in overalls unloaded a truck parked outside its wide doorway while another man, this one all in black, watched with folded arms. Rick paid the taxi and walked to the guy in black.

"I'm looking for Father Galeazzo."

"You've found him, my son. You must be Signor Sanguinetti."

"No, Father, I'm his interpreter, Riccardo Montoya." They shook hands.

"*Caspita.* The man doesn't speak Italian but has an interpreter? Must be a serious operation. Well, come on inside to my office, such as it is."

He led the way past the boxes that had been stacked just inside the doorway. Rick noticed that they were either Nutella, which the truck driver used a dolly to bring inside, or breadsticks, which he carried in his arms. An image of priests dipping breadsticks into Nutella jars jumped into Rick's head. Beyond, on one side, were floor-to-ceiling shelves stocked with various food items, in front of which was parked a small forklift marked with the papal seal. What looked like a cold locker ran along most of the other side, leaving room for a niche with a desk and three metal filing cabinets that Rick took to be the office. A crucifix hung on the wall next to a calendar. The father pointed to a tall wood box in front of the desk.

"I was only expecting one of you, so if you could pull over another box, I'd appreciate it."

Rick found another box that was strong enough to hold him, dragged it next to the other, and perched himself on top. No sign of Juan Alberto, and he was starting to become concerned. "It must be a complicated business, feeding everyone in the Vatican."

"I just buy the food, the sisters cook it. But you're right, it can get a bit tricky, what with priests from all over the world. The Italians, they're easy, lots of pasta. Same with the Swiss Guards, they like their carbs, but you have to give them fondue at least once a week or they get cranky. You don't want those guys cranky, what with those big spears they carry around."

Rick couldn't be sure if the man was trying to be humorous, given the flat delivery of the lines.

"You have to cater to national tastes to a certain extent, I suppose."

"You got it. The Americans always want peanut butter available, though it's something I could never understand." He glanced at Rick's cowboy boots. "Not that there's anything wrong with it, of course. We have a few vegetarians, but we can work around that by always having a side dish of macaroni and cheese. The sisters make it from scratch. The Holy Father, though, he's not a vegetarian, not by a long shot."

Rick shifted on his box, which was starting to get hard. Where was Juan Alberto? "The Argentinians love their red meat. Do you have to import it for the pope?"

"No, the local beef is good enough. But we do have to bring in chimichuri sauce. He puts it on everything. I'd never heard of the stuff until he became pope. Can I get you some water? I've got cases of it in the walk-in refrigerator."

"Thank you, Father, I'm fine."

"The last pope, he was a different story, and of course he brought a bunch of Germans with him who had the same tastes." He jerked his thumb toward the refrigerator. "I had half the cooler filled with bratwurst and sauerkraut, and the other half with beer." He looked at his watch with no subtlety.

"Juan Alberto should be here momentarily," Rick said. "The traffic is pretty bad today."

"I hope he gets here soon. I've got a shipment of vegetables coming in from the south that I'll have to give my full attention. These Neapolitans are amazing, what they try to get away with. You'd think they'd be on their best behavior, this being the Vatican, but no." He shook his head, either in disgust or wonderment.

"Let me give Juan Alberto a call." Rick reached for his cell phone but at that moment a taxi stopped in front and out stepped the Argentine holding a bottle of wine. After what appeared to be a small argument with the driver, Juan Alberto paid his fare and walked to the doorway where Rick met him.

"*Hola*, Reek," he said, as if he had arrived on schedule.

Rick switched into Spanish. "Your lateness is not going to help you make a sale, Juan Alberto."

"Late? In my country this would be considered early. Are we in Italy or America?"

"We can discuss that later. Come meet Father Galeazzo."

Juan Alberto shook hands with the priest and put the bottle on the desk. "*Mucho gusto, Padre.*"

After the greetings, Rick went into his interpreter's routine.

"Just tell him, Reek, that the pope should have wine from his homeland."

Rick turned to the priest. "Signor Sanguinetti thinks the wine will make an excellent addition to the Vatican's wine cellars."

"There's a lot of wine around, what makes his so special?"

"Father Galeazzo would like to know what makes your wine so special."

"It's from Argentina, Reek. Doesn't he know the pope's from Argentina?"

"He says it is one of the finest wines in the country, Padre."

"Well, Signor Montoya, let's give it a try." He opened a drawer and rooted among hammers, screwdrivers and other tools before coming upon a corkscrew and pocketknife. Rick swallowed hard as Galeazzo cut off the plastic stop with the knife and carefully inserted the corkscrew. He turned it several times, until the screw was deep into the cork, then stood and pulled. It opened with a pop. Another drawer was rifled and out came three plastic cups. "Will you join me?" said the priest, holding up the bottle.

"None for me, thank you," answered Rick.

"*Si, claro,*" was Juan Alberto's reply.

Two cups were filled halfway, one passed to Juan Alberto.

"*Salute,*" said the priest before taking a sip.

Rick held his breath. The stuff was probably plonk.

Galeazzo took another taste. "*Non c'è male.*"

"What did he say, Reek?"

"He says it's not bad."

"Just not bad? What does he know?"

They were interrupted by Padre Galeazzo. "What about the grapes?"

Rick translated into Spanish.

"Grapes?" said Juan Alberto. "They come from Argentina and they grow on Argentine vines in Mendoza which is in western Argentina. I don't bother with such details, Reek, I'm here to be sure that our pope has a good glass of wine with his meals,

wine from his homeland. Did I mention that the pope is from Argentina?"

Rick rubbed his eyes and tried to gather his thoughts. Juan Alberto was not making this easy. He looked up and saw the bottle sitting on the desk where the priest had placed it after pouring the two cups. The rear label was facing him. He leaned forward slightly, hoping Galeazzo wouldn't notice.

"Signor Sanguinetti says that it is a premium blend of Malbec with other specialties of the Mendoza region, where high altitude and low soil salinity create a smooth red with a hint of fruit that combines perfectly with cheese, meats, or pasta, but can simply be enjoyed by itself, sitting by a fire with your closest friends." He leaned back from the bottle.

The priest took another taste. "*Va bene*, tell him we'll take twenty cases."

Fifteen minutes later the bottle was empty, Father Galezzo was overseeing the delivery of Neapolitan vegetables, and Rick and Juan Alberto were walking down the street looking for a cab.

"I knew that would be easy, Reek. I hope you learned something about salesmanship, it might come in handy for you some time."

Rick spotted a taxi and waved. "You're really good at it, Juan Alberto."

"What can I say? It's a gift."

• • ● • •

It would be sandwiches two days in a row, Rick thought as he came up the elevator to his floor, but even sandwiches might soon be out of his price range if he didn't get some work. He had calculated that his savings would last him two to three months, but every time he walked past a store window he noticed the prices, and they weren't like Albuquerque. The money from the countess for the translations would help, and taking these

Americans around today should pay well too. Perhaps he should take up Giulia's offer to do some guided tours. He might ask her more about it tonight at dinner, if the subject came up. No, that would be tacky.

He dropped his phone and keys on the table, and had the eerie feeling that he wasn't alone. Glancing up at the window, he saw Fellini's gray figure sitting patiently on the ledge. Rick debated whether to let him in or not, a difficult decision since once again he had nothing for him. And he certainly did not plan on sharing his luncheon meat with a cat. He heaved a sigh and opened the window.

"Sorry, Fellini, I have let you down once again. But I must say you don't appear to have missed many meals. Strong body, shiny coat; I think you're doing all right. But I promise to have a treat for you on your next visit."

He turned on his laptop computer, logged in, and went into the kitchen to make his sandwich. The wine was now chilled, and he decided that a glass with lunch would not be a luxury. It was Rome, after all. When he returned to the table with his sandwich and wine, Fellini was sitting on the chair staring at the computer where the screensaver had kicked in, bouncing balls off the sides. Rick picked him up and placed him on the windowsill.

"I'd let you sit on the table, Fellini, but if my mother ever found out, she would give me a tongue-lashing."

The word *tongue* prompted Fellini to begin giving himself a bath, leaving Rick to scroll through his e-mails as he ate. Most were from Albuquerque, friends asking for news on how the move had gone and if he was missing them terribly. Eventually he got to one he wanted to see, a request to do a translation for a university professor in Trieste. The paper was attached to the e-mail, and she needed it in two weeks, a reasonable deadline. The thought of some income made the sandwich taste better.

When he finished eating and put his plate and glass in the kitchen sink, he walked back through the living-dining space to

his bedroom. It was better to err on the side of being too formal for his afternoon guide duties, so he put on a blue dress shirt and a tie, and pulled his blazer off the hanger. When he returned to the other room, Fellini was nowhere to be seen. Rick looked in the kitchen and the few corners of the apartment and assumed that the cat had gone back out to the roof and off to parts unknown. When he turned around after closing the window, he noticed that the mouse from his computer was dangling from the edge of the table. Rick shook his head, put it back next to the laptop, and left the apartment.

On the bus ride he thought about the day that Carmella had picked him up and realized with horror that she would be dressed the same. The jeans and red sneakers would not make a great impression on the wealthy church donors, and it might get back to Lidia's—that is, Sister Teresa's—boss, and she could be in trouble. Why hadn't he thought to say something to Carmella? He was still stewing when he got off the bus near Piazza di Spagna and walked toward the Spanish Steps. As he got closer, the horde of tourists thickened, almost hiding the sunken ship fountain. Starting up the steps, he carefully picked his way through the foreigners, their numbers enhanced by young Romans trying out their English on the American girls. Halfway up he stopped and looked back down Via dei Condotti, site of the city's most elegant stores, its pavement obscured by shoppers.

At the top the facade of the Hotel Hassler appeared. Black cars, their grilles pointed outward, were lined up on either side of the entrance. One was Carmella's shiny Alfa Romeo, with her leaning against it on the passenger side. She wore a dark blue suit over a white shirt, with black flats, and her hair was brushed into place. Picking up a groggy Rick at Fiumicino was one thing, driving for someone staying at a five-star hotel was clearly another. He had worried himself sick for nothing.

"*Ciao*, Carmella. You're looking quite, uh, professional."

"*Ciao*, Riccardo. What did you expect? I assume this job will

be lucrative, if they can afford to stay here. How did you get in on this?"

"A friend of mine from school."

"The one whose name you can't get straight?"

"Yes, that one. I'd better go in and find these people."

"You do that."

Rick walked past the doorman, up the steps, and into the plush lobby. He located the reception desk, behind which stood a man wearing a blue suit with the hotel name embroidered into his jacket. He was checking the screen of a computer.

"Mr. and Mrs. Field?"

The desk clerk answered Rick in English. "Let me see if they're in." He turned to the rows of boxes behind him and checked one. "Their key is here, so—oh, there they are. They must have been expecting you." He pointed his chin toward an elderly couple sitting in one corner of the lobby. The man was reading the *International Herald Tribune* and the woman a small paperback. She wore a print dress and her gray hair looked like it had been done that morning. Her husband was more casual, a burgundy blazer over a white golf shirt, slacks, and tasseled loafers. Rick crossed the lobby to where they sat.

"Mr. and Mrs. Field? I'm Rick Montoya. Shall we be on our way?"

Mrs. Field looked up over her half glasses. "Oh, my. Sister Teresa said you would be a handsome young man, and she was right."

"A complete waste," grumbled Mr. Field.

"Don't mind my husband, Mr. Montoya, he's talking about the sister. He thinks all nuns should be homely. Come along, Lambert, you can check your baseball scores when we get back."

He heaved a sigh, folded the newspaper, and rose to his feet. "The Eternal City awaits," he announced, with an air of resignation.

Outside Rick introduced them to Carmella, got them into

the backseat, and took his place in the front passenger seat. He turned his head. "Sister Teresa told me you have already decided what you'd like to see?"

Mrs. Field took out a piece of paper from a small purse. "That's right. I've heard so much about San Clemente church, if we could go there first, please."

"Basilica di San Clemente," he said to Carmella, switching to Italian.

Carmella turned on the engine and pulled into the street. "Anything new on the case?"

"I thought you were on your day off and didn't want to talk police business."

"I was curious."

"I'll bring you up-to-date later. Let me try to earn my pay." He turned toward the backseat. "We are on Via Sistina, named for Pope Sixtus the fifth, who had it built."

"Like the Sistine Chapel," said Mrs. Field.

"Actually, that was Sixtus the Fourth."

"Was there a Sixtus the Sixth?" Mr. Field asked.

"I don't know, let me ask our driver. Carmella, *c'era un papa Sisto Sesto?*"

"Are you kidding? What pope would want to take that name? It sounds like something out of a tongue twister."

"No, Sir. The fifth was the last."

The Alfa Romeo dropped down to Piazza Barberini, where Triton blew a jet of water into the air through a conch shell, before the car started climbing another hill. There were more ups and downs before they came up behind the Santa Maria Maggiore Church and drove along its side into the busy square in front. That put them on the tree-lined Via Merulana going in the direction of San Giovanni in Laterano. After a sharp right and a few more blocks, Carmella wove her way through a series of one-way streets to the curb next to the doors of San Clemente. The doorway was ornate, but set in a long wall with no decoration, and judging from the look on Mr. Field's face, he was unimpressed. In contrast, Mrs. Field was glowing with anticipation.

Fortunately, Rick had been to the church many times when he was growing up. When someone from the States came through Rome and had time to see only a few sights, Rick's father usually brought them to San Clemente. It was the perfect place to demonstrate the layers that made up the city, and after so many visits, Rick hoped he would still remember much of his father's monologue.

"In the seventeenths century, Irish priests took over the care of the church, and they remain here to this day," he said as they got out of the car and walked to the door. He pushed it open and stood aside while the Fields entered, then followed behind. All three crossed themselves a few steps in.

"This is magnificent," said Mrs. Field.

"Here at street level is the twelfth-century church, with additions and improvements made over the years, but always keeping the original layout, including the *schola cantorum*, and of course the cosmatesque floor designs. The tile decoration above the apse is especially beautiful." He felt like a tour guide, and realized that this afternoon that was exactly what he was. He also found he was enjoying it. The Fields walked toward the apse and Rick was about to follow them when he felt a tug on his elbow.

"What's new in the case?" said Carmella.

The Fields appeared to be happy walking by themselves and gazing at the church decoration, but he stayed a few steps behind. "I went back to the street and talked to some of the people again. I asked Avellone why he didn't tell us that his mother was the harp teacher, and he shrugged it off. He said the count had noticed a harp he was restoring, and that's how he'd recommended his mother for the lessons."

"So nothing to go on there. What else?"

"I went back to the count's bar and found out he was there the night he was killed." He told her about the bus ticket.

Her eyebrow raised. "So who gave him the ticket, and when?"

"Also, why? Those are the questions."

They were interrupted by the voice of Mrs. Field. "Mr. Montoya." Rick walked quickly to her side. "Yes, ma'am."

"Lambert was wondering about these columns. They don't all match and they look Roman."

"It was very common when constructing churches to recycle materials from ancient buildings, and especially columns. You can find Roman columns holding up ceilings in churches all over Italy."

"Fascinating." They continued walking toward the altar.

"What did she ask?" said Carmella.

"They wanted to know if the columns were Roman."

"This is Rome, everything here is Roman. Did they think they'd be Neapolitan?"

"Carmella, when Americans say Roman, they think—oh, never mind. Do you want to know what else I heard on Via Anacleto?"

"Fire away."

"Pina, the *salumaio* lady, said something I found very intriguing. On that last day he was there, the count told her that we can learn from history, and history can repeat itself. I think there could be something significant in those words."

"Significant would be if he'd told her that Avellone had threatened him with a knife. You're grasping at straws, kid. That was just babble from somebody who wanted to make people think that his little hobby was important, when it was really just a waste of everyone's time."

Rick tried not to show his disappointment. "Maybe you're right." He moved up and walked around the church with the Fields, pointing out details he remembered, until they had made a complete loop. Carmella stood near the door.

"This has been wonderful, Mr. Montoya. I have a couple more churches that had been recommended to us to see."

"But Mrs. Field, we're not finished here." He took them to a ticket window at the opposite side of the church from the door, and after Mr. Field got passes for all of them, including Carmella, they descended a long stairway and found themselves in a dark, musty space with a low ceiling. Lights on the ground lit their path through stone and dirt.

"The church above was built on top of the original fourth-century church we are in now. Over there on those pillars you can see frescoes on the life of Saint Clement, but even after careful restoration they're pretty faint. Still, when you consider that you're looking at artwork done fifteen hundred years ago, it's quite striking. Be careful walking, the path can be very uneven."

Mr. Field held his wife's hand and they took in the representations of the saint's life. Rick stood back with Carmella.

"You ever been here, Carmella?"

"On a school field trip in the third grade. This was my favorite part. So what else?"

"I met Ludovico, the middle generation of the Stampatelli clan."

"The one who is fooling around with Pina."

"I didn't ask him that directly. He was less than cooperative, and I didn't get much out of him other than that he didn't really warm to the count, nor think much of his history research."

"Can't blame him for that, but was it enough to murder the guy? That's the question."

"Something else. I got the sense that his son was almost trying to cover for Ludovico. Like the kid knew there was something going on that the police, we police, shouldn't find out."

"That is interesting. Was it his father spending too much time with Pina, or something more sinister?"

"Hard to tell. Maybe it's nothing, along with the count's comments on history repeating itself."

The Fields returned.

"Mr. Montoya," said Mrs. Field, "this is so different from

the church above but equally fascinating. To think that people worshiped here that long ago, it shows how the faith has grown over the years. Shall we return to the main church?"

"There's more," Rick said.

"Another church below this one?" said Mr. Field, laughing. He had momentarily forgotten about his baseball scores.

"You could say that."

"Lead the way."

They went down more steps, but these were narrow and dark, cut into the earth below the upper church. At the bottom they found themselves in a long passage with openings on both sides, and lit by lights set into the walls and ground. If going from the main to the lower church had taken them centuries back in time, this final descent carried them even more into the past.

"We have several things at this level," said Rick in a low voice appropriate for the atmosphere. "That includes fifth-century tombs, catacombs, if you will. Most fascinating to me is that centuries earlier, this space contained a room used for ritual banquets by the pagan cult of Mithras. If you peer in there you can see an altar used by the cult, carved with an image of Mithras himself slaying the bull."

"A church built atop the ruins of a pagan temple. There's a message there."

"The Romans loved such symbolism back then, Mr. Field. They still do."

Two hours and three churches later, Carmella pulled up at the door to the Hotel Hassler. The Fields thanked Carmella and asked Rick to come inside, since Mrs. Field had left her money at the front desk, not wanting to go out into the city with much cash. She bustled over to reception.

"That was a very interesting tour," said Mr. Field. "As this entire trip has been. Unfortunately, it fell just at a week when my team is playing a key home series, but there was nothing to be done about it. The important thing is that Mrs. Field is happy."

At that moment she appeared, holding an envelope. "Mr. Montoya, I trust this will cover you and Ms. Lamponi. It has been a delightful afternoon and we are most appreciative. I have the card you gave me and will certainly recommend you to any of my friends coming to Rome."

Rick hoped that he'd be doing interpreting, not guiding tours, but thanked her just the same. "It has been a pleasure, and I hope you enjoy the rest of your stay."

"We're here until the end of the week," said Mr. Field with a touch of sadness.

They shook hands and Rick walked out to where Carmella was waiting. He opened the envelope, took out the four notes, and handed two to her.

"Half to you, half to me, Sergeant."

"*Accidenti*, I usually have to drive for three days to get this much."

"Americans are generous people, Carmella. And now I will not feel constrained about what I can order on my dinner date tonight."

"Are you going out with the one whose name you can't remember?"

"No, that was Teresa, the one who got this job for us today. Dinner is with someone else."

"Well, please thank Teresa next time you see her." She stuffed the money into her pocket. "Can I drop you somewhere?"

Rick thought for a moment, and realized that it was all downhill from there to his apartment. "No thanks, this is a nice time to walk. I suppose I'll see you tomorrow?"

"Whatever the *commissario* says. He'll probably want to go over what we've found regarding the case since our last meeting. He's very meticulous, but you must know that since he's your uncle."

"That reminds me, I forgot to tell you that I met again with Syms-Mulford. I wanted to ask him where he was the night of the murder." It was of course Syms-Mulford who wanted to tell Rick, but she didn't need to know that, nor the fact that Syms-Mulford thought Rick was a spy.

"And I forgot to tell you that I went back and talked to the harp teacher to ask her the same thing," said Carmella. "It appears that we both neglected to ask that key question."

"What did she say?"

"That she was with Syms-Mulford."

Chapter Ten

Rick worked his way down through the clumps of foreign tourists milling all along the Spanish Steps, enjoying their Italian experience while surrounded by non-Italians. At the bottom he opted to avoid Via Condotti, turning instead to the left and walking to Piazza Mignanelli, where a giant column was topped by a statue of the Virgin Mary. At the corners of the base sat four Biblical patriarchs who, if concerned about the shorts and tank tops walking by, didn't show it. Rick looked up at Moses before turning into Via Frattina. While it did not boast any of the big names of Italian fashion found two streets over, its shops were just as elegant and almost as expensive. Rick only glanced at the windows, not because he couldn't afford what was behind the glass, but because he was still thinking about what Carmella had told him. If Signora Angelini was telling the truth, it threw out his theory that Syms-Mulford and the count were arguing because Syms-Mulford was paying too much attention to the countess. Were both men fooling around with the tattooed harp teacher? Could it be that the crafty Brit was in relationships with both her and the countess? Rick tried to wash that image from his mind as he crossed Via del Corso and entered Piazza San Lorenzo in Lucina, with the church of the same name. He recalled going there as a kid and being shown the gridiron on which Saint Lawrence was martyred. It had made an impression. As he came to the end of the square his phone rang. He recognized the number.

"*Ciao,* Giulia."

"*Ciao,* Rick."

"I'm looking forward to dinner. I have reservations at a place on Via dei Coronari. I made sure we have a table outside, and the weather looks perfect for it."

"Rick, that's why I'm calling. I'm so sorry, but something has come up and I won't be able to make it. I feel terrible about this."

"Business?"

"Yes, of course, and you know how it is when you're running your own operation."

He didn't, at least not yet. "Of course, Giulia, I understand. We'll do it another night."

"Thanks, Rick. I'll call you."

They said their goodbyes and Rick slipped the phone back in his pocket and started along Via Campo Marzio, named for the fields where the Roman legions trained back in the old days. Now it was another shopping street, with a few stores where he could almost afford to shop. But even those would be out of his price range until he got some meaningful work. He stopped and looked at himself in the glass of a shoe store window. What is happening with you, Montoya? On the murder case, nothing was happening. In his love life, the same: nothing. His former sweetheart was a nun, and Giulia was too busy to give him the time of day. Worst of all was his interpreting business. Not much there either, and he'd been in Rome for almost a week. The only aspect of his life that was moving along briskly was time, and with it, his savings. He took a deep breath and it came to him that there was something that could get him out of his funk. It had never failed him when he'd lived in Italy as a kid, and it would work now. He was sure of it.

Gelato.

Fortunately, one of his favorite *gelaterie* was just ahead. When

he walked in and pre-paid at the cash register, he found he was
the only customer there. Too close to dinner for the Italians, and
the tourists had started to abandon the historic center for the
day. The man behind the counter looked down at Rick's cowboy
boots, took him for a tourist, and checked his watch. Rick began
to study the metal pans of gelato behind the glass, moving his
eyes along under the gaze of the server. Life was full of decisions,
as Rick was well aware. He'd learned once in a college class that
the more difficult it was to make a choice between options, the
less difference it would make when the choice was finally made.
The statement always seemed nuts to him, which is the way he
recalled the professor of that course. It was a psychology class.

He stared at the glass, and, wracked with indecision, tried to
weigh the advantages and disadvantages of each option. It was
not easy, but it never was in La Palma. He moved to the left, and
more choices came into view, which certainly didn't help. The
man staring at him, small cup in hand, was the embodiment of
patience. Since Rick was the only one in the place at the moment,
the guy could afford to be patient.

"I think I know which three I want," Rick said, his eyes still
scanning the shining stainless steel pans of *gelato*, "I just need
to decide which order to put them in the cup."

The man behind the counter nodded, silently confirming that
the sequence was important. He also realized, both from the
fluent Italian and the statement itself, that this was no cowboy
tourist, boots or no boots. The sign of a true connoisseur, he
knew, was choosing not only the right flavors, ones that complemented each other without being overpowering, but also placing
them in the correct order inside the cup. A fruit flavor on top of
a chocolate, could ruin the enjoyment of both. A disaster.

"Start with the *gianduja*," said Rick. "Then *riso*, and finally
pesca." It was a combination he'd not had before, but would
work well. The peach on top would be consumed first, a light
palate cleaner, followed by the rice with its crunchy pieces, and

ending with the hazelnut and chocolate flavor of the *gianduja*, like Nutella, but with a more subtle bouquet. The man behind the counter followed Rick's instructions to the letter, inserted a plastic spoon, and passed it across the glass with an approving nod. Rick took it, dropped a coin in the dish, and headed for the door. Italians were not known for eating on the hoof—food was meant to be consumed in a civilized way—but *gelato* was the exception to the rule.

It helped his mood, but only marginally. After considering and rejecting the idea of swinging by the elephant statue, he dropped his empty cup and spoon into a trash bin on Piazza Rondanini and walked toward Piazza Navona. It was getting late now, the time when Romans were leaving work and squeezing onto buses to get home, or if they were fortunate, walking there. Soon they would be sitting in front of their TVs complaining about what was on the newscast, while the pasta water was put on to boil. Which reminded him that he would be eating alone that evening, and the cupboard was bare. Fortunately, the *salumaio* would still be open, so he pointed himself in its direction.

The woman who had helped him the last time was behind the counter taking care of a customer, and once again he tried to recall where he had met her, if indeed he had. Wait a minute: could she have been the one behind him on the passport line when he was arriving at Fiumicino? He tried to remember the face, but all he could think of was how groggy he'd been that morning, and the embarrassing rebuke for being in the wrong line. But it had to be her; why else would he be so sure he'd met her? How could he subtly ask? From a side door on the right an older woman wearing an apron appeared, bearing a resemblance to her coworker. Mother and daughter? Rick remembered the guessing game he'd played with his uncle at dinner and decided his instincts on this one would be flawed as well. They were probably sisters. The older woman said something to the younger, picked up an empty tray from behind the glass, and exited stage left. The younger woman took the customer's money, bagged up what she'd bought, and handed over the purchases. She looked up and saw Rick waiting. The pleasant smile returned and Rick smiled back.

"You finished your sandwiches," she said.

"And they were so good I am back."

"Another sandwich?"

"No, this will be dinner, so something more substantive. And I need some other basics as well, so let's start with them. Prosciutto, about three *etti*." He watched as she heaved a ham leg onto the slicer and went to work. When it was sliced and wrapped she placed it on the counter in front of her and looked at him, awaiting the next order.

"Do you travel much?"

"I don't understand."

"Sorry, I thought I might have seen you recently. In the airport." It had sounded like a clumsy pickup line. He might as well have asked her if she came here often.

"The last time I was in the airport was to pick up my mother, and that was a year ago. I never travel anywhere."

"It wasn't you then. Anyway, a box of spaghetti and one of those jars of sauce." He pointed to some tomato sauce on a shelf. She picked up both and put them next to the prosciutto.

"A piece of *grana*?" He formed a triangle with his fingers.

She held up a chunk of the cheese, and when he nodded she wrapped it up.

"Olive oil, good but not expensive."

She took a bottle off the shelf. "It's what I use." She put it next to the other items and flashed the smile again. "What else? Wine? Did you finish that bottle of *bianco*?"

"No, but I should get a bottle of red. Again—"

"Good but not expensive. How about this one?" She pulled one from the row of bottles and showed him the label.

She was finishing his sentences. That had to be a good sign. "It's what you drink?"

"I've tried it and liked it. What else?"

"Just dinner. I was admiring that platter of lasagna. Could you slice me one portion, *per favore?*"

She produced an aluminum dish and cut a square of the lasagna to fit in it. "This is excellent. My mother made it this morning and it's what we'll probably have ourselves tonight if nobody takes the rest."

So she lives with her mother, Rick thought. And she knows I live alone since I asked for only one portion. "I think that will do it."

She started adding up the items on a small machine, pushing them aside one by one.

"Wait, there's something else I almost forgot. I need a can of tuna."

She finished with the last item but before hitting the total button walked to a shelf where various cans were stacked. She reached up but then stopped and turned back to Rick. "Water pack or oil pack?"

It was either the words, or the way she said them, but it finally registered.

"Which does Fellini prefer?"

First she frowned. Then her mouth dropped open, revealing a perfect row of teeth. Finally she laughed, which Rick thought was even better than her smile, but she tried to stifle it with her hand.

"It's you, the one who called me."

"Since I came in here the first time I was trying to remember where we'd met, since you seemed so familiar. When you said water pack or oil pack, I finally got it. Do you have a name, or do your friends just call you Fellini's Mom?"

She giggled. "Gina."

"I'm Riccardo." They shook hands after she wiped hers on her apron.

"I wasn't very nice when you called, Riccardo. It was especially hectic here that day."

"And you've felt guilty ever since and wished there were a way you could make up for it."

"Well—"

"Then how about this, Gina? I'll put my lasagna in the

refrigerator for tomorrow and you'll let me take you out to dinner."

"I would enjoy that."

"Your mother won't mind eating alone?"

"She'll watch TV. And Fellini will keep her company."

• ● ● ● •

Gina had insisted that Rick cancel the reservation at the other restaurant so they could go to a place close by. You must get to know your neighborhood, she'd said, and he had to agree. This *trattoria* was not someplace he would have stumbled upon himself, hidden as it was among the back streets off Piazza Navona, but apparently enough people knew the way.

The first waiter they saw knew Gina, and he pointed them with his chin to an empty table as he balanced several steaming plates. They got the last two chairs at what seemed like one long table, but was really several pushed close together. The seating provided a good way to meet people, even if you didn't want to, but from the noisy conversations, that didn't appear to be a problem. One narrow aisle ran the length of the room, barely big enough for the waiters to get past one another as they carried food and wine out from the kitchen and empty plates back. Rick and Gina squeezed past chairs and took their places facing each other. A waiter reached across the table, dropped menus in front of them, and asked for their drink order. She asked for mineral water and a liter of red, turning to Rick for agreement. He nodded approval, and the waiter rushed off.

"This is exactly the kind of place I envisioned coming to when I was planning my return to Rome."

"There are no restaurants like this in—what was the city again?"

"Albuquerque. We have local places that serve New Mexican food, and are somewhat noisy and friendly, but they're different."

"I want to hear all about it. We have American tourists in

the shop all the time, but I never get to ask them about their country since they don't speak Italian. They just point at things and I wrap them up."

The water, wine, and bread arrived with a thump, and the waiter, seeing that the menus were still sitting unread in front of them, went on to another table. Rick poured them each a few fingers of the *vino* and they clinked glasses before tasting. Gina was dressed casually, as would be appropriate for the restaurant, with a simple print blouse over blue jeans. Her hair was brushed out more than it had been at the shop, and she'd added a touch of makeup. A gold chain was visible around her neck but the blouse was not open enough to see what dangled at its end. Rick imagined a medallion. He turned his attention to the menu.

"What's good from this kitchen, Gina? You seem to know everyone who works here, which I assume includes the chef."

"He's a distant relative. I'd suggest Roman specialties. If they have *maialino al forno* tonight, that's what I'd like. But you should try their *saltimbocca,* it's wonderful. For pasta, if you're hungry you might want the *spaghetti al'Amatriciana.* I think I'll just have some *antipasti* and skip the *primo.*"

"You haven't even glanced at the menu, so I won't either and just go with your suggestions."

A different waiter appeared, greeted Gina by name, and she ordered for both of them, including "my usual" for the antipasto course. If she was trying to impress him, she succeeded. Rick pushed his chair forward to let someone squeeze by and bumped his knees with hers.

"Sorry about that."

"It's all right, Riccardo, it comes with eating in this place. They have about a dozen more tables than they should have, for the amount of space. But it adds to the atmosphere." She patted his hand. "Now tell me about America."

He did, but began by explaining that it was not a single entity, despite chain restaurants and connecting highways. New Mexico was about as different from Maine as Tuscany was from Sicily. He told her that the country's size was something that foreigners could not understand until they went there, that Italy's square kilometers would easily fit inside New Mexico. And given its size, the state was really many different regions and climates, from desert to mountains to plains.

She was fascinated.

The first of the food arrived, a plate of antipasto for her and the *spaghetti al'Amatriciana* for him. Rick peered over to see what "the usual" was, and saw a single roman artichoke, a few small balls of mozzarella, and two paper-thin slices of prosciutto. He nodded his approval and checked out his spaghetti. The *Amatriciana* sauce was what he'd hoped for, thick and ruby red, with chunks of crisp *guanciale*. He sprinkled cheese and each wished the other *buon appetito*.

"How long have you had Fellini?" he asked when there was a pause in the eating.

"A few years. My mother found him on the street under a car. She thought at first he was feral, like so many cats in the neighborhood, but he came right up to her so she realized he was a stray and brought him home. He immediately took over like he'd always owned the place."

"It sounds like he owns the whole block."

"He loves to walk around on the roofs, and yours is one of the few apartments that he can get into. I'm sure the person who lived there before you fed him, so he expects you to do the same."

"Now that I have tuna, I will."

"Don't spoil him. We just give him scraps from the table."

"Which from the looks of that lasagna are better than canned tuna."

She laughed and cut into her artichoke, tender and coated with oil. "You said you are looking for business, Riccardo. How does that work?"

He dipped some bread into his sauce and took a small bite.

"I just have to get the word out that I'm here, make contacts, that kind of thing. I did translations from America for several professors in universities here in Italy, and I'm asking them to let their colleagues know I'm available. The interpreting may be difficult to break into, but once I do a couple jobs and people know me, it should be easier."

"Not just in Rome, then."

"No, I'll go anywhere in Italy where somebody can use me."

"Do you have a car?"

"No, and I'm not planning to get one. Do you?"

She finished her artichoke and sopped up the oil with a piece of bread before popping it in her mouth. "Goodness, no. If I have to go outside Rome I take the train, and in town I use the bus."

"That's what I'm planning to do."

"Be sure to always have some bus tickets with you. You never know when you'll need to get on the bus, and you don't want to be caught by an inspector without one."

"I'll do that tomorrow. Would you like to taste my *Amatriciana*?"

She didn't hesitate; her fork darted out and she pulled a few strands from his bowl to her mouth. "Yes, as good as ever. Some prosciutto?"

He held up his hand. "No, thank you. These spaghetti are filling me up and I have to save space for my *saltimbocca*." He inserted his fork. "When you do travel, Gina, where do you go?"

She held up her hand as she finished the last mouthful of antipasto. "In the summer, when we close for two weeks, we rent a beach house near Rimini."

"Fellini goes too?"

"Of course. He hates the ride on the train, but loves it once he's there."

The empty dishes disappeared, and Rick topped off their wine-glasses. Despite the murder case going nowhere, the broken date with Giulia, and the anxiety that had earlier begun to creep in about whether he'd made the right decision by moving to Rome, he was in a decidedly good mood. It was helped considerably by wine, good food, and the company of a charming woman. Wasn't there a poem about that?

The *secondi* arrived.

The strong aroma of rosemary wafted off Gina's suckling pig, right out of the oven with a few crisp potatoes next to it. The meat fell easily off the bone when she touched it with her fork. Rick's *saltimbocca* was almost ready to jump into his mouth, as the name suggested. Two thin pieces of veal were topped with thinner slices of prosciutto and sage leaves, all secured by toothpicks. They had been sautéed in butter with a splash of Marsala, giving the dish contrasting, yet complementing, sweet and salty flavors.

Conversation, after comments on their choices for the main course, turned back to Gina. She was an only child, growing up in the same apartment where she still lived with her mother. When her father died she dropped out of the university, taking his place at the *salumaio*. Somewhat to her surprise, she found she enjoyed the work, from ordering the merchandise to dealing with clients. Most of the customers lived or worked nearby, and she realized that the store was more than just a place where people bought food; it was important for supporting the human fabric of the neighborhood.

They passed on dessert, but lingered for a while over empty plates to finish the bottle of wine before Rick reluctantly called for *il conto*. Exiting the row was difficult, but the neighboring tables pushed their chairs in and they were able to make it to the central aisle and walk to the door. When they got outside there was a line waiting to get in.

"Thanks for suggesting this place, Gina, it certainly is popular."

"Yes, for those of us who know—" She stopped in mid-sentence when she saw the people in the line. Toward the back was a couple about their age, she an attractive brunette, he with long black hair and a fashionable stubble on his face. As Gina approached the man he looked up from his conversation, noticed her, and smiled.

"I didn't know you were back in Rome," she said.

"It's been a few weeks. I was going to call you. The job didn't work out."

"I...I'm sorry it didn't work out."

As Rick watched, the two continued to talk, all the while standing still and staring hard into each other's faces. He couldn't tell if the look on Gina was anger or relief, but whichever it was it was mixed with affection. He felt a tap on his arm.

"I think we're invisible."

Rick glanced to his side where the woman who'd been in line was now standing, and he could not help noticing that she was not at all unattractive. "It seems that way. Do you sense that there might be some history between them?"

The woman rolled her eyes as only Italian women can, though she seemed especially good at it. "This may take a while," she said. "Fortunately, I'm not very hungry."

"It's worth the wait," said Rick. He held out his hand. "By the way, my name is Riccardo Montoya."

She took it and held on for longer than necessary under the circumstances. "*Piacere*, Riccardo. I am Erica Pedana."

Chapter Eleven

During the night the sky had changed. High-level winds carrying tiny grains of Sahara sand had moved north from Africa, blowing over the Mediterranean and Sicily, then continuing up the boot until they were now over Rome. The system had stalled, and sat like an evil presence over the city. When the Romans awoke and looked upward they saw the sun filtered through an ugly brown haze. It was the *scirocco*, bringing headaches, respiratory problems, an increase in automobile accidents, and a general heightening of irascibility in a city which, even on a normal day, was not known for the equanimity of its residents. Many of them recognized the signs and stayed in bed.

Rick awoke to itchy eyes and wondered if the cottonwood allergy could possibly have followed him from Albuquerque to Rome. A shower made him feel somewhat better, and while shaving he vowed that this would be a productive day. Why not write down all his thoughts about the Zimbardi case? That's what the cops always did in the British crime shows, and usually some thread appeared which when followed broke the investigation wide open. He would gather his thoughts over coffee and a *cornetto* at the bar around the corner before coming back and putting them to paper. Then it would be off to his uncle's office to review everything and decide where to go next. After that, if time could be spared from the investigation, he would drop by the university and see a couple of contacts about possible translation and interpretation work. Yes, it would be a productive day indeed. He dressed in business casual, with a blazer and his best cowboy boots, and was walking to the door when his phone rang.

"*Buon giorno*, Uncle."

"Buon giorno, Riccardo. You seem in good spirits despite the *scirocco*."

He glanced out Fellini's window and noticed the dark sky. There was no sign of the cat, who clearly was smart enough to stay inside. "Is that what it is? No, I'm just fine. I was going to drop by your office this morning to talk about the case. Will you be there?"

"That's why I was calling. I very much appreciate what you've done regarding the Zimbardi investigation."

This is not sounding good, Rick thought.

"But it is time for you to get on with your real work, Riccardo. Sergeant Lamponi and I will be meeting today to go over where we are, and I'm going to assign another officer to the case as well, to get a fresh viewpoint. Before that, I wanted to ask you if there is anything new you've found out, I mean since we talked about it over dinner."

Should I tell him I want to stay on the investigation? Rick was getting to know his uncle better, and the way Piero had started the conversation indicated that his mind was made up. No doubt he was having second thoughts about getting Rick involved beyond the translation of the count's papers. The *commissario* was correct, of course; it was time for Rick to work on his business full time, especially since he hadn't been much help in smoking out the killer. Well, being a cop was fun while it lasted.

"The only new development since our dinner is that I spoke again with the Englishman, Syms-Mulford." Rick decided to omit the details of how the meeting transpired. "He confessed to me that he was with a woman the night of the murder."

"What woman?"

"He wouldn't say, but I was sure it had to be the countess, and he was trying to protect her good name as well as his own. But Carmella spoke to the harp teacher, who claimed that she was with him that night."

"This is starting to sound like daytime television. But the harp teacher? Is she some kind of *femme fatale*?"

"I would not have used that term to describe Signora Angelini."

Piero's deep sigh was audible over the phone. "I have a meeting with the countess in the afternoon, at her request. I wasn't looking forward to it before, and certainly am not now. She has friends in the Ministry of Justice who could make my life difficult."

"Sorry I have not been able to help you very much, Uncle."

"You have been of immense help, Riccardo, and I am most appreciative. We will have lunch when this is all resolved."

After they said their goodbyes, Rick put his phone in his pocket, picked up his keys, and left the apartment. When he came out of the elevator, he saw Giorgio wielding a broom around the courtyard, pushing into piles the usual dirt from the street, today mixed with specks of sand from the sky. The *portinaio* was not in a friendly mood, which was fine with Rick since at the moment he wasn't up to engaging in small talk about movie westerns. He nodded at Giorgio and left through the back door, walking in the direction of what was becoming his regular bar for morning cappuccino.

Coming out of the canyon formed by the narrow street, he emerged into Piazza Navona where the sky was a canopy of orange malevolence. The always calming smell of brewed coffee greeted him as he came through the door, and moments later he had a cup of it in his hands, along with an almond *cornetto*. After two bites and two sips, he felt considerably better. He promised himself that once this *scirocco* blew over he would go back to starting each morning with a dawn run around the neighborhood. He was a morning person, and with the jet lag gone, he could resume his normal schedule. The thought of jogging around an empty Piazza Navona boosted his morale even more, but the sting in his eyes brought him back to the present. He rubbed them, but it didn't help. Gina's image came to mind when his eyes were closed. The evening had not ended like he'd originally hoped, but it was probably for the best, especially for Gina herself.

"Nasty out there, isn't it?" said the barista. "I had to rinse my eyes when I got here this morning."

"It's pretty bad," said Rick, "but work has to go on." He recalled his conversation with Gina about getting around Rome. "Is there somewhere nearby where I can get bus tickets?"

"The *giornalaio* on the other end of the *piazza*." He moved over to take care of another customer, and Rick finished his breakfast while continuing to think about the previous evening. He drank and ate slowly, trying to avoid the air outside for as long as he could. Reluctantly, he put down the empty cup, dropped a coin on the counter, and walked to the door.

Outside, a group of intrepid tourists stared at the fountains in the square while the locals rushed to get where they were going. Rick walked to the newspaper kiosk where inside it a man's head was framed by reading materials. The arrangement was standard: daily newspapers lay in rows closest to Rick, magazines were stacked behind the dailies, other magazines hung from clips, and some paperbacks lined up behind the man's head. It was a paper recycler's dream. Rick looked down at the headlines of the dailies and his eye was caught by a story of a strike by healthcare workers. Under the headline was a photo of the hospital next to which the count had met his attacker. He was reading the first few sentences of the story when he was interrupted by voice of the *giornalaio*.

"You gonna buy something?"

"Oh. Uh, bus tickets."

The man produced a wad of them. "How many?"

"Give me ten, please."

He deftly fanned through them with his thumb until reaching

the right number, then tore them off and stretched his hand over the stacks to Rick. "Fifteen euros."

Rick paid him and dropped the tickets into his jacket pocket. He thought about getting a bus route map, but quickly decided he didn't want to be taken for a tourist. For where he was heading, the university main buildings, he was sure a bus would be found on the Corso, so he walked in its direction. After a few steps he stopped.

That's it. It has to be it. Why didn't I think of that sooner?

He pulled out his phone and scrolled through the numbers before punching one.

"*Si*, Riccardo."

"Uncle, something just hit me, and I think it could be important for the Zimbardi murder. We'll need to check something."

"I could certainly use a break in the case. What is it?"

Piero listened carefully to Rick's explanation.

"I'll have Sergeant Lamponi get on it immediately. It shouldn't take long. I'll call you as soon as we know something." He hung up. Rick stood in the *piazza* and stared up at the menacing sky, thinking that he wasn't off the case yet. How long would it take to check on his hunch? Certainly more than enough time to have a second cup of coffee and even another *cornetto*, since he was suddenly hungry again. When he entered the bar, the barista did not appear surprised.

"You found the *kiosko*?" he asked as he made a second cup for Rick.

"Yes, thank you." He drummed his fingers on the bar, lost in thought. When the coffee arrived he added sugar and stirred, watching what he was doing but not seeing.

His phone buzzed and he ripped it from his pocket.

"Zio?"

The reply came in Spanish. "Reek, it is me. How are you this lovely morning?"

"Kind of busy, Juan Alberto, to tell you the truth."

"Busy? Me as well. I wanted to let you know, Reek, that all the paperwork on the sale I made has gone through. The Vatican is very efficient. Not what I expected."

Did he say *his* sale? "That's great news, Juan Alberto. So I imagine you'll be flying back to Buenos Aires. Nice of you to call to say goodbye." He looked at the clock on the wall over the coffee machine.

"No, no, Reek. You'll be glad to know that I have decided to stay longer. Another business opportunity, a local one, has come up."

Rick rolled his eyes heavenward. "Something in the tourism trade, I'm guessing."

"You are correct. I must tell you all about it."

"But not now. I really must go. I'll call you in a few days."

Rick hit the "end call" button, stuffed the phone away, and shook his head. So that's where Giulia was last night, why she couldn't have dinner with him. She was wining and dining the Argentine Lothario so she could use him to set up the business to bring in South Americans. Well, he had only himself to blame since he had put them in contact in the first place. If only he'd had some inkling that it would end up keeping Juan Alberto in Rome.

His phone rang again, and he snatched it back out of his pocket.

"Riccardo, you were correct. Sergeant Lamponi is on her way."

"I'll meet her there," Rick said.

● ● ● ● ●

Rick considered trying to find a taxi, but immediately decided to walk, taking off at a fast pace. The sky had turned a darker yellow, even more menacing than when he had left his apartment, and the thick air dried his nose and mouth as he strode across the square into a side street. Buildings squeezed in on both sides, diminishing the little sunlight that penetrated the clouds. His heart beat faster, but he wasn't sure if it was merely from exertion, or the possibility that the Zimbardi case could actually be resolved. Or was he just out of shape? He picked up his pace, and the sound of his boot heels hitting the cobblestones echoed like a horse trotting through a canyon.

He arrived at one end of Via Anacleto at the same time that Carmella pulled up in a patrol car and climbed out of the driver's seat. A uniformed policeman emerged from the passenger seat.

"I've got another patrolman at the other end of the street," she said without a word of greeting. "I hope everyone is here today." She instructed the other cop to stay at the corner. "Let's go," she said to Rick, her tone indicating that his lieutenant status had been rescinded.

They walked together past Pina's delicatessen and Signor Avellone's furniture restoration shop. Rick glanced through glass and saw Pina behind the counter. She also saw him, and a look of concern darkened her face.

"Look at that, Riccardo. They're at the pizza parlor. How very convenient."

Rick looked, and saw all three Stampatelli generations standing just inside the open front of Ahmed's pizza establishment. They were empty-handed, indicating they had just arrived and were about to place their orders. From the mechanic's shop, directly across from where the printers stood, came the noise of a hammer on metal. Signor Leopoldo was back, and at work. When Rick and Carmella reached the entrance to Ahmed's, Silvio, the youngest of the Stampatellis, noticed them and tugged on his father's sleeve. Ludovico looked at his son with annoyance and then saw the police uniform.

"Well, look who's back," he said. "A slow work day?"

"I could ask you the same question," said Carmella.

"We always come here at this time of the morning for a slice of pizza to hold us until lunch." Ludovico raised his index finger to the sky. "And today we had to complain to Ahmed for bringing us this damn weather from his country."

The youngest Stampatelli giggled at his father's comment, but Ahmed didn't seem to notice. "Would you like pizza?" he asked Rick and Carmella.

"Not for us today, Ahmed," she answered before turning to Rick. "Lieutenant?"

It seemed that he had retained his rank and was expected to do the talking. Or if his theory turned out to be wrong, he would be the one with egg on his face. He swallowed hard and considered getting a soft drink from Ahmed to get the dust out of his throat.

"What is going on?"

The voice was that of Pina, who had seen Rick and Carmella and rushed down the street behind them. She stepped into the store and grasped the arm of Ludovico Stampatelli. Even Leopoldo had abandoned his broken Vespas and was in the street rubbing his greasy hands on an even greasier rag while watching the proceedings. They had a quorum.

"Some new information has come to light in the case," said Rick using his most official-sounding voice.

"You've found Umberto's murderer?" asked Pina before covering her mouth with her free hand.

Ludovico's face turned hard and he stared at Rick. The old man's eyes widened. The kid looked scared. Leopoldo blinked. Ahmed's expression had not changed from his normal polite smile.

"Let me finish, Signora. The night of the count's death he took a bus most of the way to his residence. We are not sure where he got on the bus, but we do know where he got off, at Tiberina Island."

"That's not new," Ludovico said. "We all read about it in the newspapers."

Rick thought about what a real cop would do and decided he should continue as if he hadn't been interrupted. "The count crossed one bridge, then traversed the island and walked onto the Ponte Fabricio for the final meters to his home. It was on that second bridge that he met his end."

Pina sniffed. "Poor Umberto."

"It was interesting what we did not find on the count's person." Rick glanced at Carmella, who was beginning to show impatience. He didn't care; he was getting into his role. "His wallet. His wristwatch."

"So it was a robbery," piped up Leopoldo, still rubbing his hands on the rag. Everyone looked back at him and then returned their attention to Rick.

"Or the murderer wanted us to believe that, Signor Leopoldo. But there was something else that we did find, and it was in the count's pocket." Rick reached into his own pocket and very slowly pulled out what appeared to be a small piece of paper. Everyone squinted to see what it was.

"It's Umberto's bus ticket," said Pina, trying hard to hold back her tears. "His very last bus ticket. Most people would have thrown it away when they got off the bus, but not Umberto. He was very tidy. It was one of his virtues."

Ludovico Stampatelli was not interested in hearing about the count's virtues, especially from Pina. "So he kept his ticket, what does that have to do with anything?"

"Ah, but it has everything to do with the case," Rick replied. "The count kept a journal, and during the final week of his life he recorded some concerns on its pages. He had encountered something which bothered him greatly, something that went against his sense of decency, something which—"

"And what would that be, Lieutenant?" Carmella was ready to cut to the chase.

Rick help up the ticket. "It's all in a common bus ticket. But was it really so common?"

Eugenio Stampatelli stepped forward. "Let me see that." Before Rick could react, the oldest Stampatelli snatched the bus ticket, peered at it, and suddenly stuffed it into his mouth.

"Grampa, what are you doing?" said Silvio.

"Papa, are you *pazzo*?" said Ludovico.

After two bites it was on its way down, but it became obvious to everyone that it did not settle well. He held his stomach, his face turned a color similar to the morning sky, and he sank to one of the benches with a low groan. Ahmed reached under the counter, pulled out a cold can of Coke, and passed it to the elder Stampatelli who took a few sips. His color stayed the same.

"That will be two euros, please," said Ahmed.

"Why did he do that?" said the moped mechanic, staring at the old man.

"It's very simple," said Rick. "When the sergeant and I first came to the street, we spoke with Eugenio and Silvio Stampatelli. Eugenio told us about how his father had used the family business to fool the Nazis during the occupation of the city. Do you recall that, Silvio?"

"I've heard the story a million times." The boy kept his eyes on the ground.

"Do you remember telling us, Signor Stampatelli?"

"I'm not saying anything," answered Eugenio, taking a sip of the Coke. It seemed to help settle his stomach.

"It was this morning," Rick said, looking at Carmella, "that we recalled that story, and put it together with the bus ticket which," he paused for several seconds, "is counterfeit."

"Papa," said a horrified Ludovico, "so that's why you were staying late in the shop. How could you?"

Rick replied for the old man: "He could and he did. But somehow the count found out and must have insinuated that he was going to the authorities. Is that what happened?"

The man's reply was a belch. The carbonation was doing its work. "But you don't have any evidence now," he said in almost a groan, while smiling and pointing to his stomach.

"The ticket you ate is one I purchased this morning," Rick answered. "The one found in the count's pocket is still back at the *questura*. Sergeant?"

Carmella pulled a set of handcuffs from her belt and walked toward the old man.

Ahmed, sporting his standard grin, looked at the other two Stampatellis. "You still want pizza?"

• • ● • •

Rick held the phone to his ear and talked with his uncle as he walked. "I wasn't sure which of the three Stampatelli was printing up the tickets, but suspected it was the kid. Fortunately, Eugenio, by snatching and eating the one in my hand, answered the question."

"I'll reimburse you for the ticket out of petty cash, Riccardo."

"No need, just buy me a coffee sometime. Was it easy to tell it was not a real ticket?"

"Our counterfeiting specialist confirmed it almost immediately. You have to wonder how many of them are in circulation, but that's not my problem. What I have to do is get the old man to confess to doing in the count. If we find his prints on the ticket, though, it will be all we need. They're checking it now."

A clap of thunder exploded close to Rick, and the phone connection was out for a split second. "Are you there, Uncle?"

"Still here. It sounds like Mother Nature is going to clear the air of the *scirocco*. You'd better get somewhere inside. Thanks for your work on this. It's going to make my meeting with the countess considerably easier."

"I'm glad to hear that, Uncle."

"You really should consider taking the police exam, Riccardo."

"Let's not start on that again. I'm perfectly happy with my career choice."

"We can discuss it at our next lunch."

They said their goodbyes and Rick noticed raindrops beginning to fall. Rather than make a dash for his apartment, he decided to duck into a building, and realized that O'Shea's Pub was just around the corner. Would it be open at this hour? He loped toward it as the drops became larger, and he was pushing through the door when the heavens opened up. Guido was at his place behind the bar. He glanced up at Rick and then went back to what he was reading. The rest of the bar was empty except for one table where Alan Firestone sat, immersed in the musical scores spread out in front of him. Apparently the guy used the pub as his studio. He looked up.

"Oh, hi, Rick." He seemed genuinely pleased, perhaps he needed a break from whatever he was working on, and waved a hand toward an empty chair next to him. "Join me. You want to order something?"

"No thanks, Al. I just ducked in here to wait out the storm."

"Storm?"

"Didn't you hear the thunder?"

"I guess I was concentrating on my work." He put on a sheepish grin, and Rick made a mental note to look up why sheeps had grins. It was the kind of thing a translator should know.

"Did your friend get in touch with Signora Angelini?"

"Oh, the harp teacher? Yes, Al, he did. Thanks again for the information."

A rumble of thunder rolled in the distance, the main part of the storm was approaching.

"I don't know if she's a good teacher, Rick, but she is an excellent performer. I saw her in a concert of the symphony a few weeks ago and one of the numbers had a very demanding harp part. She nailed it. I went backstage afterward since I know some of the musicians, and I saw her sitting alone. She looked exhausted."

"You must go to a lot of concerts."

"Not as many as I'd like. That one was a special performance to celebrate the founding of Rome. It's a big deal around here, apparently, though I don't know how they can be sure of the exact date. Not that it matters."

204 David P. Wagner

Rick had been slouched in his chair but now sat up straight. "Al, are you sure it was that night?"

"Absolutely, the girl I was with speaks English and she was telling me all about Romulus and Remus. They teach all that in junior high school here." He watched as Rick pulled his cell phone from his pocket. "You need to make a call, Rick?"

•• ● •• •

Rick kept to the side of the street, ducking under the overhang of buildings in order to keep somewhat dry. The rain had subsided, but its clouds still hovered over the city, cleaning both the air and the streets. The Romans were beginning to emerge, looking to the sky to see if it remained the same brown color, and were pleased when they saw the gray of a normal rainy morning. Wet weather that would normally elicit grumbling was now welcomed, and he could almost feel the collective relief as every surface was cleansed. His own throat was still parched with Sahara dust, and he was thinking how a cool glass of mineral water would hit the spot. Fortunately the Bar Il Tuffo was just ahead.

When he entered, Syms-Mulford was standing at the bar, chatting with Gilda. In front of him was a large cup and a small glass of water. The bar was almost empty, save for two gray-haired women at one of the tables, and a well-dressed man at the far end of the bar reading a newspaper and sipping an espresso. Rick brushed some moisture from the shoulders of his jacket and walked to the bar.

"Good morning."

Syms-Mulford looked up quickly and smiled at Rick. "Good morning to you, Mister Montoya. I was happy to get your call and the news that the crime has been solved. It was very decent of you to offer to tell me about it, an unexpected courtesy." His British accent seemed especially strong, perhaps it came with being in a good mood. "Someone on that infernal Anacleto Street, I suppose? But let's get you something. What will it be?"

"A glass of mineral water would be perfect. I need it for the dust in the air."

Syms-Mulford gave the order to Gilda and turned back to Rick. "Damned nuisance, that *scirocco,* it puts everyone out of sorts. Thank goodness for this rain. So, are you permitted to tell me the details, or is it still hush-hush? My guess is that it has something to do with that woman. Some hot-blooded Italian male didn't appreciate the attention Umberto was giving her?"

Rick's water arrived and he took a long drink. "Not exactly. The count discovered some illegal activities being carried on by someone working on Via Anacleto."

The news elicited a furrowing of the brow. "Oh, dear." He glanced over his shoulder at the man at the other end of the bar who was still reading his paper. There was little chance that the guy understood English, but he lowered his voice anyway. "So Umberto stumbled into something and had to be silenced?"

"It appears that way, though the man refused to talk. He is in custody now."

Syms-Mulford thought about that for a moment. "You police have your ways to bring out a confession, I suppose."

Rick took another sip of the mineral water and the bubbles felt good on the way down. "We can't make someone confess to a crime if he didn't commit it."

"Whatever do you mean? You just said that Umberto had found out that the man was committing a crime. Is there a question about that?"

"No, we are sure that he was doing something illegal, and we are sure that the count discovered it. But putting it together with the murder is something quite separate. So we are still trying to tie up loose ends, which is why I wanted to talk to you again."

"I don't see how I could be of any more help. But have at me if you must." He held up his arms in a mock defensive gesture.

Rick finished his glass and signaled to Gilda for another. "To begin with, tell me about where you were the night of the murder."

The question was not expected. "As you well know, Mister Montoya, I was with Signora Angelini. What we did that evening is of no importance to your investigation, and I do not see what it has to do with this malcreant on Via Anacleto. Signora Angelini confirmed that we were together. You police found out from her, as you will recall."

"The police just interviewed her again, and she decided quite quickly that she was mistaken about the night in question. Apparently, when you saw her a few days ago and talked about it, she got confused. Perhaps it was the excitement of receiving that lovely diamond brooch from you. She recalled that on the night of the count's death she was playing in a symphony concert, and went home immediately afterward. It must have been another evening when you were with her, which is understandable since she says you have been seeing a lot of her in the last several weeks."

Syms-Mulford shut his eyes tightly. "Frailty, thy name is woman."

Rick watched the new glass of mineral water being placed in front of him, then bore in. "And you didn't want the countess to find out since you have been—how shall I say this?—very attentive to her as well. You are quite the ladies' man, Sir."

"She has gone through too much anguish, with Umberto's death, she needs no more of it."

"Very noble of you. So tell me where you really were that night, though I think I can reconstruct the scene myself."

"Perhaps you should do just that, Mr. Montoya. I am finished with attempting to assist you."

Rick took a drink from his new glass and patted his lips with a paper napkin. "Perhaps I will. The count was out that evening, playing cards in this very place with his friends. Like a good husband, he phoned his wife and told her he would be home soon."

Syms-Mulford's eyes bore in on Rick, but he said nothing.

"The count usually called when he was on his way, as a courtesy to the countess, and his habit was very helpful to you, wasn't it?"

"I don't know what you mean." His tone had an unconvincing gruffness.

"His calls always gave you time to make your escape. And on that night, since you assumed he would be arriving home as always in a taxi, and you didn't want to run into him, you decided to walk across the river and find one for yourself on the other side. But instead, your old friend had taken a bus and was himself crossing the island. It was an awkward meeting, to say the least. Especially since you had argued with him that day, in this very spot, about your relationship with the sess."

"You seem to have it all figured out, Mr. Montoya." He was breathing deeply in an attempt to keep himself under control. It wasn't helping.

"What exactly happened then on the bridge I can only guess. You being the larger man, I suspect that when the argument started, you threw him to the ground."

Syms-Mulford exploded. He slammed his hand down next to his cup and glass, upsetting them both and startling both Gilda and the man at the end of the bar. "That's not true! It was completely unintentional, we struggled and he slipped, but I did not throw him to the ground. You must believe me." He lowered his voice to almost a whisper. "He was my oldest and dearest friend."

Rick looked past Syms-Mulford and nodded to Commissario Piero Fontana, who folded the newspaper and put a coin on the bar.

Chapter Twelve

The rest of Rick's day went very well—perhaps even better—than the morning, since he'd succeeded in getting a foot in the door at the university for some new translation work. That could be the start of getting his name out in the Italian university community and going on to the next step in his business plan, breaking into the interpreter circuit. His father had suggested contacting the public affairs office of the embassy, since they needed interpreters on occasion, and he would do that tomorrow. Perhaps this really could work. The crisp air added to his good mood. A pastel red dominated the late afternoon sky, taking over from the dirty layer that had covered the city before the cleansing rain. The price paid by the Romans, at least those who owned cars, was the thin layer of brown mud that covered every vehicle left outside. He walked past an old Fiat, its back window scrawled with the Italian equivalent of "wash me." In the next few days the car washes would be as busy as shops selling fresh pasta. Though the *scirocco* was a rare weather phenomenon, Rick added it to the list of reasons not to get his own car.

He pushed open the door to O'Shea's Pub and immediately went from Rome to Dublin—or to a pseudo-Irish city populated mostly by Americans and other non-Irish. The place was starting to grow on him, and he no longer found fault with the anonymous member of his class who, in the distant past, had picked it as a gathering place. Leave the chic wine bars to the native Romans, Guido's unpretentious pub served its purpose for the alumni of the American Overseas School. Rick adjusted his eyes to the dim light and spotted Art at his usual place. His friend was alone with his beer glass, but two dishes of greasy french fries sat in the middle of the table.

"Is someone sitting here?" Rick asked as he reached the table.

Art looked up. "Aha. Our resident sleuth. Sit, sit. My drinking companion is wandering around the room, talking to people about the baseball game." He gestured at the screen above them where an outfielder, unaware that a camera could be on him, was scratching where he shouldn't. "Tell me what has been happening in the life of Rick Montoya. It will be more exciting than this athletic contest. We'll get you a beer if Guido comes back out from the kitchen. Someone, no doubt tourists, foolishly ordered the day's special, and he is in the back preparing it since yesterday he fired his cook. Always a drama in this place. Have a french fry in the meantime."

Rick looked at the plate. "I don't want to spoil my dinner."

"I can't blame you. Guido's food has a way of doing that. So, have you and your uncle solved the crime of the century? Can we once again walk the streets of the city without fear?"

"As a matter of fact, you can, Arturo." He told him about the criminal activity of the eldest Stampatelli, and how Count Zimbardi must have stumbled upon it.

"What a great idea. It's like that guy I read about once who counterfeited one-dollar bills. Nobody prints up dollar bills in their basement, the bad guys always go with higher denominations. But that's what this guy did, and since they only check fifties and hundreds in stores, he got away with it for decades. Did your guy sell the tickets, or just use them himself?"

"You seem to think that printing the bus tickets is a more interesting crime than murder."

"Absolutely. Murders are a dime a dozen. So this counterfeiter murdered the count to keep his activities from the eyes of the police."

"No, in fact the count was bumped off by his oldest and dearest friend, to quote the murderer."

"With oldest and dearest friends like that, who—"

"My thoughts exactly, Arturo."

"I want to hear more about this. How about we get a pizza after this and you can fill me in."

"No can do, Art. I am having dinner with a young lady."

"Aha. Let me guess: the lovely and talented Giulia Livingston?"

"No. We were supposed to dine last night, but she canceled at the last minute."

"Bummer. So you dined alone."

"No, in fact I went out with a lovely girl from my new neighborhood."

"Excellent. And things went so well you're meeting her again this evening."

"Wrong again. The evening went well until she ran into an old flame and dropped me like a hot potato, if you'll excuse the use of two similar figures of speech in the same sentence."

"Ouch. You deserve a drink." He looked toward the bar. "Where's that Guido? How can he make any money in this place if he's not around to serve his clientele? So who is it tonight?"

"Her name is Erica, and I think she's a college professor."

"Let's hope this new relationship lasts more than twenty-four hours. What about your Argentine friend? Has he managed to sell his wine to the Vatican?"

"He did," answered Rick, without going into details.

"So he'll be on a plane back to Buenos Aires."

"No, he's going to work with Giulia in the travel business."

Art held up a hand. "Wait. Is that why she—?"

"I'm quite sure, yes."

Again Art looked for Guido. "Where is that guy? You really, really need a drink bad."

"No, I'm fine, Art. In fact I had an excellent day, starting with solving the murder case. I made some progress on my business as well, and now I will dine with a lovely woman. How could it be any better?"

"You failed to mention having a drink with your oldest and dearest friend, if Guido ever appears to serve it to you, but I'll let your oversight pass. I hope this woman breaks your streak."

"Streak?"

"I'm referring to your love life. You've been here barely a week and your high school sweetheart turns out to be a nun, another high school friend scorns you for a so-called friend of yours from South America, and a lovely lady from your neighborhood longs for her old boyfriend. Zero for three is a bad streak."

A voice boomed from behind them. "Our best hitter is O for three tonight, is that who you're talking about?"

Rick turned to see a familiar figure standing behind him with a bottle of Budweiser in hand.

"Rick," said Art, "let me introduce Lambert Field, a visitor from America."

"We are already well acquainted, Art. It was Rick who called and gave me the name of this wonderful establishment. It was like being thrown a lifesaver after falling off my yacht. But I do not see any libation in front of you, Rick." Field caught the eye of Guido, who had finally made an appearance. "Innkeeper, a flagon of your finest ale for my companion."

Guido nodded and reached for an empty glass.

Food and Wine

In this book Rick once again manages to eat well, as would be expected since he finds himself in Rome at meal time. But his first lunch on these pages is set in Albuquerque, when he dines with his sister before leaving for Italy. He has a local specialty, the green chile cheeseburger, topped with green chiles from Hatch, New Mexico and served with french fries. The Alien Ale he drinks as an accompaniment was inspired by the UFO landing in Roswell, south of Albuquerque. When in New Mexico you should try both; Rick would not steer you wrong.

The first dinner out with his uncle in Rome is at a neighborhood restaurant, where Piero orders an unnamed "dark red from Piemonte." The Piedmont region, of which Turin is the capital, boasts a number of quality reds, including Barolo, Gattinara, Barbera, and Dolcetto. All are readily available at good wine shops in the States. To go with the red wine Piero orders soup while Rick has one of his favorite Roman pasta dishes, *spaghetti alla gricia*. It is one of those recipes that looks simple to make but never tastes as good at home as when you have it at a restaurant in Rome. Meat is next, with Piero getting a traditional steak while Rick orders *carpaccio*. The paper-thin raw steak that Rick has can be served with various toppings, but the traditional one is shaved Parmigiano-Reggiano cheese drizzled with olive oil.

Their next meal is at Giggetto in the Ghetto, what the Romans call the Jewish neighborhood of the city, which was indeed a ghetto in the worst sense during the Middle Ages and afterward. (The word is from the Venetian dialect going back to the original ghetto in that city.) Appropriately, the two have Roman/Jewish specialties to start the lunch: crisp Jerusalem artichokes and rice balls stuffed with cheese, both deep-fried. Rick follows with *parmigiana di melanzane*, which bears no resemblance to eggplant parmesan you get in restaurants in the States. Piero has porcini mushrooms, which can be grilled like steaks, but in this case are roasted in the oven. The one word that can truly describe these grilled mushrooms is "rich." To accompany this repast, and stay relatively local, Piero orders a Velletri Rosso, produced around the town of the same name south east of Rome at the edge of the Alban Hills.

Once again Piero mixes a local wine with local food when they lunch in a Ligurian restaurant. I don't name it in the text, but I had Taverna Giulia in mind when I wrote this. It was the best place to get Ligurian food in Rome when I lived there, and it is found near the eastern end of Via Giulia, a street Rick walks at one point in the book. You can't get a more Ligurian pasta dish than *trenette al pesto*, which is what Rick orders. I should warn you that the problem with ordering pesto in Italy, especially in the towns near Genova, is that when you get back home the pesto will taste terrible in comparison. I could say that about many things you get in restaurants in Italy compared with the States, but pesto is perhaps the most extreme example. (It and mozzarella cheese. See *A Funeral in Mantova*.) Piero has *pansôti* as his first course, but it also goes well with the white they drink with the meal, Cinque Terre. It comes from vines on hills around the five (*cinque*) towns (*terre*) just down the coast from Genova, which have become a tourist mecca. Compared to other Italian regions Liguria does not produce many quality wines, or really many wines at all, but that is simply because it is much smaller in area.

Rick's last meal in the book is a dinner with Gina in a very informal restaurant near his new apartment. The place I had in mind when I wrote this was da Francesco, a short walk from Piazza Navona. Without a GPS it's hard to find in the matrix of streets that make up that neighborhood, but it will be worth the effort. Rick's choices here are classic Roman specialties, *spaghetti al' Amatriciana* followed by *saltimboca*. The pasta's name comes from the town of Amatrice in the mountains east of Rome, where it originated. Their wine for this meal is specified only as "red." When one so orders at *trattorie* in Italy the waiter will bring the house wine, more often than not in an open carafe, and refill it as needed. It can be ordered in a quarter liter, half liter, or full liter, depending on how many of you there are. Obviously, the restaurant orders the house wine in bulk, and where it comes from is not specified. Though I've never asked, I'm sure the waiter will tell you what kind of wine it is, if you are curious. Let me state that I have never been disappointed by a house wine in Italy.

Author's Note

I am most grateful to my editors, Barbara and Annette, for suggesting a prequel to the Rick Montoya series, as well as for urging that it be set in Rome and encouraging me to put in more humor than the first five books. I enjoyed writing it and am excited that something which could be described as "Montoya Lite" is going to press. To my regular readers I promise that, in the next one, Rick will leave the big city and again find himself in another of those wonderful small Italian towns.

This book allowed me to poke around some of my favorite places in Rome and have some fun with the foibles of both residents and tourists. Having spent six wonderful years there, I feel like I'm allowed. I hope my Roman friends agree. Rome's historic center is, to use an Italian phrase, *a misura di uomo.* That can be roughly translated as, "the measure of a man," meaning that everything's easily reachable on foot. Rick does take buses and taxis, but most of the time he walks, and doing so allowed me to show that strolling around the city's ancient streets is a joy open to both locals and visitors. It is what I miss most about living in Rome. Well, that and the food.

While the plot and characters are complete fiction, all of the main streets and sites mentioned in the book are very much real. That includes Bernini's delightful elephant statue, the Vatican press office, and La Palma *gelateria*. Another is the Torre Argentina *area sacra*, a required stop for those interested in ancient Roman ruins as well as for cat lovers. One can spend hours watching the felines strolling around the temples. There is not a Via Anacleto in Rome, though an anti-pope of that name did exist, and the description of his life that I wrote is accurate. For Anacleto's history I consulted one of my favorite references, *Lives of the Popes*, by the late professor Richard P. McBrien.

Rick's Rome apartment, in both layout and location, is roughly based on that of my good foreign service friends Joe and Barbara Johnson, when we all lived in Rome in the mid 1980s. I hope they don't mind that Rick borrows it. I also thank two old buddies from New Mexico, Art Verardo and Alan Firestone, for the use of their names. Perhaps they will think of Rick the next time they have a green chile cheeseburger.

A big *grazie mille* goes, as ever, to my son, Max, for his support and ideas. Both he and Rick Montoya attended the American Overseas School of Rome, and are better people for it. Of course my wife, Mary, was again instrumental in keeping me on track with his book, always providing encouragement and excellent ideas. I couldn't have written it without her.